Mystery
at
Apple Tree
Cottage

BOOKS BY CLARE CHASE

Mystery
at
Apple Tree
Cottage

CLARE CHASE

bookouture

Published by Bookouture in 2020

An imprint of Storyfire Ltd.
Carmelite House
50 Victoria Embankment
London EC4Y 0DZ

www.bookouture.com

ISBN: 978-1-83888-527-4
eBook ISBN: 978-1-83888-526-7

To Warty

PROLOGUE

Early April

Any local looking at the woodland between the village of Saxford St Peter and the heath that led down to the coast would know the season. Beneath the evergreen Scots pines, bluebells formed a glorious dark-cobalt carpet, peppered here and there by white-petalled wood anemones, their centres decorated with yellow anthers. Leaf-burst for the oaks was still a month or so off, but beneath the gnarled old trees, wood sorrel grew from the moss clinging to fallen logs and branches. Its purple-veined white flowers dangled from the slenderest of stems, marking the progress of spring.

From a distance, the scene looked reassuringly familiar.

In the deepest part of the wood, a figure crouched next to a fine silver birch with plump catkins hanging from its branches. The forest floor was teeming with life. But at his feet, amongst the flowers that promised the return of warmth and hope, lay death – brutal and simple.

Ashton Foley had been shot through the head.

In the countryside, the sound of a gun firing wasn't so unusual. The shot hadn't brought anyone running, and Ashton's corpse lay a good way from the nearest house. All the same, the man kneeling by the body was on high alert, pulse racing, leg muscles trembling. It was early, but dog walkers would be about. With a quick glance over his shoulder, he leaned forward and investigated each of Foley's pockets in turn. The leather jacket was easy, but the jeans were tight, and it was a challenge to check inside. He rolled the dead man awkwardly up onto one hip, and then the other, looking in his back pockets now. *Aha.* There was the wallet. But it was almost empty – just some cards and loose change.

He wiped the leather with a clean tissue, replaced it, then paused a moment. None of the pockets contained a door key. That was odd…

CHAPTER ONE

Four Weeks Earlier

Eve Mallow arrived at Monty's teashop, with its bay windows and colourful bunting, looking forward to her shift. Working with her friend Viv, who owned the place, complemented her real profession perfectly. As a freelance obituary writer, she interviewed the living to unearth the secrets of the dead, but also spent hours researching her subjects. Wanting to understand people was hardwired in her. Regular shifts in Monty's ensured she stayed solvent, but the work was also sociable, and an additional people-watching opportunity.

She still felt slightly surprised to find herself installed in a Suffolk village. As a city girl, born and raised in Seattle, who'd moved to London as a student and stayed for thirty years, she'd assumed rural life wouldn't suit her. It was a working vacation in Saxford St Peter the previous summer which had changed her mind. Life there had a lot to offer. You got to know people properly. The chance to really understand them was appealing. Eve's beloved dachshund had been delighted by the move too. Pelting along the beach, leash-free, was a lot more appealing than sniffing lamp-posts on Kilburn High Road.

Viv was serving as Eve walked through the teashop door. After hanging up her coat in the office, off Monty's kitchen, Eve joined her friend behind the counter.

'How's it going with your dead poet?' Viv asked.

'Fascinating. I'm almost done, and I'll be sorry to leave her behind. Apparently she sat in the nude with the windows open for an hour each morning to reconnect with the world.'

Viv shuddered. 'I rely on a cup of Darjeeling for that, but each to their own.'

A pair of middle-aged women had just arrived and taken seats at a table in the window. The early spring sunlight slanted in, falling on the daffodil-yellow tablecloth, which matched Viv's hair colour this season. The table was topped off with sparkling silverware and a jam jar, decorated with a purple ribbon and full of hellebores.

Eve recognised one of the newcomers: a woman of around sixty, with brown hair, streaked with grey. She'd been in Monty's before, and though she was always kind and polite, she usually looked rather buttoned-up, as though life had taken its toll, and she'd put up barriers against further upset. Today, things were different. She smiled and eased off her coat, sliding it over the back of her chair, and relaxed, her shoulders down, chest out, as though she'd just taken a deep breath. She made Eve think of a flower whose petals had opened in response to the sun. In a moment, the woman with her said something, and she leaned forward to reply, beaming and animated.

'That's Betty Foley,' Viv said in an undertone, following her gaze. 'She lives in Apple Tree Cottage, down in the woods. It's nice to see her looking so happy. I wonder what's up.' A moment later her thoughtful expression was replaced by one of panic. 'Oh no – the scones!' She disappeared into the kitchen.

Eve went to take Mrs Foley's order. She was pushing the boat out; Monty's tea-time selection was a substantial treat. A moment later, Eve ferried a collection of stylishly mis-matched crockery over to their table. It was a trademark of Monty's, along with the brightly coloured tablecloths and seasonal wildflowers. As she approached, she picked up on the pair's conversation.

'So, Ashton's going to be here for some time?' the friend said to Mrs Foley, leaning back so Eve could put her plate down.

Betty Foley nodded, her eyes bright. 'That's right. Four or five weeks *at least*, he said. The work's quite complicated – a lot of planning and design and then there's actually "siting" the plants. That's what he called it.'

'I can't believe he's working for a pop star! But then I suppose he's a celebrity himself these days.'

Betty blushed as Eve laid their places. 'Well, that's right. He is really. It's a hugely successful business now, and they've worked for actors and models, even some of the minor royals.'

'Wow!' The friend let the word out on a sigh as she relaxed in her chair.

Eve retreated to fetch a cake stand, laden with tiny cucumber sandwiches, apricot and white chocolate blondies, chocolate truffle cupcakes and lemon shortbread. The man called Ashton was still the topic of conversation when she returned.

'People seem to find it very therapeutic to have more plants in their homes,' Betty was saying. 'And it's not just the type of pot plants we might have. His company puts in trees and climbers.' She paused and then said in a rush: 'Everyone who's anyone wants to buy Ashton's services. The company's waiting list is a year long!'

Her friend's eyes widened at sight of the cake stand. 'Goodness, what a treat!' She smiled at Eve, then turned back to Betty. 'But I can see why you're celebrating. You must be so proud.'

'I am.' Betty blushed again. 'And I can hardly believe it. It only seems like five minutes since he was in school.' For just a second, a shadow seemed to pass over her, but then she brightened again. Ashton must be her son. Eve could tell Betty was practically bursting with pleasure, but equally that it went against the grain to boast. She was obviously a bit bashful about sharing her happy moment. For a second Eve felt quite unreasonably emotional on the woman's behalf. But she knew that feeling of joy; when her own twins called to relay good news, she felt elated and proud too.

'No wonder he's not able to come home often,' the friend said, 'he must be rushed off his feet.'

Just before Eve turned back towards the teashop's kitchen, she caught another tiny flicker of distress in Betty's eyes, but it was quickly gone. 'That's right. He has no time at all, poor thing. It'll be so nice to have him around for a while at last.'

Eve went to fetch the pair a pot of Assam tea. By the time she returned with it, together with milk and sugar, Betty's friend was speaking.

'Very expensive, I presume?'

'Oh yes,' Betty said. 'Not for the likes of us!' She chuckled and shook her head.

'Well, please let me know when he arrives and introduce me!' the friend said.

Betty nodded, her glow increasing, her hands clasped to her chest. 'I will.'

A moment later Eve was back behind Monty's counter with Viv. 'Were the scones okay?'

'Perfect.' She wasn't one for false modesty, something which Eve appreciated. 'So, what's Betty's news?' she added in an undertone.

'It sounds as though her son's coming back to Saxford to do a job for Billy Tozer.' Unsurprisingly, there was only one pop star in the village. The rapper had moved into an architect-designed millionaire's playhouse, close to the beach.

'Mrs Foley can't wait to see him, that's for sure. She's nice, isn't she?'

Viv nodded and folded her arms. Her expression had turned sour. 'She's a gem.'

'Why the grim look then?'

She glanced at Mrs Foley and then down at her watch. 'What about a glass of wine after we finish? I'll fill you in.'

*

By the time Eve and Viv had seen the last customer out of Monty's, prepared the tables for the following day and cleaned the kitchen, it was a respectable hour for a pre-dinner drink.

The sun was low in the sky and the wind had risen. 'What about a glass of red,' Eve said, 'to keep out the chill? I've got a bottle of Cabernet Sauvignon back at Elizabeth's Cottage.'

'Perfect,' Viv said.

They skirted the village green to reach Eve's road, Haunted Lane. Its entrance was bordered by a majestic old oak on one side, its trunk swathed in ivy, and a dense hawthorn hedge on the other. Beyond, hers was one of just two cottages. After that, the tiny lane petered out into a path, which led to the marshes and the estuary. As they walked, a great white egret swooped overhead. The abundance of wildlife surrounding her new home still took Eve's breath away and feeling close to nature grounded her. But Haunted Lane had a turbulent past. Elizabeth, the village heroine, had lived in Eve's cottage in the 1720s. She'd hidden a local servant boy there, to save him from the gallows after he'd stolen a loaf of bread to feed his starving siblings. He'd escaped in the end, but it had been close. The lane was named for the sound of thudding feet you were meant to hear late at night: echoes of the men sent to hunt the boy down. They were said to be an omen of danger. Eve often thought of the story as she returned home, and now, as the sky grew darker, and the wind stronger, it made her shiver.

'Let's get inside and light a fire,' she said, opening the garden gate in her thick privet hedge. Already she could hear Gus just inside the cottage, jumping at the door. Her dachshund would be in seventh heaven when he realised Viv was there too.

They shimmied round him, shut out the cool air, then bent to tickle his tummy as he rolled over, a giddy look in his eye.

'He's so much more rewarding than my cats,' Viv said. 'They're insultingly disdainful. Anyone would think they feed me, not the other way about.'

Eve already had kindling and logs banked up in the inglenook fireplace. Viv had coached her on how to do it, having grown up in Elizabeth's Cottage; it had belonged to her parents before Eve moved in. She put a match to the wooden fire starters she'd laid under the kindling.

'Nice work!' Viv said, walking over to warm herself.

There was nothing more comforting than the thick-walled, beamed room on a chill evening, with the smell of woodsmoke in the air.

'I'll get the wine.' Gus trotted after her, knowing supper would also be on offer.

After getting him sorted, Eve poured two glasses of red and emptied some cashew nuts into a blue crackle-glazed bowl. She put everything on a tray, then carried it back to the living room and set it on the coffee table. She and Viv sat either side of it, on the twin couches Eve had bought with the cottage, close to the warmth.

'So,' Eve said, 'what was bugging you, back in the teashop?'

Viv heaved a sigh. 'Seems like Betty Foley's building high hopes for Ashton's visit. I don't want her to be disappointed.'

Eve took a nut. 'You think he's likely to let her down?'

Viv shrugged. 'He's younger than me, so I didn't really know him when he lived in the village, but he's been back briefly since, and the gossip about him is pretty consistent. Though I've heard most of it through a single source…'

'Moira?' The village storekeeper was expert at extracting information, dramatising it, and passing it on.

Viv nodded, edging closer to the fire. 'Obviously, I know she'll have homed in on the most scandalous elements of his story. She says Ashton was a tearaway when he was a teenager.' She waved a dismissive hand. 'That's nothing, of course. My three had their moments.' Her boys had all left home now. Her youngest was on a gap year before university, travelling the world. 'But – unusually for Moira – she came across with several concrete facts. He was caught thieving, getting other kids into trouble, and then finally he got sent to a young offenders' institute for dealing cannabis.' She shook her head. 'Clearly, there was someone older involved, who used him. And from his point of view he was just passing on some weed to his friends in exchange for cash. I guess he wouldn't have seen it as dealing, but he probably took a cut, even if he passed most of the proceeds to his supplier.' She shrugged. 'Moira was scandalised, naturally.' It was a state the storekeeper seemed to enjoy. 'And the authorities took an especially dim view, because he wouldn't say who'd recruited him.'

Eve sipped her wine, watching the reflection of the flames in the glass. 'I guess he might have been scared to name them.'

Viv nodded. 'You'd think so. But Moira says he came across as cocky, which wound the magistrate up. Apparently, Ashton said he knew he'd been used, but Moira reckons he didn't like the police any better than his supplier, so he kept schtum. Just claimed he didn't know where the cannabis came from, and that he'd been approached by a stranger in a bar, after which it was all anonymous drop-offs and pick-ups. But the person in the bar was never found, and everyone reckoned he was lying.'

A lot of the gossip Moira had passed on must be on public record, Eve guessed, but she decided she should wait and form her own opinion, assuming she got to meet Ashton. It had all happened a long time ago, when he was very young, and people could change. 'What did he do when he was released from the young offenders' place?'

'From what I can remember, it wasn't long before he went off to live in London. Slept on an older friend's floor. He'd have been around eighteen, I guess.'

Eve had moved to London when she was eighteen too – after what now seemed like her daring decision to study abroad. Her mom was American, her dad British. He'd encouraged her to spread her wings. She loved the UK's capital, though nothing could replace home; visiting her parents on the Pacific coast was always a tonic.

'Moira says Ashton managed to get work as a roadie for a couple of bands, one of which became a chart topper. Then, after that, he got his big break in business.'

'So what's his line then? Mrs Foley and her friend were talking about plants.'

Viv nodded and took another handful of nuts. 'He runs a company called Outside In. You've not heard of it? They always seem to be splashed over the pages of some glossy mag or other these days.'

'The name rings a bell.' Eve read the obituary columns first, and kept up with news and reviews too; there wasn't always time for homes and interiors.

'They bring the outdoors into your house to improve your well-being and quality of life.' Viv snorted. 'I can't imagine why you'd spend thousands of pounds to fill your house with temperamental greenery, when you could spend a couple of quid in Monty's eating fine cakes and talking to your friends. I would have thought that would be a lot more beneficial.' Her mission was to provide soul food for the village – and a place to pause, relax and take stock.

Eve had a feeling Viv felt more strongly about Ashton's plant obsession than his misspent youth. Once again, she decided to reserve judgement. She liked plants, but the idea of letting someone else decide where she should put them sent shivers down her spine. After years of having to negotiate how she organised her living space with her know-all ex-husband Ian, she was holding on fast to her autonomy. Tranquillity was key when it came to her surroundings and there was nothing tranquil about losing control.

'The firm must be pleased about the contract for Billy Tozer.' He'd have a lot of money to spend and it would be good publicity too. 'I wonder if Ashton knows him through the band he worked for.'

Viv sipped her wine. 'There's a rumour going around that Ashton's first clients at Outside In were people he sold drugs to – after he was prosecuted, when he moved down to London. He might still be at it now, for all I know. Maybe *that's* how he and Tozer bonded.'

'Is that why you think he might cause Betty problems?'

Viv nodded, her daffodil hair reflecting the firelight. 'I'm just not sure how much he's changed. He hardly ever comes back to the village, but the one time I saw him, he made me nervous. I think he's trouble.'

CHAPTER TWO

It was a few days later when Eve first saw Ashton Foley in person. She was sitting in the Cross Keys pub, halfway down a glass of Coke, having finished a session with an interviewee. The inn and the teashop were useful venues for her work. A squally spring shower was flinging itself against the seventeenth-century building's sash windows; the March evening had come on early, thanks to the weather. For a second, she glanced outside. She could barely see the village green through the murky air. It made the pub's interior feel even more cosy and comfortable. To Eve's left, vast logs glowed orange in the ancient soot-blackened fireplace, and flames licked the bricks at its rear.

Jo Falconer, the pub's lead chef, was just bringing out the first evening-meal orders. There was a look of challenge in her eyes as she set them down, which morphed into a gracious smile as the recipients gushed about the amazing smell. Gus, who had been sprawled under the table, pressed himself against Eve's legs as Jo walked past. Hetty, the pub schnauzer, was sitting to attention over by the bar too. They both relaxed again as Jo went back behind the scenes. One of the drinkers said something and Matt Falconer, Jo's husband, roared with laughter. The hush that had briefly fallen was broken again. The husband-and-wife team ran the pub jointly with Matt's brother, Toby, but Jo was just a little bit more in charge than the others.

Gus pottered out from under the table and looked up, his appealing brown eyes on Eve's. She glanced at Toby Falconer, Hetty's owner, and he nodded and gave her a smile.

'Go on then!' Eve said to Gus. 'You can go and say hello to your lady friend.' She'd had to stop him when she was interviewing – it was too unprofessional. 'But play nicely! Quietly, Gus. Quietly!' He'd gotten to know the rules now. Once the place filled up, serious rough and tumble was out.

Eve decided to stay for another drink, so Gus could have his fun and she could finish her notes. She wouldn't rest until she had everything nailed down. She ordered a glass of wine and took it back to her table.

She was still scribbling details, and ideas on how to frame her piece, when the pub door opened and a tall man with shoulder-length dyed-black hair entered. He was wearing a knee-length black leather coat and biker boots with large silver buckles. He held the door open theatrically, allowing the chill wind and spots of rain to blow in, and a moment later Betty Foley entered. She was followed by a man who was probably in his sixties, like her, with pointed features and flyaway grey hair.

Betty laughed and blushed as she walked inside. 'Ashton! You're making a scene.'

'Nothing wrong with treating my mother like royalty!' He gave a mock bow.

Ashton let the door drop just before the older man was properly through it, so that he had to put out a hand to avoid it knocking into him. The older guy glanced to left and right, but no one was looking apart from Eve, and she cast her eyes down just before he caught her at it. All the same, she continued to monitor the group surreptitiously as she sipped her wine. She was sitting side-on to where they were now, at the bar.

'I'll get them.' The older man leaned forward over the counter, next to Betty, but he hadn't taken out his wallet. He sounded strained and his cheeks were tinged red.

Betty put a hand on his arm, her kind eyes on his.

'No. This is most definitely my shout.' Ashton's voice carried across the pub, despite the level of background chatter. 'It's not often I get to treat you, Ma!' His gold and black credit card was in his hand.

The older man opened his mouth, then closed it again. He was tall like Ashton, but gaunt, and somehow, he seemed smaller.

'What do you fancy?' Ashton put an arm round his mother's shoulders. 'I know you were always a gin and tonic fan. What about the orange-flavoured one?'

Eve happened to know it was one of the pub's most expensive drinks. She was a gin fan herself, and had sampled it as a treat, the evening she'd moved to Saxford.

'Well, if you're sure.' Betty sounded breathless.

Ashton turned; Eve could see his mischievous brown eyes now. 'Of course I am!'

A short while later, Gus and Hetty had played themselves out, and the dachshund pattered back across the bar. Ashton spotted him from where he'd sat down with his mother and her companion.

'Cute dog!' He bent for a moment to make a fuss of Gus, who was anybody's for a ruffle of the fur round his neck or a tickle on the tummy. Then he watched as the dachshund pottered on to his destination, and finally raised his eyes to meet Eve's. Ashton Foley gave her a look that made her feel awkward, coupled with a lingering smile. She guessed he was in his early thirties, whereas she was forty-nine, but his expression made nothing of the age gap.

Eve felt a blush come to her cheeks and bent rather stiffly to say hello to Gus. After that she busied herself with her notes again, but she risked glancing up occasionally.

Ashton and his mother's companion sipped pints of Adnams as they talked. So this was the owner of Outside In. His body language was expansive as he relaxed back in his chair, arms open. He was telling them about a previous client, the owner of a chain of department stores who lived down in London. Eve caught bits of their conversation.

'The guy had two rooms devoted to clothes. Must see all the latest fashions come into stock and then can't resist them. And let me tell you, I found some very odd items in his bedroom when I was measuring up there!'

'Really?' Betty Foley was laughing.

The stern companion wasn't saying much, but when she looked at him anxiously, he sat forward. 'How long does it usually take to plan a job?' he said, after a moment.

Betty smiled, and under the table, Eve saw her squeeze the older man's hand.

As the conversation went on, Eve applied herself to her work. There were still some free tables, so she wasn't blocking anyone, but she'd almost finished her wine and it was time she got home. Gus had eaten his supper before they'd come out, but she'd yet to cook hers.

She'd picked up her bag, and was just packing her writing gear away when Betty spoke.

'And guess what I've cooked for your homecoming supper! Beef and ale casserole with a cobbler topping.' Her smile became more uncertain as she watched her son's face. 'Is it still your favourite?'

Ashton leaned over the table and squeezed her shoulder. 'Cooked by you? Always. But Ma, you should have told me! I can't eat with you tonight – I've got to catch up with some of the old gang.' He laughed. 'You know how it is! So many people to see and so little time. After all, my days are going to be full. Tozer's place is enormous, and he wants the works.'

Eve saw Betty's face fall – literally, her features sagged – but she mustered a smile in a fraction of a second, her hands clasped under the table.

'Of course. I should have checked. It was thoughtless of me not to tell you my plans.' Eve knew that reaction. Taking the blame was less painful than acknowledging the other person had treated you badly. She'd seen interviewees do it, and recognised it easily because she'd done it herself, too. For years she'd made excuses for Ian's behaviour. It was only when he'd finally walked out that she'd gotten some enforced perspective. It had been freeing in the end.

'Don't be silly!' Ashton glanced at his watch. He was half standing, his pint empty, one arm inside his leather coat. 'I should have asked you. But right now, I've got to dash.' He pulled his coat on properly. 'Tell you what, though – if there's any casserole left, I could heat some up later when I come in as a midnight snack!' He bent to give her a hug. 'That would be some treat!'

His words softened the blow, Eve could see that. Betty's smile was gradually becoming more natural, but the set of her shoulders and her eyes still gave away her emotions. Eve felt for her. You could just say it was a breakdown in communication, but he might have thought. Her kids wouldn't have behaved like that.

'I'll see you in the morning then. Promise I'll let myself in quietly!' He gave a wicked grin and then swept out of the pub.

His mother and her companion followed him, and Eve was ready to leave now too, so she and Gus were just behind. Eve pulled up the hood of her yellow mac as they exited – a fashion house answer to what a former city dweller like her ought to wear near the coast. The rain was like a fine mist now, hanging in the air.

As Eve attached Gus's leash, Betty turned left out of the pub and her companion followed her. He rushed to deploy an umbrella to shelter her from the weather, then put his arm around her waist. As he tried to draw her in close, she twisted to give her son a final wave.

Ashton waved back and Eve was glad he'd noticed and responded, for Betty's sake. She guessed her companion would share the beef casserole she'd prepared. It was good she had company. She wondered if he lived with Betty. She hadn't seen him in Monty's.

It looked as though Ashton was going in her direction. He glanced over his shoulder at her for a second and, after accidentally meeting his eye again, she decided to give him a head start. Small talk wasn't something she fancied right now. She was always curious about people, but she didn't want to flatter his ego. She pretended to check a message on her phone, leaning forward to shield its screen from the rain. Gus disapproved of the delay and was tugging in the direction of their cottage, casting her frequent accusing glances.

She let his extendable leash out as soon as Ashton was a safe distance ahead, and started the short walk up Love Lane towards her road. To her left, the damp village green was deserted, but on three of its four sides – Love Lane and two others – it was bordered by thatched and tiled cottages with brightly lit windows. They looked snug, as though they'd hunkered down against the weather. The only buildings in darkness were the village store and Monty's teashop, both of which were closed for the night. On the fourth side, opposite Love Lane, St Peter's church rose tall and dark against the indigo sky.

Up ahead, on Eve's route home, Ashton turned, opened the low wooden gate of one of the houses facing the green, and knocked at the door. Through a sash window, Eve could see a table lamp and the glow of yellow walls.

A moment later a woman with glossy chestnut curls opened up. 'Ashton!' Her bright brown eyes sparkled.

He grabbed her round the waist, then pulled her in close. Eve thought he was going for her lips, but in the end he kissed her on both cheeks.

She laughed. 'You're such a tease. What *do* you think you're doing?'

'I've come back home on serious business!' He paused for a moment. 'And not just over at Tozer's place either.' His voice had suddenly turned sober, but a second later he laughed, as though trying to shake himself free of the thought that had struck him. 'So allow me some fun! We're meeting round at Sue's and your presence is required!'

Eve was just a few feet away from them now. The woman was lit by a lamp over her front door. Her eyes were dancing, but she was holding back a little. 'Well, I don't think Dave will be too keen somehow.'

'Dave is more than welcome to come too. How could you doubt that?' Ashton had his back to Eve, but she could hear the humour in his low, suggestive voice.

The woman put her head on one side. 'Yeah right – I'm not sure that'll convince him. His presence didn't seem to cool your ardour all that much last time!'

'That was down in London. I'm so much tamer when I come home to the countryside. That said' – he took a step towards her – 'I'm only human, so I can't make any promises! With that in mind, are you coming? It's going to be quite a party, and you can stop being so coy; a little bird told me Dave's out of town right now.'

The woman gave a deliberate sigh, but a slow smile was spreading across her lips. 'Oh they did, did they? They're well informed. Well, all right then – just let me grab a bottle!'

So it wasn't just his mother's feelings Ashton was careless of, Eve thought, as she walked on towards her home. What kind of stories would 'Dave' come back to? He and his partner's tiny cottage looked so cosy and comforting in the fading light. Maybe it was an illusion and the couple weren't happy, but Ashton's dangerous presence could only make things worse. Eve sensed he was on course to smash their carefully constructed home life to smithereens.

CHAPTER THREE

In the days that followed, Eve saw Ashton Foley several times around the village, but more often than that, she heard other people talking about him.

'He was there until four, apparently! The life and soul. I don't know how he does it when he's up again early to work at Billy Tozer's house.'

'Fancy seeing inside. Can you imagine?'

'... thinking of inviting him over for our do next week. Harry's not keen, but it sounds like I'm missing out!'

'... not sure his business manager approves. She was looking daggers at him.'

But Eve had also seen him on the beach with his mother. They'd been striding over the pebble-strewn sand together, the sun sparkling on the sea behind them, one weekend morning as she'd walked Gus. He'd had his head bent towards her and she could see he was listening as well as talking. Betty was wearing what looked like a new coat – a well-cut quality wool number, though it was a little big on her. It didn't look like her usual style and Eve was betting Ashton had brought it with him from London. Betty's cheeks had colour in them, and though it might have been down to the clear sea air, Eve didn't think that was the only reason.

It was around ten days after Ashton's arrival when Betty Foley came in to Monty's again. She was with the man who'd accompanied her and Ashton to the pub. Eve noticed her tense shoulders and the dark circles under her eyes. The man had his arm around her again, and this time she wasn't shrinking away.

Angie, one of Viv's college-student helpers, saw the pair to a table.

Eve was watching them from the crafts section Viv had established at the teashop a few years earlier. She and her friend were rearranging the display and Eve would have to photograph the new layout once they'd finished. Viv had a creative eye and made the whole teashop look original and inviting, but she wasn't so hot on organisation. Eve had a system which involved keeping a photographic record of what was where, so she could see what was missing. That way she knew at a glance what had been sold and which artist needed paying, even when Viv had forgotten to write it down. Long term, she was trying to get her friend to use a notebook to record the codes Eve attached to each piece. (*It's just three characters, Viv…*) It was an uphill struggle. Viv had recruited her for her organisational skills, so she had to be strict; there'd be no point otherwise. Besides, she longed to bring order to the place for her own personal satisfaction.

Eve was holding a beautiful verdigris-green ceramic jug, the work of Daphne, one of her neighbours on Haunted Lane. She put it onto a beechwood stand and sidled over to Viv.

'Is Betty okay?'

Her friend let out a sigh. 'Not very. Has she come in?' She peered round the corner into the main teashop, then turned back to Eve. 'Her aunt's had a stroke – I only heard yesterday. She brought Betty up, from when she was seven or something, so' – she put her hands up to her face – 'you can imagine how she's feeling. They don't expect her to live, and on top of all that she emigrated to New Zealand ten years back; she's in Auckland, so it could hardly be more difficult, geographically.'

'Oh no. Poor Betty.'

'She's got a last-minute flight out there later today, and she's in bits – mainly because of her aunt, of course, but she'll miss the rest of Ashton's stay too.'

'Who's the guy with her?' As they watched, he put a hand on Betty's arm and gave it a pat, leaning forward, his eyes on hers.

'Howard Green. They've had a thing going forever. Betty was widowed when she was young, and she and Howard got friendly when Ashton hit his teens.' She chewed her lip. 'I don't know the ins and outs, but he and Ashton have never got on. I've seen them all together since Ashton came back though. I suspect Howard's been making a supreme effort for Betty's sake, but the fur flew between them in the old days. I get the impression that's why he and Betty have never moved in together. She'd consider it disloyal. They see a lot of each other, but Howard keeps his house on Dark Lane, and Betty's hung on to Apple Tree Cottage.'

'Even though Ashton hardly ever comes home?'

Viv shrugged. 'The bond between Betty and Ashton's pretty strong, by all accounts. And Moira says Ashton made her think it was Howard's overbearing attitude that caused him to rebel when he was a kid, so Betty's felt guilty ever since. But Howard's an old-fashioned sort of guy and he's always been very protective of her.'

It sounded as though Betty was caught in the middle, keeping the peace, putting her own needs last.

'Howard's going to take Betty down to Stansted to catch her flight,' Viv said. 'She's got to go via Dubai or somewhere. Cheapest route. I invited her to come in for tea and cakes on the house to set her up for the journey. I felt so sorry for her when I heard, and there's nothing else I can do.'

Both Monty's and the Cross Keys were like second homes for a lot of the villagers – providers of comfort and sustenance.

'It was a lovely idea.'

Viv walked through to where Betty and Howard were sitting, and Eve followed so that she could express her sympathy. Betty was so agitated that Viv recommended some plain shortbread rather than anything more fancy.

'You can take it with you if you don't want it here.'

Betty thanked Angie when she arrived with a pot of Darjeeling, but she was clearly distracted. She kept looking out of the window, her eyes damp, then glancing at her watch. When she did it for the third time, Howard took her hand and she turned to face him instead.

A second later, the old-fashioned bell over the teashop door jangled and Betty started as Ashton rushed in, as full of jumpy energy as ever.

Howard had to let go of her hand as Betty stood. A moment later, Ashton was giving her a hug.

'I'm so glad you came,' she said, looking up at him, but a moment later she glanced over her shoulder at Howard again.

'Of course I came! And I started work early at Tozer's so I can take you to the airport now as well. Car's waiting outside.'

'Oh!' Betty's cheeks flushed. 'It's just that Howard was going to—'

'I know. But now I can save him the trouble.'

Betty looked anxiously at the older man. 'I—'

Howard reached out to hold her hand again. 'You know I only want what's best for you.' He put a very slight emphasis on the word *I*, Eve noticed. He stood up. 'Call me? When you arrive?'

'Of course.' Betty sounded relieved. They embraced awkwardly as Ashton waited by the door, car keys in hand.

CHAPTER FOUR

Eve was partway through a shift at Monty's the following Thursday afternoon when Ashton Foley beckoned her over to his table at the back. He was sitting opposite his business manager. She was called Marina Shaw, according to the village grapevine; Eve hadn't been introduced to her yet, despite taking their order earlier. To be fair, she'd distracted Ashton by asking after his mother. (She'd arrived safely, and her aunt was still holding her own. The doctors said it was touch and go.)

Marina and Ashton looked like a proper rock-star couple: she with her high cheekbones, leather jacket and heavy black eyeliner, he with his shoulder-length raven hair and cool confident expression. He wore a pendant: a silver claw hanging from black cord. If someone had asked her to guess their profession, horticulturalists would have been well down the list, but Eve knew of old that you couldn't judge a book by its cover.

'What can I get you? Would you like another pot of tea?' Eve's head was still full of the times she'd seen Ashton so far – and the knowing look he'd given her when he'd caught her watching him in the Cross Keys.

Marina's eyes were unfriendly, but Ashton gave her a lazy smile.

'I just wanted to ask you a question,' he said. 'A little bird told me you write about dead people. How cool is that?'

Despite the green nature of his work, he was dressed from head to toe in black, down to his edgy biker boots. She had a feeling the idea of an obituary writer might appeal to his gothic aesthetic.

'What makes you work here as well?' Marina asked. There was a very slight smile tilting the edge of the woman's lips now. She probably guessed Eve wasn't successful enough as a writer to do that full-time. But journalism was an uncertain business these days. Not many people had secure careers based on freelance work alone.

'She's in it for the free cake,' Viv said. Eve hadn't spotted her, dashing past with a tray laden with exquisite-looking miniature lemon curd tartlets, decorated with edible flowers. 'Also, I nagged her mercilessly until she agreed to help me. She has special powers when it comes to organisation.'

Ashton Foley stretched back in his chair and laughed, staring after Viv. 'Cool hair.'

The daffodil yellow she'd chosen had only recently replaced her winter colour – a sort of mistletoe white. Eve could never work out how her hair stayed so glossy, despite the constant dying. Her own mid-brown pixie crop never gleamed in quite the same way.

'Did you know Viv when you lived here as a child?'

'I do remember her a little.'

She'd be at least fifteen years older than him, but Eve wasn't surprised. Viv was memorable.

'I used to live here too,' Marina said. Her lips hardly moved as she spoke.

'I hadn't realised.'

'My parents moved away.'

That explained why she was lodging at the pub. Ashton was staying on at his mother's house, while she was away in New Zealand. Eve imagined he was making good use of having her cottage to himself. He could play host, and she had a feeling playing was his forte…

But as she had the thought, she remembered he'd said he had some kind of business in Saxford too – beyond the job for Billy Tozer. He'd claimed it was serious when he spoke to the woman she'd seen him visit – and just for a second he'd sounded like he meant it. What had that been about?

Eve could see that other customers needed her attention. 'Can I get you both anything else?'

Ashton smiled. 'Just the bill, thanks. You know, you should consider writing about me. I've a good story to tell. I know I'm not dead yet, but I enjoy living dangerously. And I like the idea of someone like you taking on the job. *Icon* magazine want to cover my work for Tozer, but they're going to send some middle-of-the-road hack of their own. I'll tell them I'm not interested unless it's you.'

Maybe he felt her involvement would add a certain mystique. A lot of people had a morbid fascination with obituary writers. It struck Eve as crazy. She wrote about people's lives: their achievements, their relationships, their highs and sometimes their lows. There was nothing creepy about it. It was frequently life-affirming and always compelling.

'You might want to read some of my work before you say that. And besides, obits are my specialty. Writing a biographical feature of a living subject takes a different set of skills and I'm too old to switch now.' What a load of boloney; the older you were, the wider your knowledge. But she didn't want to write about him; he made her feel uncomfortable, and he'd have expectations too. The only issue was turning him down without giving offence.

She went to prepare their bill so that they could settle up. After leaving it on the table she returned a minute later and found Ashton had left what was due, together with a ridiculously large gratuity.

He was halfway to the door now, but he turned on his way out. 'You don't look too old for anything.' His roguish dark eyes were on hers.

If Marina's expression had been cool before it was nothing to what it was now. But Ashton's comment was pure soft soap. Eve was almost old enough to be his mom, and she wouldn't be his type, anyway, nor he hers. She smiled inwardly. She was immune to being buttered up; when you spent years studying people you got to know when you were being played.

'I hope you'll think about my suggestion,' he said, as he left the teashop, Marina striding out in his wake.

'His *suggestion*, eh?' Viv said, hurtling past her again. 'And what might that have been? Will Simon be jealous?'

Simon was Viv's brother. Eve had only been out with him on five dates, and one of those had been a memorial concert for a murder victim. Things had fizzled out pretty quickly. Eve rolled her eyes. 'I've already told you we're just friends now.' *Have been since January…* 'He's still sowing his wild oats. I'm well past that stage.' Simon was six years younger than her, charming, friendly and flirty. Viv had warned her about that last quality from the start, but now seemed unwilling to let go of the idea of Eve as future sister-in-law.

'It just seems like a shame.' She cocked her head. 'I'm sure Simon's ready to settle down now. And he's looked very subdued lately.'

'You have a vivid imagination. He looks like a dog that's been let off the leash each time *I* see him. Can you please stop talking about us like we're star-crossed lovers?'

She got an exaggerated pout in response. 'Whatever. But moving back to Ashton's suggestion?'

'He wants me to write about him.'

Viv put a pot of tea down on a nearby table and drew Eve to one side. 'You don't sound very keen.'

'Writing about people who can answer back isn't my scene.'
She laughed.

'Seriously. When I produce a piece, I'm always truthful. It's unprofessional not to be. But I have a feeling Ashton Foley has a very firm idea of the sort of man he'd like me to portray. He'll want a puff piece rather than anything too perceptive, I'd guess.'

'You'd get to see inside Billy Tozer's place,' Viv pointed out. 'Meet him, probably.'

And that was the trouble: curiosity was already gnawing at Eve's gut. She wasn't star-struck – that wasn't her style – but all people were interesting. Finding out more about the rapper, as well as Ashton Foley and even his business manager – who appeared to have a chip on her shoulder – was a tempting prospect. Why was a man like Tozer paying to have his house filled with plants? And how on earth had a pair such as Ashton and Marina started their quirky business?

Viv gave her a knowing look. 'And as well as seeing all there is to see, you could probably name your fee for the work. Ashton's not short of a bob or two these days, and he's got plenty of influence. Even if he's not paying personally, he'll be calling the shots.'

A decent fee would be the icing on the cupcake…

'And of course,' Viv went on, 'if you went for it, you could give me all the inside information in advance of writing your article.'

'Hmm. It was you that implied he was trouble, before I even met him. You can't blame me for hesitating now.'

'But you never go by what I say; you always make up your own mind.'

'I look for concrete evidence. What I've seen so far is making me cautious.'

Viv put her hands on her hips. 'You're always cautious.'

'And it's served me well.' Though it hadn't stopped her getting into some sticky situations in the past.

'Well, you'll get another chance to observe him on Saturday afternoon.'

Saturday was the day of the Outside In raffle draw. Since he'd arrived in the village, Ashton had agreed to help raise funds for the church roof. He might be causing a stir with his partying and extravagant behaviour, but he was putting himself back on the map in other ways too. His role was to provide the prizes for the draw, as well as selecting the winning tickets. He was offering three 'lucky' people an Outside In consultation, with the chance that one might be picked to undergo the full company makeover, and feature in his new television series. She and Viv were catering for the event, but she'd donated, rather than buying a ticket. The possibility of having Ashton and Marina as temporary house guests didn't appeal.

She'd have to consider Ashton's request to write about him between now and then, and use her judgement when she'd had more time to think. He wasn't backward about coming forward and he was clearly used to getting his own way. If he pushed her, she ought to turn him down on principle, and besides, everything about him made her nervous. And yet she *was* curious. The strong desire to know more battled with a feeling of uneasiness in the pit of Eve's stomach.

Watch and wait: that had to be her motto.

CHAPTER FIVE

'I've run a lot of events in my time, but never one like this.' Viv was standing at one end of Saxford St Peter's church hall, under a high arched window, watching the hordes of locals who'd come in to see Ashton Foley performing the Outside In prize draw.

The tables in front of Eve were covered in bright sea-green cloths they'd raided from the supply of spares at Monty's, and crowded with platters of the teashop's cakes. The serving dishes were an array of the beautiful but mismatched crockery Viv favoured. It made you feel as though you were having tea with friends, and was one of the things Eve had admired the very first day she'd visited Monty's. She'd been curious to meet the creative person who'd managed to source items that complemented each other so well.

People were helping themselves to food and putting donations for the church roof into pretty honesty boxes made from recycled tea cartons. Opposite where Eve and Viv were standing, the church's hot water urns sat on a long trestle table. They looked as though they'd been doing service for generations, but the stuff that came out was steaming reassuringly. More honesty boxes, tea, coffee, milk and sugar sat next to them, together with Viv's mix-and-match cups and saucers.

The whole layout looked great against the backdrop of the cream walls. The sun helped: shafts of light from the leaded windows fell across the room's occupants.

'What's different about this event?' Eve turned her attention to her co-worker.

'You, you ninny. Look at us. We're just standing here. Well, okay, I'm keeping an eye on Jonny Bates, who appears to be pinching more cakes than he's entitled to while his mother's not looking. But overall, I'm not sweating blood, with my heart rate shooting up into the stratosphere. That's a first. I mean, I miss the adrenaline rush, obviously, but there are upsides. It's almost as though I'm one of the guests.'

Eve felt a little glow inside which she hoped wasn't transferring itself into a hint of smugness in her expression. 'Do you admit I was right to insist we got here an hour and a half ahead of time?'

Viv gave a dramatic sigh. 'All right. Yes. I'm sorry I whinged about it. And before you say it, you were right about the ingredients lists too. They don't look institutional when they're printed on that card and in that font. So, hooray for your weirdly organised nature.'

'And for your cooking skills. I'd love it if I could bake as well as you.'

'Heavens no, that would be awful! I'd be redundant. You can go off a person, you know.' Viv laughed. 'So what drives your life of meticulous organisation? Were you studying the finer points of project management when I was learning how to dye my hair?'

'No!'

Viv opened her eyes wide. 'I was kidding!'

Eve kicked herself. Six months on and she still hadn't managed to switch off her knee-jerk responses to Viv's 'jokes'.

'I like to be prepared, that's all.' She tried not to sound defensive. 'It's satisfying.' As soon as she knew what needed doing she'd twitch until she was tackling it. It was the same with her obituary work. She researched the heck out of her subjects before she started writing about them.

She was just wondering what she'd find if she investigated Ashton when he appeared at her elbow. He looked even more dramatic today than he had at the teashop, having added a black top hat to his outfit. Its brim was decorated with feathers, sharp animal teeth and bits of bone, making her think of voodoo.

'Good to see you again,' he said, staring into her eyes until she felt uncomfortable. His smile convinced her that he was well aware of the effect he was having. 'This all looks amazing.'

'Viv's work entirely.'

He turned to her friend. 'I have a feeling you're the reason the crowds are here. My part's just an added extra.'

'Flatterer!' said Viv. 'Go on, do it some more. I love it! But sadly I have to take issue with your assertion. I've never seen Moira from the village shop look so excited. She's certainly never worn that kind of dress to eat at Monty's, so I'd say your presence has had a profound effect.'

They all glanced in Moira's direction. The lipstick she'd applied was darker than usual, toning with her dyed auburn hair, and the dress that clung to her bountiful figure was alarmingly low-cut. Eve remembered all the gossip the storekeeper had passed on to Viv about Ashton. It looked as though recent experience must have overridden her previous prejudice. She certainly seemed to be treating the draw as a very special occasion.

'I guess you remember Moira from when you lived in the village,' Viv said.

A slow smile spread across Ashton's lips. 'Oh yes. I remember Moira.'

The storekeeper had made an immediate impression on Eve too, the moment she'd entered her premises that first time. As well as squeezing information out of the unwary, a lot of her comments were unthinkingly passive-aggressive. Still, Eve was already starting to feel a weird kind of bond with her. And there was no doubt she was a useful source of gossip.

Ashton's eyes were on Eve again. Perhaps he'd read something in her look. 'She's run the shop for as long as I can remember. She and Paul are village institutions.'

Eve could see Paul now, standing hunched near the exit, looking as though he'd like to disappear through it.

'I'd better go and get ready for the draw,' Ashton said. 'But you and I need to talk about that article, Eve. I can put a copy of *Icon* magazine and some details about Outside In through your door.' He raised his eyebrows. 'Then you can have a think.'

She paused. That would mean giving out her address, but it would sound weird if she asked him to bring the package to the teashop instead. What was it about the man that made her so uneasy? Was it just the way he flirted with her, or was there something more sinister setting her alarm bells ringing? Before she could answer, he spoke again, his smile back as though he'd read her thoughts.

'I know you're at Elizabeth's Cottage on Haunted Lane. You've moved into the most renowned house in Saxford St Peter.'

It was true. Each successive occupant of her house was known by the villagers as its 'keeper', and Eve was no exception. It was weird, but she liked the feeling of history it gave her and the thought of Elizabeth's noble deeds; they were something to live up to.

'Right. I'll look out for the package then.'

He nodded and turned towards the stage at the far end of the hall where Saxford St Peter's vicar, the Reverend Jim Thackeray, was busy with a boxful of raffle tickets and a portable mic, which was making ominous crackling noises. After a moment, Jim sang into it, his grey hair quivering slightly, and for a second the villagers were treated to the opening of 'Non, Je Ne Regrette Rien'. Moira Squires pursed her lips. The vicar's rendition was every bit as powerful as Edith Piaf's; his height and bulk probably helped with projection.

A moment later, Ashton mounted the stage in one quick, agile move. The vicar didn't have to call for quiet; the effect of the guy's presence seemed to travel as fast as a wave of light across the room. The crowds drew closer to the stage, cakes and tea in hand, their eyes on the action. Even the children in the room were silent. It struck Eve that Ashton might look a little frightening, towering on the stage in his tall black hat with its feathers, teeth and bones.

The vicar introduced him as the artistic director of Outside In. Eve was struck by the rector's expression. He was wryly jovial as usual on the surface, but there was a knowing look in his worldly eyes. Maybe he was aware he was part of Ashton's PR campaign. The church roof appeal enabled him to position himself as a philanthropist to villagers who might otherwise focus on his past as a lawbreaker.

'It's so good to be back at home,' Ashton said, to immediate applause from several female members of the audience, including Moira Squires. Her reaction continued to surprise Eve. She was always keen to present herself as a moral guardian of the local community, and wasn't known for letting bygones be bygones.

'You've no idea how long I've dreamed of this,' Ashton went on, his voice low, eyes mischievous. 'To come back to Saxford having seen the world, when at one time I was locked up here in Suffolk.' There was an audible intake of breath at that. Her neighbours hadn't imagined he'd tackle his past head-on, Eve guessed. 'To return having achieved something, with an innovative business to my name, that changes people's lives.'

He made it sound like he'd solved world hunger. Still, you couldn't deny he'd come good – as far as anyone could tell.

'For all you young ones out there,' he went on, 'the take-home point is that it's never too late to change course. You just have to be creative if you want to achieve your goals. It's important to do things on your own terms.'

His eyes were far away for a moment, and Eve had a feeling he was thinking of some very particular and personal ambition. Was this all about Outside In? Or was there something else going on?

'And now,' Ashton's voice dropped lower still, 'it's my great pleasure to do my bit to support St Peter's, and the man who presides over the place.' He shot a sidelong glance at the vicar. Jim Thackeray's look in response was ironic, but Ashton didn't see it. He was still gazing down at his audience. 'So, let me cut to the chase, and draw the first winning ticket.' The vicar held out the box that contained the raffle slips and Ashton turned away to pick one. A moment later he crouched down so that he was at the same level as the adults in the audience and let his eyes drift over the room. 'It's blue, number seventy-two,' he said, turning it over. 'Aha! Moira Squires, you are a winner!'

A rosy glow showed under the storekeeper's carefully applied make-up. 'Oh my goodness! How exciting!' She turned to her fellow audience members, her hands held up to her face. Her husband, Paul, gave an audible grunt and raised his eyes to heaven.

'We'll talk, Moira,' Ashton said. 'Fix up a time for me to come and visit you.' His voice was like treacle, his tone suggestive. 'So, next up' – he turned back towards the vicar again, put his hand in the box and glanced at the slip of paper now held between his fingers – 'we have a pink ticket. It's number ninety-one.' He crouched down again, and when no one raised their hand, he turned the ticket over. 'Hey, this is like a trip down memory lane. Amber? Amber Ingram?' He stood up tall again and Eve watched as some chatter started, not far from where she and Viv were standing. Several people were looking at a pretty woman with long, wavy copper-coloured hair, wearing a marine-blue dress. Eve guessed she'd be in her early thirties, similar in age to Ashton. An old school or girlfriend, perhaps?

Eve moved forward and shifted her angle slightly so she could see Amber's face. No one would notice her interest; all eyes were either on the woman she was watching or on Ashton.

There was a guy standing with his arm around Amber: a man with blond curls, styled to look rakishly ruffled but entirely immobile, so clearly relying on a lot of wax. It was only a split second before his voice rang out. 'Great to know we'll see more of you, Ashton. We can reminisce about old times.'

'Sounds good, man.'

The star of the show smiled that lazy smile of his, but Eve's attention was divided between him and Amber Ingram, whose cheekbones were blotchy and red. She was rubbing the back of her neck with her right hand and Eve saw her swallow.

The man she was with turned to her, but without really paying her proper attention, Eve noted. 'This is excellent, darling. Well done! How many tickets did you buy?'

But she didn't answer, and he didn't appear to care. He was too busy looking pleased with himself, cool in his blue shirt, navy waistcoat and trousers.

Eve raised her eyes to Ashton Foley again, whose smile hadn't faded. She had a feeling he hadn't missed a thing as he stood there, looking down on his audience.

'So,' he said, after a moment, 'time to draw the last ticket. And' – he turned to the vicar for the final time – 'it's pink again. One hundred and four.' He turned the slip of paper over. 'Oh wow! This is going to be a special one for me. Tina Adcock, where are you?'

A blonde woman – in her fifties, Eve guessed – lifted her head slowly. She was standing just a few feet to Eve's left. Great figure, good cheekbones too, and a sort of insolence in her look, as though daring anyone to cross her. She had a man with her who appeared significantly less enthusiastic about her win than Amber's companion had been about hers.

'Most of you probably know I was taught by Tina and her husband when I was at secondary school,' Ashton said. 'And Carl' – he looked at the man next to Tina – 'or Mr Adcock, I feel I should still say, I have to thank you.' He paused for a moment and Eve watched Carl's wary eyes. 'It was your words that came back to me, when I was trapped inside the young offenders' institute. You told me I'd never make anything of myself. I vowed right then and there to prove you wrong. If you hadn't given me that impetus, who knows what might have happened. I certainly might not have founded such an amazing and fulfilling business.'

Eve was suddenly aware of Ashton's manager, Marina Shaw, looking on from the sidelines with a stony face.

'I feel that working on your house will give me the chance to pay you back in some small way. I'll contact you to arrange a time for your consultation.'

As he leaped down from the stage, Eve and Viv moved to parcel up some of the uneaten cakes. They'd decided to invite the villagers to take them home in return for an additional donation. Eve was tying each box up with ribbon when Amber Ingram and her partner walked past them. The guy had his hand on Amber's elbow, guiding her towards the door, which would have irritated Eve.

'What a successful evening,' he said, as they moved on in the direction of the exit. 'If we end up getting picked to go on his TV show, just think what excellent publicity it will be, with prints of my designs up on all our walls. It'll showcase my work as much as his!'

Once again, Amber Ingram said nothing.

CHAPTER SIX

The week after the prize draw, Eve saw most of the players in what seemed to be the drama of Ashton Foley's life. Before, they'd been unidentified Saxford St Peter residents, but now she was able to pick them out: anxious Amber Ingram and her puffed-up blond partner; insolent, sexy Tina Adcock and her husband and fellow teacher, Carl.

It was Marina who came to drop off the package of information Ashton had promised, containing a sample copy of *Icon* and a brochure about Outside In. Eve glimpsed her through the window and instinctively ducked out of sight, startling Gus, who leaped back himself and hit his rear on the coffee table.

It wasn't until Wednesday that she saw Ashton himself. She was in the village store, where everyone in Saxford was destined to cross paths sooner or later. As she entered, he was already in the queue, wearing a black velvet coat that toned perfectly with his raven-coloured hair. She gathered the vegetables, cheese and crusty loaf she wanted quietly. She guessed he'd start asking about the article again as soon as he saw her.

The smell of the fresh bread filled her nostrils as she took her place in the queue. Toby Falconer supplied it to Moira. Although Jo cooked all the evening meals at the pub, its bed and breakfast operation was his baby. He made loaves for the Cross Keys' guests each morning, and extended his batches so the villagers could buy his wares too. Happily, breakfasts at the pub were open to non-residents as well. Eve was planning another visit there soon: Toby's full English platter set her up for the day like no other meal.

Ashton had reached the front of the queue.

'So, we're on for tomorrow, Moira?' He made it sound like a date, but Eve presumed it was the storekeeper's turn to take up her prize. She was all of a flutter now.

'Oh yes, Ashton, I'm expecting you. Paul will hold the fort here at the shop while I show you round.'

Eve made a mental note to avoid the store the following day. Moira's husband hated customers, especially those not born in Saxford, let alone anyone from outside the county of Suffolk.

'Great to know I'll have your undivided attention,' Ashton said, in that low, caressing voice of his.

Moira giggled.

'I'll be visiting Amber and Justin Ingram tomorrow too.'

Justin was probably the puffed-up blond guy, then.

The storekeeper's smile faded slightly.

'Not before you, of course,' Ashton added, leaning forward. 'I've pushed them back to the afternoon to make sure we have plenty of time together. And I'm not bothering with Tina and Carl Adcock until Friday.'

Moira simpered again.

'As for Amber and Justin, their visit might be a challenge. They say you should never work with children and animals.' He laughed. 'And they've got a son, haven't they?'

Moira nodded eagerly, clearly pleased she had all the right information at her fingertips. 'That's right – Leo. But you needn't worry, he's growing up into a nice young man.'

'Ah, but kids hate you encroaching on their territory, and they're not usually interested in indoor plant design.'

Moira smiled. 'He's not at that rebellious stage yet. Amber came in here for ingredients a couple of months ago when she was baking for his birthday party. He's only just turned seven.'

She probably knew his shoe size too…

'Oh, I see.' Ashton laughed. 'Well, I'll keep my fingers crossed then.'

Moira smiled indulgently. 'You might finish before he gets home from school, anyway. It's still term time. The youngsters don't break up until next week.' She raised her eyes to heaven. 'Paul and I are always well aware when the school holidays start. The children are all in here, tearing around and knocking things over.'

'How much do I owe you?'

'Let's see. Fourteen pounds ten. Very many thanks, Ashton.' She took the fifty pound note he handed her and scrabbled around in her till for the change, seeming to manage the task without taking her eyes off him. 'Until tomorrow, then…'

It was only then that Ashton turned and saw Eve, two people back in the queue. 'Hello again! I hope you got my package? I'm looking forward to hearing from you. Maybe you could let me know by Sunday? I've already told *Icon* I don't want anyone but you.'

She wasn't busy at the moment, but a fascinating obituary subject could turn up at any time. It wasn't like you got advance notice. She didn't want to neglect her real work to flatter Foley's ego. Curiosity vied with a feeling that she'd regret it if she gave in to his demands.

'Sure. I'll have another read through and let you know.'

He gave her a slow smile, and finally turned to make his way across the store, manoeuvring round a stand housing newspapers and magazines. Before he reached the exit, the bell above the door jangled and Betty's partner, Howard Green, walked in.

'Howard!' Ashton said. 'How very delightful to see you in here. Following me around?' There was an edge to his voice, and Howard said nothing in reply. A moment later, as the two men passed each other, Ashton let his right shoulder knock hard against Howard's. The store wasn't that cramped; Eve was certain it had been deliberate. All pretence at being polite to his mother's boyfriend had clearly dropped since Betty had left the village. Howard was still reining in his feelings, though. It couldn't be easy. Eve guessed he must really mind about Betty.

She was forced to turn away from the spectacle at that moment. Moira was ready to take her goods. The storekeeper didn't pass comment about Howard and Ashton, but her eyes spoke volumes. She caught Eve's look for a second, then raised her gaze over her shoulder, whereupon her eyes widened slightly. Then she focused on Eve again. She was dying to pass on some nugget of gossip, Eve was sure, but was thwarted, given one of the subjects was still in the store.

'That's eleven pounds ninety, dear,' Moira said, pursing her lips after one more glance over Eve's shoulder. 'And we'll see you again soon, I hope.'

Yes, desperate to offload.

As Eve turned, she realised there was something about Howard Green that had increased Moira's level of interest. Now that she could see him head-on, she noticed there was a dark bluish bruise visible on his left cheekbone. She made her journey to the door as slow as possible. Moira was bound to ask the question.

'Good morning, Howard. Whatever's happened to you? You look as though you've been in the wars!'

'It's nothing.'

'Witch hazel is the thing for bruises,' Moira said, 'but it does look nasty…' Her voice was heavy with curiosity.

Just as Eve was letting the door swing shut behind her, Howard spoke again: 'There was a sheep in the road. Had to pull up suddenly. Face hit the steering wheel.'

CHAPTER SEVEN

On Friday, an hour into her afternoon shift at Monty's, Eve had nipped into the food prep area to sample the results of Viv's new recipe: an Earl Grey tea-flavoured cupcake topped with an orange glaze. Delicate strands of peel lay on top, interspersed with tiny slivers of fresh mint.

'Heaven,' Eve said. 'They'll look beautiful on the tables, alongside the hellebores.'

Viv smiled. 'Thank you! How's it going out front?' She walked over to the doorway to survey Monty's eating area.

Eve's heart sank. She'd been hoping Viv wouldn't emerge from the kitchen any time soon. A second later, her friend's eyes opened wide. She turned and walked swiftly towards Eve, a look of irritation mingled with sympathy on her face.

Eve began counting to ten.

'I'm so sorry,' Viv said, shaking her head and patting Eve's arm. 'He is such an idiot!'

Simon, Viv's brother, was in Monty's having tea with Polly Cartwright, a comely PR professional who lived in the village.

Eve thought about pretending not to understand, but that would only spin the conversation out. 'Please stop treating this like an unresolved emotional cliffhanger in a soap opera. I know I seem like someone with limitless patience, but I'm having to work at it.'

Viv looked puzzled. 'You don't mind?'

Please take the comment to heart this time. 'Now you're getting it!'

Eve had just gone back through to join Angie, who was helping out again, when the teashop door was flung open, sending Monty's bell ringing hectically. The rush of air lifted the yellow tablecloths nearest the entrance and the man she recognised as Justin Ingram, husband of Amber, rushed in. His blond, carefully tousled curls were falling about the place in a way they weren't meant to. This was a guy that used a lot of wax; if his locks were shifting, something was up.

His eyes ran over the room as Eve went to close the door behind him. She could already see a woman pulling on her cardigan, an indignant look in her eye.

After a moment, without glancing at Eve, Angie or any of the other customers, Justin marched to the far end of the teashop. Amber was sitting there with a friend. Her blue eyes were on her husband, confusion and anxiety written all over her face.

'We need to talk.' Justin had reached her table now. Eve had seen trouble brew up in pubs near where she'd lived in Kilburn, before she'd moved to Suffolk – had had a man land at her feet on the pavement outside one particular establishment, in fact – but brawls weren't usual in Monty's. Yet Justin had that air about him. Eve tensed, and exchanged a look with Angie, who nodded. They were ready to intervene if required.

Amber gripped the table in front of her, and the friend she was with put a hand on her arm.

'I said we need to talk.' Justin spoke through gritted teeth. 'Now. In private.'

Amber stood up and fumbled in her bag for money to leave for her bill. Her hands shook as she put it on the table, ignoring her friend's offer to pay. There was a blush spreading up her neck as she turned to face her husband. He gave a sharp nod towards the door and Amber walked ahead of him, through the hush of the shop, with all eyes on her. This was ridiculous. Eve wished she could do something to make everyone carry on talking, but she couldn't think what. Amber kept her gaze straight ahead, but her blush deepened as she pulled the door open slowly and walked out into the cold. Justin strode after her and grabbed her elbow as they crossed the lane to the village green.

That evening, Eve took Gus out for a stroll, down Haunted Lane and towards Elizabeth's Walk, the path that led on towards the marshes. As they reached the estuary, gorse bushes gave way to banks of reeds, which shifted in the light breeze. Eve drew her navy puffer jacket more closely around her and did up the zipper. It was the coat she wore for warmth when the weather was dry; less self-advertising than her yellow mac. The tide was high. Ahead of them, moonlight lit the water, picking out the shapes of roosting wading birds out on the saltings.

Eve could hear creatures rustling in the undergrowth, so she kept Gus on his leash, though she let it out so he could investigate all the smells on offer without getting into trouble. Her mind had been on Justin Ingram's outburst in Monty's. It had left her uneasy. She'd watched him and Amber walk away from the teashop, to check he had his temper under control. Now her thoughts turned to Ashton Foley's run-in with Howard Green, two days earlier at the village store.

'You know, Gus,' she said, following him almost into the reeds as he followed his nose, 'Howard's excuse for his bruised cheek doesn't sound at all likely.' She could only see the dachshund's rear, but she told herself he was paying her rapt attention, even if he appeared to be focused on something down in the mud. 'Surely he'd have been wearing a seat belt? And even if he wasn't, he'd likely have had his hands braced against the steering wheel as he pulled up. I can't imagine him hitting his head braking.' She thought of Ashton's words to Howard in the village store: 'Following me around?' It implied their paths had crossed since his mother had left Saxford.

At last, Gus tired of his explorations and they walked on again, between the marshes and the estuary on one side, and a ditch and flat fields on the other. The reeds rose up on both sides, enclosing the walkway.

The night was quiet, just the sound of the waves in the distance, and the occasional hoot of an owl, so the voices, when she heard them, were easily audible in the cool evening air.

'Your actions have consequences! Please just try to think about that. Can you imagine how it will look?'

Eve recognised Marina Shaw's voice instantly, waspish and low.

There was a laugh. Ashton. 'Get over yourself! I'm good at handling publicity anyway.'

'You're creating problems when there's no need!' Her voice had risen. 'And there's more to it than that. You don't know when to stop. Someone will end up bringing you down if you push your luck!'

They were just visible now. Shadows through the reeds, approaching quickly; she could see the tips of their cigarettes, or whatever they were smoking. The glowing ends looked too substantial for anything shop-bought. Roll-ups. Maybe with something other than tobacco inside.

The last thing Eve felt like was having to make polite conversation with them both, especially when they were having a row. She crouched down and spoke softly to Gus. 'Let's get going, buddy.'

The dachshund was also looking in the direction the voices had come from. For once, he seemed to agree with Eve. They turned and walked smartly back up the estuary path.

Marina had gone quiet. Maybe she'd seen them. If she hadn't already, she soon would, once she and Gus were back on Elizabeth's Walk, which was a straight track. Eve kept up the pace, not caring. So long as they thought she'd been on the move the whole time, a few yards ahead of them, she could pretend she hadn't heard.

She didn't want to get involved, and it hardened her resolve. Even Ashton's own business manager thought he was trouble. She didn't know in what way Ashton was 'pushing his luck' but she might find out if she agreed to write about him. It was an excellent reason for turning down his request.

The following morning, after a boisterous beach session with Gus, Eve texted Ashton to tell him she couldn't manage to work his article into her schedule. It would require too many hours.

He replied ten minutes later.

That's a shame. Why don't you pop round tomorrow at nine for a coffee and pastry breakfast? I promise I won't try to talk you round. I just want your advice on something. I'm at my mum's down on Heath Lane. Apple Tree Cottage, in Blind Eye Wood.

Blind Eye Wood covered the ground between the seaward houses of Saxford St Peter and the heath which overlooked the beach. Its name came from the days when smugglers had used it to bring contraband covertly from the mouth of the River Sax towards a quiet back lane leading south from the village. Everyone had known to steer clear of the woods if they saw a pinprick of light out to sea, or the answering signal of a lantern glowing onshore, giving the all-clear.

Going there to meet Ashton could be hazardous in a different way. Logic told her to say no, but at the back of her mind a tiny sliver of curiosity still lurked. And she was free. She had no shift at Monty's; they didn't open until after lunch on a Sunday. But if this was a ruse to try to talk her round, she'd be ready.

For all her resolve though, she didn't sleep well on Saturday night. At one point she thought she heard people running out in the lane, and a second later, Gus whined. It set her pulse racing. The legend associated with the footfalls was high in her mind. Hearing them signified danger.

CHAPTER EIGHT

Eve took Gus with her the following morning. If Ashton didn't want him in the house, that would reduce her interaction with him to a moment on the doorstep, which would suit her fine. And if he did invite her in, they wouldn't stay long. She'd want to get Gus down to the beach. She'd gone for an outfit that was rather formal for the dog walk: a woollen trouser suit with a smart overcoat. She usually found her clothes had an effect on the people she went to interview. Formal dress showed respect, but in Ashton's case it might also ensure he remembered she was only there on business.

Their route took them down Love Lane. Gus strained at his leash as they passed the Cross Keys, his mind clearly on Hetty. After they'd crossed the junction the way lost its pavement. Wildflowers grew on the grass verges, presenting a sea of pinks, purples and whites: dead-nettles, ground ivy with its funnel-shaped violet blooms and white dog violets. Eve had been looking them up; it seemed wrong not to know more about her surroundings. Gus was investigating the ground ivy closely. To Eve it smelled of tomcat, so that might explain why. He glanced at her over his shoulder and gave her a suspicious look, as though he suspected she was involved in some form of trickery.

As they neared Blind Eye Wood the road became little more than a track. Gus darted after every rustle in the undergrowth. At last Eve could see an isolated house ahead of them, on the edge of the woods. This must be Apple Tree Cottage; the garden looked like a mini orchard. A beautiful deep pink was just showing on the tips of the trees' unopened buds. The house itself was tiny but neat and painted pale turquoise, with a sea-green door and woodwork. The casement windows were made up of six panes each. Outside in the front garden sat a low log pile, depleted after the winter. If this had been Ashton's childhood home, it must feel strange coming back. She thought of the places he'd lived: here, the young offenders' institute and friends' floors and sofas down in London. But now he had freedom and lots of money. Whatever his current home was like, she was betting it was high-end compared with his mother's house.

Gus had stopped to investigate a new smell. She turned to urge him on, but he wouldn't budge.

'What is it, buddy? What have you noticed?' He was straining at his leash, his eyes on something deep in the undergrowth. For a second he glanced at her as though she was monumentally stupid not to understand and support his desire to hare off into the trees.

'No way. I'm sorry, but if I let you off your leash now, we probably won't knock on Ashton's door until midday,' she said, crouching down next to him and ruffling his fur. 'I know I'm making you miss out, but tormenting small creatures isn't on, anyway.'

When she stood up again and glanced in the direction of Apple Tree Cottage once more, she started.

Outside the house, standing under the porch, was Howard Green. She was surprised. After the encounter she'd seen between him and Ashton, she would have expected him to keep his distance. As Gus was still putting in a concerted effort to head off in a different direction, she was forced to stop mid-stride, and saw Howard without him seeing her.

She was about to call out a greeting, but something held her back. He was behaving oddly. He hadn't knocked, so far as she could tell, and now it looked as though he was about to turn away again without making his presence known. His anxious eyes ran over the front garden and Eve stepped back instinctively to avoid being seen. It meant she moved in the direction Gus had been tugging. Sensing capitulation, the dachshund pulled harder still. Eve hoped to goodness Howard didn't pick up on the rustling and sound of scrabbling paws. It would be clear she'd been watching him if Gus gave her away.

Through the leaves of a holly bush that stood between her and Apple Tree Cottage, Eve watched as Howard walked back down Betty Foley's garden path, his shoulders hunched, hands in his coat pockets, eyes still wary. However much she and Gus dug themselves into the undergrowth he'd spot them lurking there if he turned towards the village. And if she pushed her way through the vegetation he'd see their retreating backs, which would look even more peculiar. She made up her mind to brazen it out after all, and took a step into the lane, calling: 'C'mon, Gus!' over her shoulder.

But Howard Green had disappeared.

She walked up to the end of Apple Tree Cottage's front garden and saw him in the distance, already at the other side of the woods, striding over the heath. He was making for the beach instead, and he'd covered the ground quickly.

As she turned to walk up the path, she wondered whether she should tell Ashton what she'd seen, but she felt conflicted, given she didn't understand what it meant. So far, she'd witnessed Ashton winding Howard up, and Howard exhibiting restraint. Maybe she should give him the benefit of the doubt.

But when she knocked on the door, she found she needn't have wasted time worrying about it. There was no answer. It seemed, after all her worries, that she'd been stood up.

Quite annoying.

Ten minutes later, Eve was sitting in St Peter's church. She'd never been a regular attendee when she'd lived in London; she wasn't really a believer, and felt uncertain about organised religion. However, Jim Thackeray, vicar of St Peter's, encouraged all comers – of any religion or none at all – and she had a lot of time for him. He was determined to keep the church at the heart of the community, and enjoyed regular outreach sessions at the Cross Keys pub too. Eve hadn't planned to attend his service that day, given her appointment with Ashton, but she knew she'd feel more grounded if she went and listened to him talk, to say nothing of singing her heart out in a beautiful building. Dogs were welcomed. Jim Thackeray said he was happy to accommodate all God's creatures, though he dreaded special occasions when he had to deal with donkeys and the like.

She couldn't help noticing that the congregation was a little thinner on the ground than usual. As the villagers gathered outside the church afterwards, the vicar walked over to her.

'I'm so glad you came, Eve. The Lord and I are feeling a bit neglected today. No Ashton; not that I have him down as a believer, but he was here last week, and I have to start somewhere. And no Howard Green. What's more, not a single Falconer, and they're my go-to parishioners. And then, the final shock: no Viv. I hope they haven't served up dodgy shellfish at the Cross Keys or something.'

It did seem odd. She was about to say that she'd heard nothing from any of them, when her friend appeared. Eve's smile was automatic, but it faded the instant she took in Viv's expression.

'What's happened?'

Viv's face was white, her teeth chattering, her arms wrapped round her torso. The vicar rushed forward just as Eve did, concern in his kind eyes.

'Ashton Foley's been shot.' Viv swallowed. 'Jo found him less than an hour ago, down in Blind Eye Wood. She and the boys are with the police now, over at the pub.' Her blue eyes were wide with shock as she looked from Eve to Jim Thackeray. 'He was just lying there. She says he's dead.'

CHAPTER NINE

Monty's was packed that afternoon. Early online reports said the police were treating Ashton's death as suspicious. Friends and neighbours were sitting at the teashop tables, speaking rapidly in hushed tones, coming to terms with what had happened. Eve had managed to overhear the way the gossip was leaning. Ashton was a Londoner now, but he'd lived in Saxford once. The villagers suspected his killing had something to do with the trouble he'd gotten into in the past. Maybe he'd crossed an old enemy, connected with the cannabis he used to sell when he was a kid. Eve could see the use of a gun seemed to fit with that idea. Even if Ashton had only dealt with a small-time local dealer, that person might have had the right contacts to get hold of a weapon. But still Eve wondered. Ashton had ruffled plenty of feathers amongst his personal contacts too.

Moira Squires had been the first person to arrive at the teashop, soon after the doors opened.

'Anyone would think *she'd* found the body!' Viv said.

Eve looked over to where Moira was sitting, elbows on the table, dabbing her eyes with a lacy handkerchief. She'd come alone, saying she felt wobbly, and Viv and Eve had been ministering to her.

'Think she's all right?'

Viv nodded. 'I've given her the works: the intense chocolate brownies and espresso-infused caramel squares. Those and the pot of tea ought to set her right. Don't get me wrong, it's a shock for us all, but Moira? She'll be over it by tomorrow, and lapping up

all the attention she gets for being one of the prize draw winners.'
She gave Eve a look. 'She's probably only in here at all because it
keeps her in the public eye.'

The village store closed early on Sundays, so it was possible Viv
had a point.

'Cruel, but fair, Eve! I know what you're thinking, but deny it
if you can.'

She couldn't. Moira had had a steady stream of visitors to her
table. She'd sat there all afternoon as curious acquaintances came
and went.

'I still can't believe how her attitude to Ashton changed once he
arrived back in the village,' Viv said in an undertone.

'That struck me too, after all the gossip she fed you.'

Viv nodded. 'Even before he got into trouble with the police,
I remember Moira telling all and sundry what a tearaway he was,
largely because he and his mates used to go into the shop en
masse. A gang of hulking teenage boys wasn't her idea of fun. She
was pretty melodramatic about it.' Viv had been widowed young,
with her three boys to look after and a business to run. Eve could
see how Moira's histrionics in the face of minor irritations might
have irked her. 'She was always checking her stock after Ashton
had left the shop,' Viv went on, 'to make sure he hadn't pinched
anything. Everyone waiting to be served saw her at it, so it gave
him a reputation, whether or not it was justified at that stage.'

Eve remembered Moira chatting to Ashton about what a
nuisance children were during the school vacation. She'd clearly
forgotten he was once one of them, but she doubted Ashton
had. What had he thought when he'd pulled out her ticket at the
prize draw? It sounded as though he'd had difficult relationships
with both Moira and Carl Adcock. And then there was Amber
Ingram, who'd looked so uncomfortable when her ticket had
been selected…

She turned her attention to the events of that morning. 'Have you heard how Jo is?'

Viv grinned. 'You know what she's like. It was Matt who needed the stiff drink when he heard the news. An excuse for a snifter if you ask me. Toby told me Jo's been bossing the police around and keeping an eye out for Marina Shaw. They feel she's under their care, given she's lodging at the pub.'

Eve couldn't imagine Ashton's business manager welcoming the attention. She was too prickly to turn to another at a moment of crisis.

As she went through to Monty's office, ready to draw up the business's weekly plan, she was preoccupied with thoughts of Ashton. His knowing smile filled her mind. He'd given her a creeping sense of unease, but she'd never thought he'd be the one in danger – rather, somehow, that he might make trouble for others. She felt a weird sense of guilt. Had she been wrong about him? But then she thought of the argument she'd overheard between him and Marina on Friday night. Marina had implied he'd been pushing the boundaries, and she was clearly worried about the consequences. Ashton's dismissive response rang in her ears.

And then she remembered Gus as they'd waited outside Apple Tree Cottage. He'd been desperate to go into the woods. Had he known something was wrong, too? If she'd followed him, would she have been the one to find Ashton?

She'd broken the back of her work when her mobile rang. A saccharine voice checked her identity.

'Yes, this is Eve Mallow.'

'*My name's Portia Coldwell. I'm calling from* Icon *magazine. I'm so sorry to contact you on a Sunday. I was in the office, catching up with some work, when I heard the terrible news about Ashton.*'

Eve's response was a general mumble. She was trying to work out how the woman knew her number.

'*We were so delighted that you'd agreed to write the feature on him for us.*'

The day was getting weirder. Eve took a moment. 'I was actually due to talk to Ashton about that this morning. I thought you had someone on the staff who wanted to do the work.'

There was a brief pause. '*Well, we did, initially,*' Portia said at last. '*But between ourselves, we've just had to tell the person in question that we're letting them go. Restructuring, you know? Print journalism's such a tough business these days.*'

'And now they're refusing to cooperate?' Eve took a deep breath.

'*We think it's best not to involve the individual concerned.*'

They'd probably just been caught cutting up the editor's favourite jacket or something.

'*Besides,*' Portia gushed, '*as soon as we heard Ashton had convinced you to take the project on, we were sold on the idea. Only of course, the nature of the work will be more your usual line now. We can send you a fresh contract to reflect the fact that you'll be writing his obituary.*'

'A fresh contract?' She felt like a parrot.

'*Yes. If you've already signed the one we sent to Ashton, do just discard that. This one will replace it.*'

She was starting to see her visit to Apple Tree Cottage that morning in a whole new light now. He'd been convinced he could talk her round, clearly. She must look like a soft touch. The thought triggered an adrenaline rush.

'*We already have your address, of course.*' Of course. '*So I'll pop the contract in the post tomorrow.*'

'I'll need to discuss my fee,' she said at last. It was time to take control.

'*It'll be just the same as for the feature,*' Portia said, her tone soothing.

Eve didn't like to admit she had no idea what that would have been. They'd probably halve it if they knew, and Ashton was no longer there to call the shots.

*

'You agreed?'

Eve had relayed the whole thing to Viv as soon as there was a quiet moment. Angie was covering the teashop. Back in the kitchen, Viv poured them each a cup of Assam and thrust one of her mixed peel Easter teacakes into Eve's hand. The sweet orange flavour and sultanas balanced with the bite of the rind to provide the perfect pick-me-up.

Eve nodded as she took a bite. 'The pay will probably be good, but more importantly, it's my specialty.'

'You want to know what happened to him.'

'I want to know about his life. I always did.' But it was true, when you interviewed a murder victim's closest contacts, looking at the detail of their lives – past and present – you had a fighting chance of finding anyone who'd had a motive to kill them. The thought of sitting opposite someone in an interview, and suddenly seeing their guilt, sent shivers down Eve's spine. Your eyes gave a lot away, when you suddenly saw the truth. That fact had almost cost her her life just last year.

At that moment Angie appeared in the kitchen doorway. From her expression, Eve had a feeling her break might be under threat. She took a larger bite of her teacake.

'Sorry,' the student said. 'The police are here. Apparently they want to speak to you, Eve.'

Viv turned to Eve, her eyes wide. 'Blimey. If they only give you one call, make sure it's me you ring. I want to know what's going on.'

Eve gave her friend a look. 'Gee, thanks so much for your concern.'

As she walked through to Monty's main room, she saw the detective sergeant she'd met last time she was involved in a murder enquiry. It was a relief. She'd never been interviewed by him, or even known his name, but she'd seen him in action and he'd seemed all right: quick, intelligent and level-headed. But outside, beyond Monty's bay window, she could see Detective Inspector Nigel Palmer, who was the sergeant's polar opposite: lazy, pig-headed, dismissive and— But maybe she should stop. Getting herself wound up before talking to him wouldn't help. What on earth had she done to earn his presence? Surely he'd have more important people to see. But she knew he'd resented her interference on his previous big case; this was likely personal.

As she and the detective sergeant made for the door, she caught Moira Squires' look. Just Eve's luck that she was still there. The storekeeper's eyes were like saucers.

That was that then. It would be all around the village once the store reopened: *Eve Mallow, taken in for questioning.*

CHAPTER TEN

Eve's heart sank as she let DI Palmer and the sergeant (Gregory Boles, it turned out) into Elizabeth's Cottage. She'd already concluded she should tell them about Howard Green's odd behaviour outside Ashton's mother's house. Trust Palmer to get to her before she got to him.

It took a few moments to get them settled on the couches in the living room. Gus was the cause of the hold-up. He was interested in both men, but especially suspicious of Palmer. The dachshund's instincts were infallible where the DI was concerned. The weighty man looked down at her beautiful dog, a sneer on his lips.

'C'mon, Gus. You come and sit by me.' He was still looking at Palmer as though poised for attack. 'I was going to contact you.' She went straight into her story about Howard. Best to get it out of the way.

Palmer raised an eyebrow. 'So you stood in the lane, monitoring his movements?'

'He took me by surprise, and I was held up for a moment anyway. Gus was trying to sneak off into the woods. It meant I had to pause, and the more I hesitated, the more it seemed best to hold back.'

'You thought he was behaving oddly?' the sergeant said.

She hadn't wanted to plant ideas in their heads, but there was nothing for it. 'Yes, a little.'

'What makes you say that?' Palmer's tone was disparaging, as though he felt her instincts weren't worth his time.

'He was glancing around him, as though he was checking he hadn't been seen.'

'He was right to be cautious, given you were there, spying on him.'

She ignored Palmer's comment and tried not to obsess about what the detective sergeant might be writing in his notepad. 'I didn't hear him knock at the door, but I can't swear he didn't. I was focused on Gus.'

'Your impression was that he was hanging around outside Apple Tree Cottage without announcing himself?' The sergeant leaned forward.

She nodded at last.

'Could he have just let himself out of the house?'

'He could.' He might have found keys on Ashton's body if he'd killed him. But Betty Foley could have given him a set too. It was clear they were still in a relationship, even though Viv had explained he'd never moved in. And on top of that, people in Saxford had the charmingly innocent habit of leaving spare copies under flowerpots and the like. After living in London, Eve would never be so lax about security.

'It would explain how he seemed to appear from nowhere,' the sergeant said. 'And why he had no obvious mission. If he was letting himself out, maybe he'd already accomplished it.'

'And what were you doing, loitering around outside Apple Tree Cottage?' DI Palmer looked at her through narrowed eyes.

'I was on my way to keep an appointment with Ashton Foley.'

'With your dog in tow? So not a professional meeting, I take it.'

Gus raised his head and gave Palmer a challenging look.

'It *was* work related, as a matter of fact, but I wasn't planning on staying long. I wanted to give Gus a run on the beach as soon as we'd spoken.'

'Can you be more specific about the purpose of your visit?'

She knew it would come across as woolly. She explained how she'd turned down Ashton's request to write a feature about him for *Icon* magazine. And how, despite that, he'd asked her over for coffee that morning. And breakfast. And that she'd accepted his invitation.

Even Gus was looking at her in a speculative way now. Maybe her cheeks had gone pink.

'It all sounds very cosy. What was there to talk about, if you'd already turned him down?'

'He said he wanted my advice about something.'

'But not what that was?'

'No.'

Palmer raised his eyes to heaven. 'Are you sure you said no to the job?'

Seriously? 'It's not something I'd get wrong.' She took her phone from her jeans pocket, keyed in her passcode and showed him their text exchange.

Palmer looked disappointed. 'It's clear he still hoped to win you round. We're here because we found a contract he had, ready for you to sign.'

'That figures.' She told him about the call she'd had from *Icon* that afternoon and wished she could see the paperwork Palmer had. It would give her an idea of the fee, but it seemed too callous to ask.

'I shall want to hear any relevant information you receive in the course of your work. And an assurance that you won't go beyond your brief, or interfere with the police operation.'

She didn't answer. He'd built his last case based on the evidence she'd gathered.

'Is there anything you want to share with us now?'

Eve spooled through the people she'd seen interacting with the dead man. From his disagreement with Marina Shaw, to the odd dynamic with Amber Ingram and his old school teachers. But she had nothing concrete, and they'd be sure to interview them all in any case. Thoughts of Ashton's aggression towards Howard pulled her up short though. If she told them, it would be another hint Howard might be guilty, even though he'd been the one to stay calm.

Palmer's eyes met hers. There was nothing for it. She related the scene in the village store. 'But Mr Green was very restrained in response.'

The DI and his sergeant exchanged a look.

'And what were your own relations with Ashton Foley?' Palmer said, after a moment.

'Pardon me?'

'How long had you known him?'

'Just since he arrived in the village.'

'Had you become intimate?'

Heck, Palmer had a vivid imagination. 'What? No. We'd only ever spoken in public: at Monty's and in the village store. And at the prize draw too.'

Palmer was looking at her narrowly. DS Boles, meanwhile, was looking at his shoes. They were polished to a high shine and caught the sunlight slanting through the window.

'But if you'd entered his cottage earlier today you'd have been alone together,' the DI said.

'This isn't the Victorian era. But that was one of the reasons I decided to take Gus.' Eve regretted the words as soon as they were out.

'You thought he had designs on you?'

'Not seriously. I'm sure he made all women feel that way.'

'We have a witness who was under the impression Ashton Foley had taken a fancy to you. And vice versa.'

If Eve worked out who that was... 'He was a flirtatious man, Inspector, but it was indiscriminate: admiring glances, flattering comments; it was all part of the show. He wanted me to do something for him, don't forget. But as you saw from my text, I wasn't won over. I'm almost old enough to have been his mom.'

Her thoughts ran to Betty Foley. The memory of her eager face as she'd anticipated her son's visit was vivid in her mind's eye. What must she be going through now? It was an appalling thought.

'Can you confirm your whereabouts between ten o'clock on Saturday night and two o'clock on Sunday morning?'

'I was here, in bed.' Sleeping badly, dreaming of ghosts. The knock-on effects might be adding to her tetchiness now.

'And I'm assuming no one can vouch for you?'

Eve met his look steadily. 'That's correct.' If only dachshunds could talk. Gus's melting brown eyes met hers as she glanced down. She had a feeling he understood.

Adrenaline was still coursing round Eve's body after she'd let the detectives out. She marched around the house, stamping her way upstairs to relieve the tension. Gus followed her until she relented, realising she was making him anxious.

She bent to fuss over him. 'But honestly, you do see why I'm angry, don't you? Palmer seriously imagines I might have slept with Ashton, and he has me down as a suspect too.'

It left her full of impotent rage. But she could rebel against his determination to restrict her work. As soon as she'd calmed down, she opened her laptop and set up two new files. One for information relating to the obituary of Ashton Foley, and one that focused on his murder. It felt good to spite Palmer, even if he was unaware of the fact. She entered the time-of-death window he'd provided.

And though she was working almost entirely without facts at this stage, her anger at Palmer drove her to create tabs for Ashton's contacts too: his mother's partner, Howard Green; his business manager, Marina Shaw; his old friends, Amber and Justin Ingram; and the school teachers, Tina and Carl Adcock. Methodically, she noted every detail she had about them, however small. She'd want to interview them all anyway. If she happened to find information that might be pertinent to the police enquiry, she wasn't going to ignore it.

After that, she texted Viv to let her know she still had her freedom. Her friend responded immediately, demanding to meet up at the Cross Keys that evening, so Eve could pass on her news. Things were just winding up at Monty's, so there was no need to go back. It gave Eve time to start her background research on Ashton and to think about her interview questions.

She'd been working solidly for some time when the house phone rang. The handset told her it was an international call. She picked up, but all she could hear was crying: huge, uncontrollable sobs.

CHAPTER ELEVEN

'Betty. Mrs Foley. I'm so very sorry.' Ashton's mother was trying to talk, but although Eve guessed she'd nerved herself up to call, she was finding it impossible to control her grief. Anguish tugged at Eve's core as she remembered the woman's excitement at being reunited with her son. Images of the thoughtless way he'd dashed off on his first night home, instead of having supper with her, mingled with their obvious closeness on the beach.

Eve let her cry, putting in words of sympathy, trying to soothe her when she knew there was no way to mend her pain. What time must it be in New Zealand? She looked at her watch. Wasn't it eleven hours ahead there? So it would be four thirty in the morning. She must have been up all night, having spent all day with her aunt at the hospital, most likely.

After a couple of minutes, Betty gradually regained some control, her abandoned sorrow giving way to gulps and sobs.

'Sorry. I'm so sorry. I'm sorry to bother you.'

Eve wished she was in the same room, so she could give her a hug. 'Please don't apologise. I'm so desperately sorry for your loss. If there's anything I can do…' But she knew really that there was no help for her situation. Eve was anxious to make herself available though, even if Betty just needed something practical. Maybe Ashton had been looking after a pet while she was away, or something of that sort. She guessed Betty knew her landline number because she hadn't changed it after buying the house. Viv and Simon's parents were both dead now, but they'd been friends with a lot of people in the village when they'd still lived at Elizabeth's Cottage. She wondered why Betty had chosen to contact her in particular, though she'd be more than glad to provide any support she could.

'*Thank you.*' Another involuntary sob came. '*I rang Ashton...*' As she said his name, the sob turned into another bout of crying. '*I rang Ashton on Friday, and he told me you were going to write about him for* Icon *magazine.*'

Eve didn't want to explain how her son had tried to force her hand. It didn't matter now. 'That's right.'

'*I just wondered...*' She paused and Eve heard her take a shaky breath. '*I wondered if you'll still do it now. Will you write his... his...*'

Eve clutched the phone receiver tight. This was so awful. Poor Betty. 'They have asked if I'll write his obituary now.' She'd want to talk to Betty about it of course, but she certainly hadn't intended to contact her when everything was so raw.

'*I heard you found information that helped the police, when you wrote Bernard Fitzpatrick's obituary.*'

He'd been murdered too. Eve suddenly realised the way the conversation was going. 'That's right. It was by accident though. I mean, I'm sure the police would have discovered the truth without me.' Was she sure? The thought of DI Palmer with his narrow mind and inflexible attitude filled her head.

Betty Foley was crying again.

'They'll do everything they can to find out who killed Ashton and bring them to justice.'

'*They think they already know,*' she said, between sobs.

'Excuse me?'

'*They think it's Howard.*' She lost control again as Eve took the news in. Was it because of what she'd told the police? It must have played a part.

'Is that what they've told you?' Eve said, as she heard Betty blow her nose.

'*Howard told me himself. He rang to comfort me.*'

Eve paused a moment. So between hearing the news about Ashton and calling Eve, Betty had had a call from Howard. He might have intended to provide comfort, but passing on the police's suspicions would have increased her anguish tenfold. She shook her head, damping down her frustration with him. He must be scared.

Thoughts of the part she'd played were high in her mind. She felt awful. 'Did Howard say why the police suspect him?' If it was only her report, they hadn't got much to go on.

'*They know Howard and Ashton never got on.*' Betty was speaking through her tears now. Her voice was faint. '*And I think they wonder about the gun. Howard runs an antique shop. He's got lots of contacts who sell all kinds of things. They asked him whether he'd ever dealt in weapons, and he has, so they know he'd have ways of getting hold of one.*'

Was there any chance the police were right? But as she had the thought, Betty said: '*Please, Eve. Ms Mallow. Please, can you do the same as last time and look for evidence to find out who's really guilty? Because Howard loves me. He'd never have done this. Not in a million years.*'

CHAPTER TWELVE

By seven thirty, Eve was sitting opposite Viv in the Cross Keys, the memory of the phone call weighing heavily on her chest. The pub was just as crowded as the teashop had been, the patrons huddled together, talking about the day's news.

Eve had had a quick restorative shower after her conversation with Betty Foley, changed her clothes, then headed off with Gus. A glass of wine and good company was what she needed – but the fee for the obit had better be good. She seemed to have spent a lot of time at the pub recently. She began by relaying the details of her interview with the police.

Viv sipped her Adnams IPA. 'Palmer really is a pillock.'

Gus shifted at Eve's feet, as though he'd recognised the name.

'At least I got hold of the time of death in return for my trouble.'

'I suppose.'

'His and DS Boles's visit wasn't the last surprise of the day.'

Viv's clear blue eyes opened wider under her daffodil-yellow fringe. 'I had a feeling there was something extra. What happened?'

'I was in the middle of marshalling my thoughts when the house phone rang.' Eve explained how it had been Betty Foley calling.

'That must have been a difficult conversation,' Viv said.

Eve nodded. She felt like crying herself when she thought of the woman's anguish.

'What are her plans? Is she coming home?'

Eve sipped her Chardonnay. She and Betty had moved onto that subject after the woman's bombshell request. 'Her aunt is so sick that she's staying put for now, but she's beside herself, as you can imagine.'

'Poor thing. She must be torn. I suppose there's nothing she can do if she does rush back.'

'Right.'

'So,' Viv's brow was furrowed, 'why was she calling you then?'

Eve explained what Betty had asked her to do.

Viv put down her beer rather heavily. 'That's quite a request. But I'd trust you to do the job above anyone else. And Betty probably has mixed feelings about the police, after everything Ashton went through.'

'I guess that's right. But there's more to it than that.' She explained how Howard had told Betty the police thought he was guilty, and why. 'I know his antiques business is on their minds, and Howard's past relationship with Ashton too, but I guess the evidence I gave won't have helped him.' She thought again of Howard Green, outside Apple Tree Cottage, glancing in all directions, then retreating at speed. 'I get the impression they went straight to interview him after speaking with me.'

'Not your fault.'

Eve took a deep breath. 'No. But I'm kind of glad Betty doesn't know what I said. I wouldn't want to add to her pain, and she's adamant he wouldn't have done it. So, as well as grieving over her son and watching over her aunt, she's trying to find someone who can help prove Howard Green's innocence.'

Viv swigged her drink, frowned and leaned forward. 'And you agreed?'

Eve sighed. 'I couldn't refuse her. She was desperately upset. And Palmer had me so riled I'd already started to make notes on the murder, just to spite him. I'm going to be gathering a lot of information; it would be crazy not to consider it in the light of the killing.'

Viv rested her chin on her hand. 'What do you think – about the possibility of him being guilty, I mean?'

'Each time I saw him and Ashton together, Ashton behaved in a way that was calculated to wind Howard up. But Howard's response always seemed restrained.' Eve had come across people like that who finally cracked under pressure, but if he'd done that it would have meant a sudden loss of control. It didn't seem to tie in with Howard carefully getting hold of a gun in advance, ready to carry out a planned killing.

Viv sipped her beer and nodded. 'So hopefully she's right, and you'll be able to prove it.'

'My heart goes out to her, so I really hope so. I'm going to make looking into Howard's recent activities one of my first tasks. If I can find out why he was really hanging around outside Apple Tree Cottage, that might be a quick way of showing his actions were innocent.' She'd have to do it quietly though. Betty was probably right, and Eve had no reason to think Howard was guilty, but she had some sense of self-preservation. Until she was absolutely sure of her ground, she didn't want him to know she was looking into his business. If he had anything to hide, being obvious about it could put her in danger. Her stomach clenched. 'I've asked Mrs Foley if we can talk again tomorrow morning, UK time. I'll have had a chance to think by then, and she'll have gotten some rest, I hope.' Though only if it was medically induced, Eve guessed. What mother could sleep under such circumstances?

'I shall want to hear all your updates as you work.'

'You sound like Palmer.'

Viv shot her a withering look. 'Does Palmer offer you cake in return for your trouble? Hmm. Thought not. Please don't ever compare us again. Nice dress by the way. Is it new?'

'The result of internet shopping after too many glasses of wine.'

'Russet really suits you. And it fits you like a glove.'

At that moment a hush fell over the patrons of the Cross Keys. Eve looked up to see Jo Falconer. She was bringing their food over in person. To her right, Hetty, who'd been lounging by one of the pub's sash windows, tensed. Gus crept further under their table and pressed his long body against Eve's feet.

'Smells amazing,' Viv said, as a plateful of sausage casserole landed in front of her. 'Are you all right after this morning?'

Jo nodded. 'Take more than that to floor me. Nasty sight though, and before you start, I've been pestered with questions all day. Load of press in here earlier. I ended up banning 'em.'

Viv gave her a bright smile. 'Sounds appalling. But Betty Foley's asked Eve to do some sleuthing as she researches Ashton's obituary, so if you have any information, as the person who found the body…?'

Eve gripped her wine, but after a moment Jo's eyes, which had been fiery, mellowed slightly. 'Well, I can't deny that we need as many minds on the problem as possible. That lazy oaf Palmer won't get there without help.'

She put down Eve's plate of poached salmon. It came with new potatoes, fine green beans and a black olive tapenade.

'If you want the low-down then I'm joining you,' Jo said. 'I can afford a minute and I'm not standing about while you let my food go cold.'

Eve felt the beginnings of indigestion before she'd taken a mouthful. Jo pulled a chair from a neighbouring table and wouldn't start talking until they'd begun to eat.

'Let's think.' The Rubenesque cook frowned and pushed her loose dark-brown curls back from her face. 'I found him deep in the woods, away from the main paths, lying on his back. I don't remember much more from the scene; I was too busy rushing off to get help. But DI Palmer let a couple of things slip.

'When I described Ashton's head wound he nodded, and said something to that sergeant of his. He's the brains behind their partnership, that's for sure.' She paused a moment. 'They were talking about the angle of the shot, and what the forensics people had said. They've concluded that the killer must have been standing close to Ashton, facing him, using a handgun. The wound was in the left-hand side of his head, so it looks as though his attacker was right-handed. There was no sign of a fight or anything like that.'

So Ashton couldn't have been on his guard then. It sounded as though the killer must have pulled the gun out quickly, surprising him before he had the chance to defend himself. If he'd run, ducked or knocked the weapon, the bullet wouldn't have caught him so cleanly.

Jo's brow furrowed again. 'What else? Oh yes. Palmer took a call halfway through interviewing me.' Eve could tell the fact rankled. 'He spoke about what was found on Ashton's body. Everything was still there, keys, phone, wallet – so it seems whoever did for him wasn't interested in his possessions. Other than that, I can't think of anything.'

'How's Marina bearing up?' Eve asked.

'Even paler than she was before. She's been speaking to the police of course. Hasn't left the pub all day. Billy Tozer sent her a bunch of lilies. Fat lot of good that'll do.' At that moment one of the casual waiting staff approached her. 'Right. I'd better see to the customers.' Her eyes narrowed as she focused on a couple of guys by the bar. 'They're not local. Journalists, if I'm not mistaken. One toe out of line and they'll be back outside.'

Eve returned to her salmon and finally noticed how good it tasted. The tanginess of the olive tapenade was the perfect pairing with the delicate fish.

'So, what's your plan of campaign?' Viv said. 'If Howard's innocent, what are your thoughts on other suspects?'

Eve swallowed her mouthful and took a sip of wine. 'Looks like Ashton had odd relationships with most of his Saxford connections, so that's worth considering. But I guess everyone's wondering the same thing. Does the gun mean the murder's linked with Ashton's criminal past? It's a long way back, but you mentioned the rumours about him selling drugs to the celebrities who became Outside In clients too. I presume the police never found out who Ashton's supplier was?'

'I don't think so.' Viv's blue eyes were serious. 'It's a good point. You will watch out, won't you? If one of our neighbours has a sideline selling cannabis, they'll have a lot to lose.'

Eve nodded. Underneath, she was just as uneasy as Viv. If the person had never been caught, they might well still be active. And if they'd killed Ashton to protect their secret, they had nothing left to lose. They'd face years in jail now.

'I'll watch out. Strictly background research until I get a handle on what I'm dealing with.'

But what then? She might not be able to prove Howard's innocence unless she took the next step, and found evidence to show that someone else was guilty.

Back at Elizabeth's Cottage, Eve messaged her twins. She'd known the press would be all over the murder before Jo had mentioned them descending on the pub. She wanted to make sure Nick and Ellen heard about Ashton's killing from her first.

Nick replied most quickly.

Is there something you want to tell us? Surely the locals are getting suspicious by now? All these deaths only started when you arrived in Saxford. (He'd ended with a laughing face emoji.)

She could see on their group chat that Ellen was typing.

Joking apart, take care, won't you? If you ever want company I'd gladly come up.

Then Nick again.

Same.

She set about replying. She still hadn't gotten the hang of touch typing with her thumbs.

Thanks both, but no need to worry. I'm surrounded by villagers monitoring my every move! (The grimace emoji seemed appropriate at that point.) *Just wanted to let you know what's going on, given it'll be splashed all over the papers. Take care. xx*

As she'd said to Viv, she'd stick to the type of questions she'd ask anyway for her obituary and see what came out. But what if that led nowhere? Would she rely on DI Palmer to crack the case? Tell Mrs Foley she was throwing in the towel?

Of course, there was always Robin, the gardener for most of Saxford St Peter. A man who many villagers thought was an ex-con. A man with a secret. She'd back his instincts above Palmer's any day. For a moment, she thought of calling him, but no – it wouldn't be fair. He kept himself to himself and that was the way he wanted it.

She'd just have to take things one step at a time.

CHAPTER THIRTEEN

Eve's neighbour, Sylvia, was standing at her elbow. They were looking out of the window of Sylvia and Daphne's home, Hope Cottage, across Haunted Lane towards Eve's house. The sky was a clear blue, the low sun streaming in towards them, and in the lane they could hear birds singing in the hedgerows and see an abundance of primroses and speedwells on the grassy banks.

Eve glanced sideways and met Sylvia's intelligent gaze. The tall woman had a long grey plait and eyes that were often mischievous. It made Eve uneasy that she looked so serious today.

'It's odd, isn't it, to look out on such an idyllic morning when something so shocking has happened? I didn't like Ashton – not one bit – but I feel it too.'

'I do wish you wouldn't say that.' Daphne was setting a pot of coffee on a round table to the rear of the living room. She was a lot shorter than Sylvia – around Eve's height – with kind grey eyes and short silver-grey hair, stylishly cut. The table was crammed: a rack of toast sat next to a pitcher of orange juice, butter, jam and orange marmalade, along with silverware and plates.

Sylvia gave Eve a look. 'I'm just being honest. And the reason I didn't like him is because he treated Daphne so badly.'

'I forgave him.' Daphne's voice faded as she went back through to the kitchen.

'Your privilege. I decided not to. Nothing I saw led me to change my mind.'

Daphne reappeared with a round pot of the anchovy paste she liked: Patum Peperium, the Gentleman's Relish. 'My mother used to have it and I love it too,' she said, following Eve's gaze. 'Unfortunately, so does Orlando.'

Daphne and Sylvia's marmalade cat was eyeing the pot with the look of an animal that was biding its time. Meanwhile, Gus was eyeing Orlando. It wasn't Eve's habit to call in on people for breakfast, but Sylvia had invited them when she'd caught them on their way back from Gus's morning airing.

Eve loved Hope Cottage. It was as traditional as her place at the front, but Sylvia and Daphne had opened it out at the back, and light streamed in over the living area from a large airy studio space. Sizeable skylights let the sun in later in the day, and through tall windows she could see the garden: including a sea of deep orange and violet candelabra primulas, with their abundant tiered flowers.

'Let's all sit down and I can explain my entirely rational opinions,' Sylvia said. 'I bumped into Viv at the village shop earlier, and she mentioned you'd be writing about Ashton.' She met Eve's eye. 'And that you might look into his murder. Don't worry – Moira Squires was out of earshot at the time.'

'Are you sure I'm not disturbing you?' The smell of the toast – made from one of the loaves Toby Falconer from the pub supplied to Moira, by the look of it – was making Eve's stomach rumble.

'Certain. Sit down, and if you don't like that muck Daphne's having there are plenty of other options to choose from.' The twinkle was back in Sylvia's eye again.

In a moment, they all had platefuls of toast and mugs of coffee in front of them. (The mugs were Daphne's work: thrown stoneware, decorated with seabirds. She sold them in Monty's craft section too.)

'I presume you haven't had the chance to interview anyone yet?' Daphne said, taking a bite of her fishy toast as Orlando looked on.

'That's right, so my knowledge is sketchy at the moment.' She wanted to rectify that as soon as she could. 'I'd gotten to know Ashton a little though. He'd already asked me to write about him.'

'That figures,' Sylvia said, drily. 'No matter that it wasn't your area. He liked to get his own way.'

Daphne gave her a pleading look.

'Shall we tell Eve the whole story from the beginning, and let her make up her own mind?' Sylvia sipped her coffee.

'*I'll* tell you,' Daphne said, turning to Eve. 'This all goes back a very long way, to when Ashton was a young teen.'

Sylvia laughed. 'Daphne is pointing out, in her own subtle way, that I like to bear a grudge.'

'We, and a large number of villagers, were over at the church hall. It was a charity art sale. I'd donated some of my ceramics, Sylvia some photographs' – that was Sylvia's profession – 'and there was a whole lot more besides. Viv and her husband had supplied tea and cake from Monty's and I was helping out in the kitchen on and off, washing up crockery and so on.' Viv's husband had died ten years earlier. It was weird to hear Daphne refer back to a world that was now lost.

Sylvia topped up their coffees.

'At some point, one of the people minding the stalls came in to tell me there was a girl who wanted to ask about my work.'

Eve could read people well enough to know that the story still affected Daphne. Her lively grey eyes were glistening. Sylvia's sparked with anger that looked as fresh now as it probably had back then. Eve wondered what was coming.

'I went out to speak to the girl.'

There was a long pause. Daphne had stopped eating her toast and Orlando was edging closer to her place setting, perched on a fourth chair around the table. Gus was at Eve's side, his concerned brown eyes on hers each time she looked down.

Sylvia took over the story. 'I'd been circulating in the hall, but at that point I saw Daphne had left the kitchen, and so I thought I'd go backstage and do my bit. The washing-up builds up horribly at that sort of do. I nipped to the loo first, and then entered the kitchen, where I found Ashton Foley.' Sylvia turned to face Eve. 'There's a ring holder on the windowsill in the church hall kitchen. It's still there, so you probably saw it when you and Viv catered for the prize draw. Daphne had taken her ring off while she was washing up and left it there. When I entered the room, Ashton had it in his hand. A hand that was on its way to being inside his pocket.'

'I still can't believe he honestly meant to take it.' Daphne's eyes were bleak. 'He did tell you he assumed someone had left it behind, and he was going to give it to the vicar.'

'He was the sort who could think on his feet.' Sylvia put her mug down on the table. 'A showman. A charmer. A trickster. You can see why I remained angry with him. What's more, it turned out the girl who'd asked to talk to Daphne was a friend of his. Amber Ingram, in fact; you know? One of the women who won an Outside In consultation. It was a put-up job, the whole thing. He was clever, I'll say that much for him.'

Eve digested the news. She couldn't imagine the woman she'd seen at the prize draw, with her presentable dress and puffed-up looking husband, running around scheming with Ashton.

'I think Amber found him rather awe-inspiring at the time,' Daphne said. Perhaps she'd read her expression. 'She was spellbound, and he was troubled.'

Sylvia snorted.

'Was any action taken?' Eve asked.

Sylvia sat back in her seat. 'Daphne wouldn't hear of it, and I couldn't prove that he was lying. A year or so later, I bumped into Betty Foley and she mentioned Ashton had been in trouble over something else. Shoplifting, I think. At that point I couldn't contain myself, and I mentioned what I'd seen him do.' She nodded. 'Betty believed me all right. Poor woman was worried sick about the way her son was behaving, but she blamed herself too. Thought her relationship with Howard might not have been helping. Anyway, she told me Ashton's lawyer had taken him under his wing. He was some do-gooder who'd occasionally go above and beyond the call of duty for hard-luck cases. Russell Rathbone, I believe his name was. I still remember because she called him Basil to start with – like the old Sherlock Holmes actor – but then corrected herself.'

Eve pulled a notebook from her bag and took down the man's name. He'd be invaluable for her obituary, and he might know more about Ashton's drugs offence too.

'I think she wanted to reassure me that something was being done. But actually things went from bad to worse, as I expect you know.'

'But he was so young when all that happened!' Daphne said. 'He made good in the end, against the odds, which was very much to his credit.' She turned to Eve. 'He had a difficult upbringing. His father died young, and his mother had some financial difficulties, I think. And then there was Howard Green, Betty's new boyfriend. I imagine Ashton probably felt out of control, and that nothing truly belonged to him. I believe that's why he stole.'

'And I believe,' said Sylvia, 'that you are too kind for your own good. As for Ashton, it was always about money and always about himself. If he'd got that ring of yours, Daphne, I'm quite sure it would have been sold on and out of his hands within a couple of days. He wasn't after it as some pretty keepsake to treasure forever.'

Suddenly, she reached across Eve and intercepted Orlando, who had extended a paw towards Daphne's plate. 'And you, my dear pussycat, are almost as bad.'

CHAPTER FOURTEEN

Eve was back at Elizabeth's Cottage by 9 a.m., half an hour early for her call with Betty Foley. It would be eight thirty in the evening over in Auckland, by the time she rang; allowing Betty to get home after hospital visiting hours.

Once again, Eve wished she could speak with the woman face to face. She'd gotten used to dealing with people in the throes of raw emotion many years earlier. They often seemed to find discussing a friend or family member therapeutic: they could pay tribute to them, or sometimes offload pent-up frustrations. But to question someone who had lost a child to murder was very different. Poor Betty.

Eve had prepared thoroughly for this follow-up call, which was her main defence against the pitfalls of interviewing. Now, she looked again at the information she'd amassed on Ashton the night before, via online research. He hadn't tried to hide his chequered past, it seemed, but wore it like a badge of honour. It might have been a long time ago, as Daphne had said, but he'd used it as part of his brand. Maybe that was the smart thing to do, if people weren't going to let him forget it anyway. Or maybe it meant he had no regrets about the way he'd behaved...

She found no mention on Wikipedia or his company website of him having done any horticultural training, so presumably the practical side of his business was down to Marina Shaw, or to contractors they brought in. Maybe he was the ideas man. He'd had a knack for publicity, too. The press had loved him in the last few years, since he'd started to make an impact with Outside In. His trademark black hat and offbeat clothes contrasted neatly with the oases of green he'd introduced into the homes of celebrities. There was no denying his charisma either; he'd charmed the birds out of the trees. Handy, whether you were talking your way out of trouble, selling drugs or pushing the latest in interior design.

There were no official news reports relating to his trial in the youth court. Eve guessed he'd been too young to be named in the press and all the details would have been locked down. However, he'd opened up about the experience himself, in interviews later on, so Eve had managed to piece together snippets that related to his misspent youth. It had been an anonymous tip-off that had led to his arrest, apparently. And in most interviews, he mentioned that his teacher, Tina Adcock, had given evidence at his trial. She'd seen a young man she didn't recognise leave an envelope on Ashton's school desk, apparently, and wished that she'd reported it to someone. Ashton said she was clearly trying to highlight the role of the dealer who'd ruined his schooldays. He said he'd always remember her contribution. Eve's mind ran back to Tina's husband, Carl, who'd dismissed Ashton so thoroughly at school. Maybe Tina had been more sympathetic than her husband. It was also interesting that Ashton had had dealings with two of the three prize-draw winners.

Ashton claimed in his press interviews that he simply couldn't help the police when he came to trial, saying his supplier had been careful about hiding their identity. But Eve found an interview with him on YouTube, and there was an odd glint in his eye as he told the story of his teenage criminal exploits. What was behind that? Eve had a feeling he knew more than he was saying. It would have made sense if he'd been scared of the person he'd worked for, and had lied at every opportunity to put the authorities off the scent. But his look in the YouTube video was cocky, echoing Moira Squires' reports. It was almost as though he was sharing a joke.

'It sounds as though Tina Adcock felt a bit sorry for Ashton,' Eve said to Gus. 'She had a duty of care, as his teacher. Maybe she felt guilty that she'd missed an opportunity to raise the alarm sooner, before he was in too deep.' She ruffled Gus's fur and felt his warmth under her fingers.

Maybe her guilt meant she'd been keen to support Ashton now, if only by buying some of his raffle tickets. And that purchase presumably indicated she'd have been happy to invite him into her home, too.

It was time for her call, and there was nothing more she could do, so she picked up the landline and dialled.

Betty Foley answered on the first ring. She sounded stunned now, as though some kind of numbness had overtaken her, to cushion her from pain. She must have had a long day after a sleepless night. '*I just can't think why this would happen now,*' she said, after Eve had expressed her sympathy again. '*When he was a teenager I was always looking over my shoulder, wondering if people I passed in the street might be his enemies, and who Ashton might owe money to. But I'd assumed his life was secure these days. Although…*'

Eve filled the pause. 'Something made you worry?'

'*When he told me he was coming home and asked if he could stay with me, in Apple Tree Cottage, he mentioned he had some old business to take care of.*' Her voice was slow, almost trance-like.

It was what she'd overheard him say herself. 'And you were concerned?'

There was another, longer pause. '*Enough to ask what he meant. But he just laughed and said it was nothing, and that he could look after himself. He sounded as though he was looking forward to it – whatever it was.*' Her sharp intake of breath carried down the line. '*And then I forgot all about it. My mind was on my aunt.*'

'Of course. It would have been the same for anyone, and you couldn't have predicted what would happen.' Eve waited a moment.

'Thinking back to the time when Ashton was in trouble for selling drugs, did he ever hint that he knew the person who supplied him personally? Or that he was still in touch with them?' He might have confided in his mom, even if he wouldn't tell the police.

'*No, but I had a feeling he suspected someone. I was always warning him of the danger he might be in, but he wouldn't listen.*'

It really did sound as though he'd been overconfident rather than scared, then. Yet he hadn't told the police what he knew, for whatever reason. Eve's mind ran back to the disagreement she'd overheard between Ashton and Marina Shaw. It sounded like she'd been warning him too.

'I read that someone tipped the police off about what he was up to.' She knew she must be bringing back painful memories, but there was no way round it. 'Do you happen to know who that might have been?'

'*He told me he'd never found out.*' Her tone was uncertain. '*In many ways he was a victim, rather than a criminal.*' Betty was crying, quietly.

But Ashton had seemed worldly-wise to Eve. The orchestrated plan to steal Daphne's ring was proof of that.

So, somewhere, the person who'd used Ashton as a runner was still out there; and quite possibly still operating too. And she was sure Ashton could have told the police more if he'd wanted, even if only about their logistics. Might he have wanted to get revenge personally, without involving the authorities? Maybe he'd withheld important information for his own use later. But why wait until now? It had been years since all this happened. Had this particular visit home offered some kind of opportunity he hadn't had before? She made a quick note in her book.

'I'm focusing on the more worrying aspects of Ashton's life because of the job you've given me,' she said, 'but I want to do him justice in my obituary too. Perhaps you could have a think about the defining moments in his life, the type of things he liked doing as a child and your memories of him.' On the end of the line, Mrs Foley took a deep breath. 'If it's easier, you could email them to me?'

'I'm sorry, I'll do that. I can't think straight at the moment, but I'd like to sit down and remember the good times.'

'Of course.' Eve thought again of Betty's excitement about Ashton's homecoming. And then had come the reality: the way he'd by turns let her down, then rushed into her daily routine like an unexpected gust of wind and swept her up again.

'I'll want some reminiscences for the funeral too,' the woman went on. *'Jim Thackeray will ask me.'*

'Of course. In that case, if you can spare a few more minutes, I'll focus on the task you gave me.' She needed to phrase her questions carefully. 'I appreciate you're certain Howard Green is innocent, but it would be useful if you could tell me about his and Ashton's relationship, even if they were' – she dismissed the word enemies – 'less than close.' Howard Green's bruises came to mind again. Could he and Ashton have had a fight before the murder? If so, it looked as though Ashton had lashed out but Howard had kept his fists in check. She hadn't seen a mark on Ashton. But if they'd fought, Eve wouldn't be doing her job if she didn't uncover the facts. She'd need them as the foundation for all the other research she'd do. She hated lurking areas of uncertainty.

Betty sighed. *'Howard's always been fiercely protective of me, and that meant he was down on Ashton for leading me a dance. He didn't understand the bond we had, and he'd forgotten what it's like to be young.'* The line broke up for a moment, then Eve heard Mrs Foley blow her nose. *'But Howard loves me, and he's loyal. I even kept a bit of distance between us, to avoid hurting Ashton's feelings, and he put up with that. It's not every man who would.'*

It always made Eve wonder when women defended their partners that way. 'At least he doesn't do x' or 'to be fair, I've been spared y'.

But at the same time, she could see Betty Foley's point. Howard must have found the situation irritating at the very least.

'I bumped into Howard recently in the village store and noticed he had a bruise on his face,' Eve said. 'Did he mention that to you, and how it happened maybe?'

'*No.*' Betty sounded puzzled. '*I suppose he didn't want to worry me.*'

Yet he'd confided in her about being the police's chief suspect. 'Have you been in regular contact with him since you went away?'

'*Oh yes. He's been calling every couple of days.*'

Eve thought back to the scene in the village store, when she'd seen Ashton deliberately knock Howard's shoulder, and noticed the older man's bruises. She guessed the marks had already been a day old by then. He'd likely rung Betty for a general chat sometime between then and the panic-stricken call he'd made after his police interview. You'd think he'd have mentioned the accident he'd supposedly had when he was passing the time of day.

Didn't want Betty to know, she scribbled in her pad.

'And did Howard mention any interactions with Ashton after you left for New Zealand?'

'*No.*' The woman paused. '*I mean, I wouldn't have expected him to really. I imagine they must have avoided each other once I wasn't around. There'd be no point in them crossing swords.*'

There was silence for a moment.

'Can I ask, does Howard have a set of keys for your house?'

'*Yes, but of course he would never have let himself in while Ashton was staying there.*'

That rang true. Eve couldn't imagine him marching in when he might find Ashton in the bath or something. Yet it looked like he might have been in Apple Tree Cottage the morning after Ashton was killed. He *might* have knocked to check before he entered, and had no reply, but it had been early. Ashton could have been sleeping. Surely Howard would have considered that.

What had made him confident enough to go inside, assuming that he had?

She had heard the conviction in Betty Foley's voice. There was no doubt in her mind that Howard was innocent, and Eve's own experience backed this up. She'd seen how protective he was of her, and how he'd managed to keep his feelings under control when Ashton had risked provoking him.

And yet, if he'd gone into Apple Tree Cottage the morning after Ashton was murdered, wasn't it most likely he knew for sure that he wasn't there, and was never coming home?

And she couldn't ignore Howard's bruises, not when she was sure he'd lied about how he got them. 'I know Howard and Ashton never got on, but can you think of any reason why *fresh* trouble might have blown up between them? I appreciate you trust Howard absolutely, but if they had a reason to argue, it's probably best to have that out in the open, even if it's irrelevant.'

There was a long pause – too long, it seemed to Eve. '*I really don't think so.*'

She might be lying; she wouldn't want to colour Eve's view of Howard. What kind of argument could have come to a head suddenly? If Howard was a regular visitor to Apple Tree Cottage when Betty was home, maybe Ashton had stumbled across something in the house that had made him mad at his mother's boyfriend.

How could she find out? She let the question occupy the back of her mind as she moved the conversation on, asking about Ashton's school, and also the lawyer who'd taken him under his wing: Russell Rathbone.

'*He was determined that Ashton could make something of himself. He got him to enrol at the Drop In, one of the local youth clubs, after he'd been caught shoplifting. And he helped me too.*' She sighed. '*Just with advice. I was never in trouble, but I had problems paying the mortgage at one point, after I was made redundant. I thought we'd have to move out, but Russell helped me write a debt management plan – that was what he called it – and the bank gave me more time to pay. He told me lawyers earn a lot and he wanted to give something back. He never gave up on Ashton and they kept in touch.'*

Once Eve thought her questions about Howard and Ashton had been forgotten, she asked about Apple Tree Cottage.

'The crime scene investigators will check your home thoroughly, but would you like me to have a look too, in case anything strikes me as odd? I could include a description in my obituary as well. It would be good to paint a picture of Ashton's childhood home.'

'*If there's any chance it might be useful then I'd be grateful if you'd look round*,' Betty Foley said. '*The police say they'll finish by lunchtime today. If you let yourself in by the side gate, there's a spare key under an iron owl in the back garden.'*

Why wasn't she surprised? The residents of Saxford St Peter had no sense of self-preservation.

She wondered if there was any danger of bumping into Howard when she went to look round.

'Is there anything I can do for you while I'm there?' she asked, feeling her way. 'I suppose Howard is watering your pot plants for you?'

Betty gulped. '*I don't have any – only dried flowers. Ashton teased me about that. He said he couldn't have me being plant-free, what with his profession. We were going to visit the garden centre together, but then I got the call about my aunt.'*

Her pain was so tangible, despite the distance between them. 'I'm very sorry.'

She heard the woman take a deep breath. '*Thank you. So no, there's nothing that needs doing at the house.'*

Eve thanked Mrs Foley and rang off. Her mind sifted through everything Ashton's mother had said. As she filtered disparate bits of information, she entered more notes onto her spreadsheet.

How did Howard get his bruises?

What was he doing outside Apple Tree Cottage the morning Ashton was found shot?

If he went inside, what was he looking for, and how could he be sure Ashton wasn't home?

Why did Betty Foley pause so long, when asked if there was a recent reason for Howard and Ashton to quarrel?

And lastly, though Howard seemed like a mild-mannered man:

Had Howard's patience with his old enemy finally run out? (Years of Betty Foley keeping Howard at arm's length, followed by close contact with Ashton, without Betty to keep the peace.)

She had to consider it, despite the old-fashioned and steadfast solicitude he showed towards Betty. For the first time, she let herself wonder what would happen if it turned out he was actually guilty. Betty Foley's pain didn't bear thinking about.

She went to join Gus in the kitchen and fixed herself a coffee.

'I don't like it,' she said to him. 'Visiting Apple Tree Cottage might give me some answers.'

She'd need to be careful though, and plan ahead; she'd rather no one knew she was there. She'd want a thorough look round, and anyone who saw her in the house might wonder what she was up to.

Especially the murderer.

CHAPTER FIFTEEN

Eve was out of cheese, so she ran over to the village store.

Inside, Moira Squires was pretending to check the vegetables displayed in the shop's box-bay window. In reality, Eve imagined she spent every customer-free moment scanning the comings and goings outside. The storekeeper bent to examine a tomato as Eve walked in, setting the bell over the door jangling.

'Oh dear, Eve! I'm so relieved to see you after you were taken away from the teashop yesterday. Are you all right?'

Eve took a consciously deep breath, and all the usual smells of the store filled her nostrils: the oranges sitting in the sun, freshly baked bread, leaf tea, ground coffee, and a waft of Moira's perfume. 'I'm fine thanks. They'd heard Ashton had asked me to write about him, that's all. They hoped I might have known him better than I did.'

Moira's pencilled eyebrows curved upwards, her eyes widened, and her cheeks turned a little pink. 'Oh, I see. I expect you must have got an idea about how the investigation's going?'

Nice try. 'Not really, I'm afraid. I think it's all confidential.' But two could play at extracting information. 'What about you, Moira? Ashton had already given you your Outside In consultation, hadn't he? I remember hearing him talk about it when I was in here last. He sounded very keen.'

Moira let out a sigh and pulled a handkerchief from her dress pocket. 'Oh yes, he was. Couldn't have been more attentive. Such a dreadful shame. Paul felt he'd been a bit intrusive when I told him all about it. Ashton took a lot of photographs, but of course, it was necessary, so he could plan the type of plants that would complement each of our "spaces", as he put it. He took measurements as well.'

'Viv mentioned he used to cause you and Paul trouble when he was younger, tearing round the shop with his friends?'

'She banned him!' Paul's voice made her jump. She hadn't seen him in the shadows.

'Oh!' Moira waved away her husband's comment. 'That was nothing. It's all long forgotten. He was a changed man!'

'A leopard doesn't change its spots,' Paul said, and exited into the store's back room.

'I've always made it my motto to forgive and forget,' Moira said.

She certainly seemed to have in his case, but had Ashton felt the same way?

'So, you'll be writing his obituary now?'

'That's right.' Eve decided not to volunteer anything. If she waited, Moira would probably parcel out information herself, to keep the conversation going.

'You'll be speaking to Howard Green, I expect?'

Eve went to open one of the glass-fronted fridge doors and picked out a packet of farmhouse cheddar. 'I think so.'

'Now, he and Ashton had an interesting relationship.'

Eve smiled to herself. 'I'd heard that too. What do you think of him, Moira?'

The woman took the cheese from her and entered the price on the till, shaking her head. No barcode scanner at the village store; it felt like stepping back in time. 'A nice gentleman. Really quite chivalrous.'

Right up Moira's street, Eve imagined. He wouldn't be Eve's sort – he sounded cloying – but she shouldn't make any judgements based on that.

'It was a shame he and Ashton didn't get on, but of course I could understand it,' Moira continued. 'Howard is *so* traditional, and Ashton was very unconventional – though charming as an adult. But returning to Howard – lately, if I'm honest, I've seen a change in him.' She leaned forward over the counter, even though they were alone. 'He's been almost brusque!'

Eve couldn't imagine him – or indeed most people – warming to Moira's inquisitive nature.

'And you'll be talking to Amber Ingram, I dare say, as a prize draw winner?'

'I hope so.' Her part in Ashton's past also made her interesting.

'She works for Howard, of course.' Moira looked speculatively at her.

'I didn't know.' That was the thing with village life: there were always connections you didn't expect.

The storekeeper smiled, clearly delighted to be the one to pass on a fragment of information. 'He's got an antiques shop, out towards Blythburgh. She's been with him several years. Just part-time, naturally.'

Moira still lived in a world where it would be inconceivable for a married woman with a child to do anything more than dabble in a career. The storekeeper leaned forward still further now, her eyes on the door.

'I do get the impression from what Amber's said that the business hasn't been running smoothly just lately.' She put her finger to one side of her nose. 'Money worries, reading between the lines. Howard lives in the cottage with the cream gate at this end of Dark Lane, but I've been wondering if he'll have to sell it.' She'd probably been monitoring his front garden for an estate agent's board.

She handed Eve her cheese. 'Oh look!' Eve turned to follow her gaze. Viv's brother, Simon, was outside the store. 'He's not with Polly today, I see.' There was a slight questioning note to her voice.

Eve resisted pointing out that the pair weren't surgically attached. Was the whole village wondering how she was feeling, now that

Simon had a new girlfriend? Would Moira use it as a topic of conversation with the next villager who walked through the door? The thought was deeply unpleasant.

She took her time paying, and was glad to find Simon had disappeared when she emerged into the sunlight.

CHAPTER SIXTEEN

Eve had offered to interview Marina Shaw at the Cross Keys but the business manager said she'd seen enough of the pub to last her a lifetime, so Eve was entertaining her at Monty's instead.

'I feel I should lay on bitter lemon cake for her especially,' Viv said, darkly, 'but in a triumph of hope over experience, let's try her with the glazed summer fruit tarts. Maybe they'll make her sweeter.'

One look at the business manager's eyes made Eve feel all such efforts would be in vain. All the same, she relished interviewees like Marina. They threw down a gauntlet, challenging you to overcome their prejudice and negative feelings. Having a mountain to climb could be invigorating, and you never knew what you'd get if you managed to reach the summit.

'Thanks for seeing me,' she said, when they were settled with the tea and confections Angie had brought over. 'I'm sorry – it must be a terrible time for you.'

Marina Shaw didn't blink as her eyes met Eve's. Eve had known she wasn't the sort to look for sympathy, but she wanted to express it anyway. The woman might be tough, but she and Ashton had worked together for years – without him, was there a future for Outside In? It was impossible to tell what feelings she was battening down.

'What did you want to ask me?' Her tone said, *Let's get this over with.*

'Maybe we could begin with how you met Ashton? I remember you said you were from Saxford originally too.'

'That's right.' Wisps of her black hair fell forward when she nodded; most of it was pulled back into a deliberately messy chignon. It suited her; the scrappy way she'd used the classic style gave it an edge. Her eyes, lined with heavy black make-up, were unflinching. 'But then my parents moved away, down to London, when I was in my mid-teens, so we lost touch at that point. After I'd finished school, I did a diploma in horticulture and got taken on as an apprentice in the garden of a stately home.

'It was just by chance that I came across Ashton again. He was a roadie for a band that came to perform in the grounds of the house where I worked.'

'Small world.'

She nodded. 'I remembered him well from school. He was rebellious, but he had a spark. I always thought he'd grow up to do something quirky and striking. When we met again, he was full of energy and looking for his next step – and I was wondering about my future too.'

So she'd been impressed with him, back when they were kids. Eve was taking notes. 'You sparked off each other? Talked about your dreams?'

Marina gave her a look. 'My plans have never been dreams. I decide what I want and then work out how to get there.'

Fair enough. Eve operated with her feet firmly on the ground too.

'Did he talk to you about the time since you'd last met? His period in the young offenders' institute?'

Marina nodded. 'A bit, but it was clear he'd put it behind him.'

Yet it cropped up a lot in the interviews he'd done. But then Sylvia had called Ashton a showman. He'd probably realised he had a good story to tell, and used it repeatedly to capture the media's attention.

'I wondered how he found life inside,' Eve said. 'I guess it must have been a tough environment.'

Marina inclined her head. 'That might be true, but he was a born diplomat. For the most part, he knew just how to get round people and keep them onside. I imagine that helped him stay out of trouble.'

Diplomat, or operator? Eve wondered what moral compromises he might have made to keep some of the trickier offenders happy. She imagined there was a hierarchy in places like that.

'I didn't see any mention of Ashton having done horticultural training?'

Marina shook her head. 'He wasn't one for formal education, but he was curious about my work. We talked for a long time, the evening we met.' A small, secret smile played around her lips. 'We explored the grounds late at night.'

After a few drinks and who knew what else, Eve guessed.

'We talked about the gardens. When we walked past the orangery, Ashton said how cool it was to have trees indoors. The idea for a business that focused on bringing the outdoors into people's homes stemmed from that.' Her eyes were far away, as though she was back in the moment.

Eve could visualise their midnight stroll clearly too. The scene would work well in Ashton's obituary. She asked Marina for the name of the stately home, so she could source images of it.

'I started a part-time course in garden design alongside my apprenticeship,' Marina went on, 'and adapted the ideas for the interiors we worked on once we set up the business. Ashton was still working as a roadie, travelling a lot, but I passed on my knowledge to him when he came back to London for good.'

She must have dedicated long hours to the project. Her own passion certainly shone through. It made Eve feel she'd gotten a little closer to Marina. 'And what about your first clients? How did you get started?' She remembered Viv saying there were rumours their showbiz contacts were people Ashton had sold drugs to, and that maybe he'd carried on dealing when he was down in London. She couldn't imagine Marina admitting to that, if it were true.

The business manager sipped her tea. 'Ashton went to a lot of celebrity parties, so he had all the right connections, and then the whole thing snowballed.' She looked down for a moment but then met Eve's eyes. 'We were making money a lot faster than most businesses.' Her tone was slightly defensive.

'It sounds amazing. And the work must be fascinating. I guess you have to get to know your clients really well, so you can assess what kind of scheme will fit with their lifestyle and their personalities?'

'Of course. It's part of the job.' Marina's gaze drifted away from Eve's. She probably thought the question was pedestrian, but Eve was interested.

'There's a bit of overlap with my work. I'm fascinated by people and what makes them tick too.'

Marina didn't respond.

'I love visiting interviewees in their homes. It's always amazing the knowledge you can pick up.'

The business manager sighed and Eve abandoned her attempts to build a rapport. 'Are there any past Outside In clients you think might be willing to speak with me?'

She took out her phone, accessed a few records and wrote down the details on Eve's pad. 'These ones have dealt with the media before. I know they're happy to be contacted.'

'Thanks. It must have taken a lot of time and effort to set the business up. And money too.'

Marina nodded. 'I managed to get a loan agreed while Ashton was travelling with the band. We were ready to roll by the time he came home.'

'You got to know each other really well, I guess, from working so intensely together.'

The woman took a bite of her fruit tart and sat back on her chair. It was hard to meet her clear-eyed stare. 'We did.' After a moment, she added, 'But we were never in a relationship. We knew each other too well for that. And if you're working with someone all day, every day, it's not conducive to having them as a life partner as well. You need some slack.'

'I guess even working relationships must have their tensions.' Eve hesitated. 'Did you see eye to eye, most of the time?'

Marina gave her a knowing look. 'You overheard us arguing, didn't you? On Friday night, down by the estuary? I saw you ahead of us.'

Eve nodded and Marina ran her finger round the rim of her teacup and looked down into the fragrant liquid. 'Ashton was good to work with: dynamic, enthusiastic, very appealing to our customers.' She glanced up again. 'We argued on Friday evening as a result of the side of his personality that let him down: overconfidence, and a refusal to take anything seriously. He'd just admitted he'd played a joke on Amber and Justin Ingram.' She shook her head. 'They're "friends" from childhood but I was aware Ashton had no time for Justin. He covered it up when they won their prize, but he's the last person Ashton would want to help.'

'Do you know why? I hope you don't mind me asking but I'll likely interview Justin too, and it helps to have the background sometimes, to avoid causing offence.'

Marina gave her a long look. 'No. I don't know. But Ashton made the most of the access he had to his and Amber's house. Justin was out when he called, so he decided to get his own back on the guy by leaving a pair of his boxer shorts just under Justin and Amber's bed.' Her face was sour. In fairness, Eve could see why, if all this was true.

'Ashton told me he went into their bathroom, took off the ones he was wearing, dragged his jeans back on and stuffed the underwear into his pocket. Then he planted the boxers when Amber wasn't looking. He thought it was hilarious, but I was livid. You can't run a company like that, paying off old scores when you feel like it. And it's my business as much as it is his.' She paused and swallowed. 'Was.' Her eyes were down on her lap now. 'I was so furious with him, but it was unimportant really – just one insignificant contact – not even a proper commission. His death's brought that into perspective.'

It led Eve on to her next question. 'What will you do now? Does Ashton's share of Outside In pass to his mom?'

Marina nodded. 'I'll offer to buy her out if she'd prefer it. I'm guessing she won't want to be actively involved. Other than that, I just have to carry on. We've got a full order book and although clients will be sympathetic, it won't override their desire to have their makeovers completed.' She shrugged. 'That's just what people are like.'

Eve was nearing the end of her shift, sorting out the kitchen, when Viv came through to join her.

'How did it go with old sourpuss?'

'Who can you mean?'

Viv gave her a look.

'It was interesting.'

'You can tell me. I won't breathe a word.' She produced a winning smile.

'Well, I think her information explains the temper tantrum Justin was having when he marched in here on Friday afternoon.'

Viv rolled her eyes. 'He's such a jumped-up twerp. What's the background then?'

'For your ears only, right?'

Viv nodded and Eve explained.

'Marina claims she was furious with him for his lack of profes-sionalism. And I can believe that.'

'But?'

'I don't know. The story fits exactly with an argument I overheard them having, down by the estuary, but I can think of other ways the situation might have played out.' Eve put down the cloth she'd been wielding. 'I'll bet Justin Ingram didn't wait until he and Amber got home to start laying into her about the underwear he'd found. He was in too much of a state. I could see he was already letting rip as they walked across the green.'

'So someone else could have overhead their conversation, meaning the story could have got back to Marina that way, rather than Ashton telling her direct?'

Eve nodded. 'It's possible. And if so, Marina might have assumed Ashton had genuinely slept with Amber, which would have been even more unprofessional. Whatever excuses Ashton gave, she might still think that.'

'So why would she lie about how the matter came to light?'

It was a good question. 'To portray her and Ashton's relationship as closer and more confiding than it really was? To imply that – although she disapproved of the way he behaved sometimes – there were no secrets between them? Or maybe to cover up underlying jealousy. She says they were never in a relationship, but she might be lying.'

Viv leaned back against one of the countertops. 'Could be.'

'Either way, I can't help feeling she has an agenda. The dynamics of their business were interesting too. Ashton called himself Outside In's artistic director, but it was Marina who studied horticulture and design. Ashton seems to have been the one to bring the punters in – and probably to schmooze the press – but I wonder if Marina felt she was contributing more.'

'You think she's a candidate for murderer?'

Eve wondered. But none of the possible tensions she'd identified seemed powerful enough as a motive, assuming they weren't secret lovers or something. And that didn't seem likely; neither of them had any reason to keep it quiet.

'Probably not. But Justin's on my mind now. He was sucking up to Ashton at the prize draw, but was probably mad as heck with him by Saturday evening. Marina says Ashton never liked him either. I'd be curious to know why. Sylvia and Daphne say Ashton and Amber used to run around together, so it could be there's some ongoing love triangle at play. But that doesn't sound quite right. Ashton hardly ever came back to Saxford, by all accounts, and his and Amber's wild schooldays are a long while ago now.' It all needed more thought. She sighed. 'Either way, the dynamic between Justin and Ashton is worth keeping in mind.'

'Interesting,' Viv said. 'What's next on your agenda?'

'Russell Rathbone, the lawyer who tried to steer Ashton in the right direction when he first ran into trouble.' She checked her watch. 'He's agreed to see me after his last appointment today. I'm hoping he might know more about Ashton's involvement in drugs. I still think his murder's most likely connected with that part of his life.'

Viv raised her eyebrows. 'Your entire project sounds so risky. Just take care, all right?'

'Yes, Mother!' Eve didn't mention her plans for later that evening; she still wanted to keep her visit to Apple Tree Cottage as quiet as possible.

CHAPTER SEVENTEEN

Eve drove to Russell Rathbone's offices at Blyworth in her Mini Clubman. She wore a mulberry-coloured dress and jacket; the weather was mild enough not to take a coat, though she'd stuck with knee-length boots.

She'd left a stoical Gus sitting on the doormat at Elizabeth's Cottage. They'd gone for a good walk over the heath before she'd left, but you wouldn't think so from the long-suffering look in his eye. At least he'd had his supper. She aimed to be back inside an hour and a half to eat hers too.

But first, she had to concentrate on her interview. From an obituary writer's point of view, Russell Rathbone was a tempting prospect. Even if he'd taken Ashton under his wing out of social duty to begin with, she guessed something must have made him stick at it, especially given his early efforts had failed. Finding out what had driven him might provide an uplifting strand to Ashton's story, and some continuity too, given they'd kept in touch. The lawyer would have followed Ashton's progress over a number of years, from a struggling youth with an uncertain future to a hugely successful businessman. And, of course, something he said might throw light onto Ashton's untimely death. He must have been more aware of his criminal contacts than most people. Mrs Foley was still on her mind; if Eve could possibly prove Howard Green's innocence, then at least Betty would have someone to support her when she came home.

The lawyer's offices challenged the senses. The frontage that faced the road was beautiful: half-timbered – Tudor, Eve guessed

– but inside, the furniture and décor were up to the minute. The clerk at the front desk sat at a wave-shaped counter, fashioned from beechwood, and the lighting came from LED panels on the ceiling, their arrangement creating illuminated geometric patterns that were ever changing.

Eve wouldn't have been able to concentrate with all of that going on. She liked peaceful decor when she was working. After a mercifully short time the clerk got up from her counter and came over to escort her from the orange seat she was sitting on (it looked like a toadstool, but with a back shaped like a tongue) over to Rathbone's office.

Inside, the scene was less aggressively glaring, but just as modern and upmarket. The seats were all retro tubular steel and purple upholstery, the desk minimalist with clean lines. It was bare except for a bottle of mineral water with two glasses, a notepad and pen and a MacBook Pro. A photograph of two teenage children, smart in blazers with school crests on their pockets, sat on a bookcase behind him.

'Welcome,' Rathbone said. 'I've been looking forward to meeting you. When something like this happens it's oddly comforting to talk to someone about the person who's died.' He shook his head. 'Of course, my relationship with Ashton was professional really, but I'd known him a long time. I'd come to mind about him and his future.'

He glanced at the bottle of water. 'Can I pour you a drink? Or I can call through for coffee if you'd rather something hot?'

'Water would be great, thank you.' She sat down in the chair he'd motioned her to, opposite his own. 'I'm very grateful to you for seeing me. It sounds as though you'll provide new insights. I know Ashton went through some difficult times. I want readers to see him in the round, and to understand the background, so they get a true picture.'

The man nodded, a rueful look in his eye. 'I applaud your approach. Once a young person gets a bad reputation it can be very hard to shake it off – however well they do later in life. I hope I can help.'

Eve turned her notebook to a fresh page and set it on her lap. 'So I gather you met Ashton quite early on. How did that come about?'

'He got caught shoplifting. I do a limited amount of pro bono work for young people from difficult backgrounds, whose families have few financial resources. A friend of a friend mentioned the Foleys to me, and I got in touch. I gave Ashton advice and managed to help him avoid a fine for the theft he'd committed. He went home with a police caution instead, though of course that still went on his record.' His brown eyes met Eve's. 'He was a character. He had so many things going for him, despite some family tensions and his rebellious nature. I think a lot of his community had written him off as a good-for-nothing child who'd always exist on the margins. But as soon as I had that glimpse of what he could be, I couldn't give up on him.'

'What made you so committed?'

Rathbone sighed. 'I think there were two strands to that. Firstly, I almost went off the rails myself as a teenager. It can happen to anyone. I got in with a misguided group of friends at my boarding school. A sympathetic teacher spotted the danger and stuck by me. If I'd been arrested it would have ruined any chance I had of a career in law.'

'And the second?'

'I could see Ashton's potential. He was charming. He often talked people round and he was mentally and physically agile. Those skills can be useful if you want to make a living from crime but they're also perfect for running a legitimate business.'

This would all work very nicely in the obituary. It linked Ashton's past with his future and it would be good to include a heart-warming human-interest angle.

'So you helped Ashton again, when he got in trouble for selling cannabis a little later on?'

'That's right. We'd got to know each other by that time and I couldn't leave him in the hands of someone who didn't understand his background. I advised him and liaised with the youth court. I don't want to portray myself as a saint. Practising in a country town can get dull, and following Ashton's progress from start to finish gave me a challenge. He was a tough nut to crack, but it was all the more rewarding when he came good.'

Eve nodded. 'I can imagine. I was looking at interviews Ashton gave, where he referred to his trial for selling drugs. He mentioned his old teacher, Tina Adcock, gave evidence.'

Rathbone nodded. 'That's right.' His eyes were far away for a moment. 'I'm sure the authorities were grateful for her input. It was a shame Ashton wouldn't give me – or the police – more details himself, but I suppose you can't blame him. He wouldn't have dared cross the person who'd supplied the cannabis.'

'You think he was scared? That seemed likely to me, but his mother implied he was overconfident, and that it worried her.'

The lawyer gave her a sad smile. 'Children can put on a good act and they have years of practice when it comes to deceiving their parents. Ashton would never have wanted to show his fear.

'Mrs Adcock's evidence pointed to a man a few years older than Ashton being the guilty party, but of course, that person would also have had his own supplier. Even if they'd identified him, it wouldn't have solved the bigger problem.'

'I see what you mean. So, what happened after Ashton was sentenced? Did you visit him at the young offenders' institute?'

The lawyer nodded. 'I wanted to check he was all right – and that he hadn't had second thoughts about passing on details that would help us to find the person who'd recruited him, of course.'

'Did you keep in touch later, once he moved to London?'

The man smiled. 'I emailed every so often, just to see how he was doing, and we met for a drink once, when I had to be in town. He shared the business idea for Outside In with me on that occasion. It was a fantastic reward to see the enthusiasm in his eyes. I was always a little worried about his work as a roadie – all that partying might have put him in drug-taking circles all over again. Outside In was the making of him, and I'm sure he was pleased to spend so much time with someone like Marina Shaw. I've seen her photograph in the papers.'

Was the lawyer just passing comment, or hinting at something? It made her wonder again if Marina and Ashton had been closer than she'd implied, and if so, whether that was ongoing. It would be good to find out more about Marina's love life.

Eve shifted in her seat. 'Thanks so much for your time. It's been really useful.'

'It's a pleasure.' But he made no move to rise from his chair. 'Look, forgive me, but I'm going to talk out of turn. I'm sure you're conscious of the danger you might be in when interviewing Ashton's old contacts. Entirely between ourselves, Ashton came to see me after he returned to Saxford. He wanted to ask my advice about something, but he also spoke a lot about Justin Ingram.'

Eve caught her breath. What was coming?

'You know he's married to one of the people who won an Outside In consultation?'

She nodded.

'Ashton was talking about the old days: his time in the young offenders' institute and the fact that his supplier had never been caught. Then, immediately afterwards, he mentioned his old "friend", Justin Ingram. I got the impression he was trying to tell me something, though he wouldn't say more when I asked.'

Eve felt a chill run through her. Was that why Ashton hated Justin? Had Justin supplied him drugs, then left him to rot when someone reported him to the police? If so, he must have been sure Ashton wouldn't name him at his trial. Maybe Ashton had no proof, and Justin looked squeaky clean. He certainly gave off that aura these days. As a teen, Ashton might have doubted the police would take him seriously. And maybe he had been frightened, underneath it all, as the lawyer suggested.

'I might be making something out of nothing,' Rathbone said, 'but when I saw the Ingrams had won the makeover in the local paper it worried me. If Ashton ended up inside their house, I couldn't help feeling he might use the opportunity to take some kind of revenge. He might have been scared back when he was a teenager, but he's been out of the drug scene for a long time now. Fear fades, whereas the desire for revenge grows.'

Eve's pen stilled on the paper. 'You've mentioned all this to the police, I suppose?'

'I called them last night. I have no evidence, just a bad feeling, but I knew I had to say something. If there was any truth to it then he might have been a threat to Ingram. I just wanted you to know. I'd hate you to be in a vulnerable situation.'

For a moment, Eve wondered if it could have been Justin who'd delivered the package to Ashton's desk at school, but presumably Tina would have recognised him, as a local. It didn't fit.

'Thank you for warning me.'

Rathbone nodded.

Eve sat in her car for five minutes before she drove home, waiting for her thoughts to settle. It sounded like Justin could have a motive for killing Ashton, but there were two oddities. If Rathbone's guesses were right, why hadn't Justin been worried when Amber won the prize draw? You'd think inviting Ashton into their house would be the last thing he'd want. Could it be that Justin hadn't been his supplier, but had been connected to them, and had no idea Ashton was onto him? But that theory didn't clear up the second oddity: the prank Marina said Ashton had played on the Ingrams. The joke seemed far too childish and petty to fit Justin's crime. Maybe Russell Rathbone had misinterpreted Ashton's words. If not, she must be missing something, but what?

She needed to interview the Ingrams and see what came out. And she could ask Mrs Foley about Ashton's relationship with Justin, too.

Her thoughts were interrupted by a text from her ex-husband, Ian.

I've just seen the news. Please tell me you're not working on the obituary of a drug-dealer-turned-murder-victim? You know my views.

Eve did, and she was supremely uninterested in them. Deleting the message felt good. Shame it wasn't so easy to delete the adrenaline rush his missives always triggered. She was so glad she'd moved to Suffolk. If she'd been back in London he'd have been on her doorstep by now. He was the one who'd walked out on her, but he still couldn't resist interfering. He seemed to feel she was incapable of running her life without his guiding hand. She was going to carry on proving him wrong, every second of every day.

She took a deep breath. Thinking time with Gus was what she needed. That and getting every fact she could muster down onto her spreadsheet.

But alongside the drugs angle of her secret investigation, she needed to keep digging for information on Howard Green. Betty believed in him, and he seemed steady, but she couldn't take that on trust. What on earth had he been doing outside Apple Tree Cottage, the morning after Ashton's death? If there was any concrete evidence he might be guilty, she'd have to face Mrs Foley with it. That evening, after she'd eaten, she would let herself into Apple Tree Cottage and see what she could find.

CHAPTER EIGHTEEN

Eve didn't want the villagers to see her entering Apple Tree Cottage. It was best if they were unaware of the job Betty Foley had given her. She took Gus for an after-supper walk up the beach, then returned him to Elizabeth's Cottage, bent to pet him, and left for Ashton's childhood home. She wore her dark-blue jeans and a navy roll-neck jumper. No self-advertising yellow macs today, and it was mild enough not to need her puffer jacket.

As she neared Blind Eye Wood, she saw a nightjar against the darkening sky, silently hawking for food. After a moment it disappeared from sight, but a second later she heard its strange churring song, rising and falling in the quiet of the evening.

The old apple trees in the garden of Ashton's mother's house were still in the silvery moonlight, their gnarled branches like twisted arms, reaching out into the night. She let herself through the side gate as Betty had instructed, feeling nervous, even though she was acting with her permission. The rusty hinges sounded loud against the hush of the oncoming night. She scanned the lane one last time for any movement before closing the gate behind her.

The back garden was home to several cast-iron ornaments, indistinct in the low light. Eve took out her phone and used its torch to sweep the lawn, picking out an ornamental hare and a duck before she hit upon the owl. It looked solid, but when she lifted it, she found it was hollow. The front door key to the cottage lay on the grass, just under the point where the owl had sat. Eve had seen similar statues cast in bronze, their solidity ensuring they were stable. This one looked cheap. Someone had wedged a bag of gravel up inside it – as a weight, Eve guessed, to stop it tipping over in the wind. She suddenly felt sad. Betty Foley had probably saved up and bought things she liked for her garden, but she guessed she'd never had a lot to spend. Now she would have the proceeds from the sale of her son's share of Outside In, but the fortune would be hollow – a constant reminder of the true value of what she'd lost.

Eve took the key round to the front of the cottage and let herself in, looking over her shoulder as she pushed the door open. Inside, she hesitated.

Howard still had a key.

It sounded unlikely that he'd visit – Betty had said there was nothing that needed doing in the house – but she still felt exposed. After a moment's thought, she slid the bolt across the door. If he tried to unlock it while she was there she'd have some explaining to do, but it felt like the least dangerous option. In another moment she'd performed the same operation on the back door.

The place was stuffy. A smell of cooking still lingered, maybe from Ashton's last meal.

Betty's home wasn't directly overlooked, but passers-by would notice if she set all the lights blazing. Instead, she took a cursory check round the house by moonlight, using her phone's torch when she needed extra illumination. As she'd expected, there was nothing that stood out: the kitchen was clear of dirty crockery and the room Ashton must have slept in didn't yield anything. A few of the man's belongings still remained; a leather jacket and a pair of boots were a vivid and eerie reminder that conjured up his mischievous smile and knowing eyes.

She'd already been certain the police would have found anything clearly connected with the crime. And if Howard Green had let himself in before they did, he might have removed evidence from the house too. His possible presence was the hardest thing to ignore, when she weighed up the chances of him being involved.

But she wasn't put off by not finding anything immediately. When she'd offered to look round, it was for the less obvious clues, the ones her professional knowledge told her might exist. What could have triggered a sudden escalation in hostilities between Howard Green and Ashton Foley? In all her years dealing with relatives after a death, money was by far the most common cause of contention.

Betty Foley was close to Howard Green, even though she'd kept him at arm's length. It was possible that their lives were more entwined than her son might have supposed. And that might include their financial arrangements. If so, Ashton could have discovered the details if he'd gone snooping in Betty's papers.

She was scanning for a filing cabinet, or something similar. During her cursory look round, she'd missed it, but on a second tour of the cottage she struck gold.

There was no hallway in the building, and the downstairs consisted only of a kitchen at the front and a living room, lobby and downstairs bathroom at the back. It was the living room that housed the filing cabinet. Its ugly grey metal was mostly disguised with a sea-green throw that toned in with the colour of the window frames. A vase of dried flowers sat on top: pink and purple statice, with a sprig of honesty.

Eve closed the door between the living room and the kitchen so she could turn on the overhead light without its glow being visible from the lane. After that, she stood for a moment, agonising, feeling out of place in the starkly lit room. When she'd asked Betty's permission to look for clues in her house, the woman probably hadn't imagined she'd go searching through her private files. But on the other hand, she'd involved Eve in a way she wouldn't have chosen, and put her in a moral dilemma, given Howard might have something to hide. And Eve had said nothing about confining her search to Ashton's belongings.

At last, she rearranged the throw and flowers to get access to the filing cabinet's drawers, but she still felt conflicted and uneasy.

She took a deep breath. She needed to know if Betty was holding out on her; her safety might depend on it. Eve thought again of the way the woman had paused when asked if she could think of any reason why Ashton and Howard might have quarrelled recently. If, as she suspected, Betty had withheld information, then her actions were hopefully excusable.

She pulled the filing cabinet drawers open one by one, scanning the labelled tabs on the drop files inside. If Ashton had gone snooping, what would he have looked for? And for what reason? If he'd been resentful of Howard still, and wondered about his mom's feelings, she could imagine him looking at her will. He wasn't short of money, but that didn't stop most people. It was the principle of the thing that got to them; the sign that a parent loved someone else as much as, or more than, them. Ashton might have looked with a view to convincing Betty to change her mind if she'd left her boyfriend anything. Or simply to enjoy feeling justified in his bad feelings towards Howard.

The will was easy to find, under W. Thankfully, it was a fairly slender and simple document compared with the few other examples she'd seen. The house went to Ashton, but she'd left a sum of money and a few specific belongings to Howard. The amount wasn't large and the possessions didn't sound valuable, but she could still imagine it making Ashton mad.

She shook her head. That might have led the pair of them to come to blows if they'd been spoiling for a fight anyway. Ashton could have punched him in a fit of anger, causing his bruises. But in that instance, would Howard have then decided to plot Ashton's murder? It didn't sound right. Eve had seen Howard's bruises days before Ashton was shot dead. It had been more than enough time for Howard to calm down and see sense.

She needed to search further, in case there was something else. She scanned the file tabs for any other subjects that might relate to finance. There was one marked 'House', which showed Betty had managed to pay off almost all of her mortgage. There was no indication that she'd done anything unusual, like putting Howard down as joint owner, and Eve couldn't imagine any reason why she should. He had his own house.

But then, as she scanned the other tabs, she saw what Ashton might have seen, if he'd been nosy and suspicious: a new tab that didn't match the rest, labelled 'Property'. The title surprised Eve. Everything she'd seen that evening told her Betty had little money to spare. Her furniture had seen better days; the carpet was worn.

Eve looked inside the file. It was all but empty, containing just two papers. The first was property details from an estate agent in Southwold for a cottage in a nearby village, valued at £300,000. And the second was an email chain between Howard Green and Betty Foley. Eve felt her pulse quicken as she scanned the details.

The messages didn't answer all Eve's questions. Betty and Howard referred to face to face conversations they'd had, so some reading between the lines was required. But it was clear that at some stage – presumably recently – Betty had received a substantial bequest from a relative. The exchange between her and Howard made it plain she couldn't invest it in the property herself, because she'd need a mortgage in addition to the capital she'd inherited. Eve thought back to the conversation she'd had with Mrs Foley. She'd mentioned she'd gotten behind with the repayments on Apple Tree Cottage at one point. Russell Rathbone had advised her and sorted out a plan to get her out of debt. It probably meant her bank wasn't keen to give her a fresh loan. The final email in the exchange was a formal message from Howard, confirming he would invest £200,000 of Betty's money on her behalf, apply for a mortgage to cover the balance, and arrange for tenants to occupy 'the house'. Presumably the one mentioned in the estate agent's information. Howard's message confirmed he would see the rent went partly to Betty and partly to pay off the mortgage on the investment property.

He'd clearly sent the email as proof that the house was hers, and she'd filed it accordingly. Eve tried to imagine Ashton's reaction if he'd sat where she was now, reading that same file. Had he even known his mom had inherited the money? She might have kept it from him and that would probably have felt like a betrayal too. And then she'd entrusted the money to Howard, and allowed him to act on her behalf.

What about the legalities? Was an email really all that was required to protect Betty's interests? And Ashton's as her next of kin? Eve thought back to the story of him trying to steal Daphne's ring. Sylvia had said it was always about money, and always about him. He might not have wanted for funds these days, but she was betting he wouldn't have liked the thought that a large sum had passed out of Betty's hands and into Howard's. After all, he'd hated Howard for years, by the sound of it.

Carefully, she replaced the papers in the files, closed the drawers of the cabinet and covered it with the throw again.

What would Ashton have done if he'd found the papers? He might have felt humiliated and angry, and she imagined he'd have gone to Howard about it.

Ashton might well have lashed out – she could see that. But why was he the one that had ended up dead?

There was something she was missing. She needed more information, both on Howard and the process for buying a house on someone else's behalf. But everything she'd found that evening deepened her unease.

She switched off the living room light, reopened the door to the kitchen, drew back the bolt on the back door and then let herself out the front. A moment later she was back in the rear garden, replacing the key under the owl.

She was still deep in thought as she made her way through the thickening darkness of the passageway back towards Heath Lane.

She expected the way to lighten as she opened the wooden gate, and caught her breath when it didn't.

A tall man blocked the way: a solid silhouetted presence that sent her heart into her throat.

CHAPTER NINETEEN

'What the hell do you think you're doing?'

He'd grabbed hold of her left upper arm with his right, his grip vice-like. She still couldn't distinguish the details of his face, but she knew who this was now.

Howard Green.

She shrank back, trying to wriggle from under his grasp as she fought to think through her panic. She guessed he had no idea Betty had asked her to try to prove his innocence. Through a fug of fear, she tried to summon up a convincing answer.

'Mrs Foley invited me to visit the house because I'm writing Ashton's obituary. It's useful to see a subject's childhood home.'

'In the dark? At night?'

'I was busy all day. You know I work part-time at Monty's, and then I had to conduct an office-hours interview and eat supper. This was the first chance I had.' Her voice wasn't quite steady.

He let go of her shoulder and shook himself, as though he was regaining control. 'I'll be checking.' His voice was still harsh. 'I speak to Betty regularly and I know her house as well as I do my own. If one single thing's out of place, I'll be aware.'

He moved to one side, but only slightly, so that she still had to squeeze past him. It was intimidating.

As Eve walked down the path from Apple Tree Cottage to the lane, her legs shook. It was understandable that she'd given him a fright, and that he was looking out for Betty's interests, but was it natural for him to seem so threatened by her presence?

And what would he see when he went inside? She tried to conjure up a precise image of how she'd left the filing cabinet, with its complicated adornment of throw and flowers. Had she gotten the positioning of the vase right? And if not, would Howard notice? She was sure he'd check carefully; he'd pretty much told her he was looking for a chance to catch her out. She made her way through the village without noticing her surroundings. If Howard guessed what she'd seen, might she be in trouble? Was it possible that Betty was completely wrong about the type of man she'd been seeing all these years? And she was worried about Betty Foley too. What would her reaction be if she found out Eve had been through her private papers?

Eve had a restless night. She pictured Howard Green examining Apple Tree Cottage, noticing a stray bit of honesty on the carpet, a bit of throw tucked into a filing cabinet drawer, a paper sticking out of a file at an odd angle… In her head his face morphed into that of the child catcher in *Chitty Chitty Bang Bang*. There was some crossover.

And what had Howard been doing, returning to Apple Tree Cottage? Had he gone back to continue a search he'd started on Sunday morning, just after Ashton's death? If so, he must have been biding his time until after the police search was over.

Whatever his reasons for visiting, he'd acted suspiciously. Going to the cottage at night suggested he wanted to avoid attracting attention, just like her. And most compelling of all, he'd been slipping round the back when she ran into him, even though he had his own set of keys. He must know he'd been seen hanging around, the morning after Ashton was killed. Maybe he'd decided going in the front way was too risky in case someone walked by again. By contrast, the route round the side of the house offered shadow, and the back garden wasn't overlooked. She shivered. Thank goodness he hadn't arrived any earlier and found she'd bolted herself in. She was sure he'd have waited for her to come out, and she didn't like to think what his reaction would have been.

Eve wanted Howard to be innocent for Betty's sake, but her doubts were much more significant now. She'd seen another side to him that evening. The dull-but-reliable figure she'd witnessed in the village had an unnerving alter ego when he was under pressure. He might love Betty and be willing to do almost anything to shield her from harm, but that didn't rule him out. Taken to extremes, his desire to protect might even have been his motive. It was clear Ashton had sometimes made his mother unhappy, and Howard could have perceived other threats to her well-being too, if Ashton was still involved with local criminals. And then there was the simple fact that Ashton had been a thorn in Howard's own side for years.

At three in the morning, looking at her shadowy wooden-beamed room through eyes that were gritty with lack of sleep, she decided to accelerate her own investigations into Howard. If she found nothing to reassure her in the next twenty-four hours, she'd explain her position to Betty. And if she found anything concrete, she'd have to involve the police too. She'd need to put off her digging for a couple of hours the following day though. She had an appointment first thing with Amber and Justin Ingram. Justin had confirmed she could visit in response to an email she'd sent. She could tell he wasn't keen though. Because he was busy, or because he had something to hide?

Early on Tuesday, she took Gus for a run along the beach to try to clear her head and returned with tiny raindrops clinging to her short brown hair. The contract from *Icon* had arrived in her absence. She ripped open the envelope as she walked through to the kitchen and scanned the contents. The magazine might be laying off staff, but the fee was still handsome in comparison to what she was used to. It might be a dangerous assignment, but at least she didn't feel used.

'Fancy a golden collar, Gus?' His look told her it was a 'no'.

After she'd had breakfast, she rang Justin to confirm their appointment. He sounded tight-lipped and a lot less bouncy than he had a few days earlier, though it might just be down to the planted underwear. She spent half an hour researching the couple. Justin was a graphic designer – the proprietor of Ingram's Designs – which explained the comment she'd overheard on the night of the prize draw. He'd hoped he and Amber would be picked to appear on Ashton's TV series, and his work would get extra exposure on the back of that. And although she couldn't find anything career-related on Amber online, Moira had said she worked part-time for Howard Green at his antiques shop.

At last, Eve changed into a neat chocolate-brown dress and jacket suitable for a formal interview. She said goodbye to Gus and let herself out onto Haunted Lane, her umbrella shielding her from the rain that was now coming down in rods from a leaden sky.

It was Justin Ingram who let her into his and Amber's cottage on Ferry Lane, a narrow, picturesque road that led towards the estuary. Today, the trees and shrubs that lined the way looked greener than usual, water pouring off them and down the lane. In the previous century, a ferryman had provided a regular service from the end of the byway, across the River Sax, north towards Walberswick – the surviving pontoon was called Arthur's Jetty in his honour. These days, travellers going in that direction had to divert inland and use the Old Toll Road bridge.

Matt Falconer from the Cross Keys had a boat moored where the ferry used to tie up, but it wasn't for public use. He liked to take Jo out for day trips as a way of sweet-talking himself out of trouble, Toby said.

The Ingrams' hall was just as she'd imagined. It matched Justin to a tee: bright, light and shiny – immaculate, but without the quirks and visible flaws that gave a place (or a person) character. Outside, the house looked almost as old as Elizabeth's Cottage, but inside you'd never know. It had been remodelled, and the beams must be hidden under a false ceiling that kept all the lines clean and straight. After what she'd overheard at the prize draw, about Justin having his designs up on the walls, she paid special attention to the works that hung there. Large poster-style images in bold colours were displayed to left and right, including one for a firm whose name she recognised. Justin Ingram hadn't been effusive in his welcome, but when he caught the direction of her gaze he smiled at last, revealing toothpaste-ad teeth.

'It was quite a coup, winning the Bannister contract. I was only twenty-five at the time. It was my first big job after I'd branched out on my own.'

He puffed out his chest and she gave him her best smile. 'Awesome!'

He took her through a door at the end of the hall and into a vast kitchen-diner. They must have extended out into the back garden. The room was made up of long lines, stainless steel, birch and brilliant white emulsion. The walls provided a good backdrop for Justin's work, but the place felt a bit like an operating theatre.

'Here's Amber,' Justin said, barely glancing at his wife. His tone was icy again. 'It's her you'll want to talk to about the raffle prize win.'

The copper-haired woman Eve had seen at the prize draw lifted herself listlessly off the high stool she'd been sitting on and offered Eve a coffee.

'Thanks, that would be lovely if it's not too much trouble. And I'd really like to speak with you both to start off.' She turned to Justin as Amber moved towards a state-of-the-art coffee machine that resembled a spaceship. 'Mr Ingram—'

'Please, call me Justin.'

'Thank you. Justin, you sounded as though you were pleased at the opportunity to reconnect with Ashton, when he drew your wife's ticket the other night. I'd love to gather some reminiscences from his childhood friends.' After what Russell Rathbone had said, she was keen to avoid him slipping away too soon.

But Justin shook his head of immovable curls. 'In all honesty, I was just being polite. Not that I had anything against the guy, but I'm four years older than him, and my parents' house was outside Saxford, so we seldom saw each other, especially as we went to different schools. I'd occasionally bump into him at the Cross Keys, but that was about it. Ashton was an underage drinker, and there was no Jo Falconer on the scene then, so he didn't get booted out.'

That was interesting. So it *could* have been Justin who'd delivered the package to Ashton in school, then. Tina Adcock probably wouldn't have recognised him. She must know him by sight now, of course, but given the previous sighting had been years back, she might not have made the connection.

'The old landlord of the Cross Keys only cared about his profits,' Justin finished.

'So there's not much you can tell me about Ashton's life as he grew up?'

'Almost nothing that you won't know already. And as that's the case I might as well leave you in my wife's capable hands. She knew Ashton, didn't you, darling? And you were the one that provided such impeccable hospitality when he visited on Thursday afternoon. Unfortunately, I had an appointment with a client. I'd hoped for a different time slot with Ashton, but *apparently* his calendar was busy.'

Amber flushed, and her eyes met Eve's for a brief moment, as though she was gauging her reaction. After her husband left the room, she made some final adjustments to the coffee maker's settings and closed the door to the hall.

'Justin was disappointed,' she said. 'He'd hoped to hear Ashton's ideas first-hand.'

He'd certainly sounded pretty peeved. Amber must have read her look and she shrugged, as though giving in.

'Ashton was very flirty. He was like it with everyone; you probably noticed. But Justin found it hard to take.' She put clenched hands up to her cheeks for a moment. 'And he was a joker too.' Her tone was tight and angry.

Might she come across with her own version of events? Eve raised her eyebrows. 'He played a joke on you?'

'One I found very unfunny.'

Eve waited.

At long last, as the machine gurgled out a small pot of coffee, Amber sighed and produced the same story as Marina Shaw. Unless she'd cooked it up with Ashton to cover their tracks, it must be true. She certainly sounded as though she was being honest.

'You must have been really mad,' Eve said, taking a sip from the cup Amber brought her. *Darn – that's really good.*

Amber nodded. 'I was.' She closed her eyes. 'I still am. I can't help it, even though he's dead.'

'Why would he have done such a thing?'

Amber was digging the nail of her right forefinger into the flesh of her left hand. 'I've been asking myself the same question.'

Could this possibly have anything to do with Rathbone's suspicions about links between Ashton and Justin, related to Ashton's dealing? And would Ashton really have used that sort of schoolboy prank in revenge for something so serious? It was weird.

At that moment the door to the hallway opened again. Eve looked up to see a boy come in, his hair a slightly darker version of Amber's.

'Do you want to watch some television, Leo?' Amber walked over and gave him a tight hug. Between her arms, Eve saw his face turn a blotchy red as he wriggled free. Amber turned to Eve. 'The Easter holidays started this week, and the wet weather's not helping.'

'Dad said I had to stop playing on my computer. He said no more screen time.'

Eve was all for fresh air, exercise and improving activities, but Justin's stipulation wasn't helpful. He'd disappeared into his study, clearly unwilling to interact with the boy, and Eve was trying to conduct an interview. She suspected he'd done it on purpose.

'Justin and I take turns to keep an eye on him,' Amber said, as though she'd read Eve's mind. 'I work part-time at Howard Green's antiques business, so when I'm not around, Justin holds the fort.'

'It sounds like a fascinating job. I love antiques but I don't know much about them.'

Amber sighed. 'My role's fairly dull, to be honest.'

'It's interesting that you're connected with Howard Green, given his link with Ashton and Betty Foley.' Eve wondered how to proceed. 'I must talk to Howard in person. Do you think he'd have useful reminiscences to pass on?' It was best to play dumb and see what came out. 'I expect he must mention Ashton to you occasionally.'

'We haven't been in touch since the murder. I'm doing odd hours this week.' She closed her eyes.

If the thought of her boss made her pull that face, Eve was guessing Moira had been right, and working with him wasn't great at the moment.

'Howard hated Ashton. You might as well know; it'll save awkwardness if you do talk.'

That was interesting. So far, Eve hadn't seen Howard show anger towards Betty's son – only vice versa – but Amber was clearly aware of the force of his negative feelings. And Viv had said their quarrels had been more obvious in the old days. She'd guessed he'd been making a big effort to stay civil since Ashton had come home, for Betty's sake. Only later, there'd been no Betty to hold him back…

Leo was still waiting for Amber to suggest some form of entertainment.

'What about drawing?' his mother said, sipping her own coffee.

Leo let out a groan, but within a minute he was up at the kitchen table with a pad of paper and felt-tip pens.

'He loves it really,' Amber said. 'Takes after Justin.' There was a hint of pride in her voice – both for her son and her husband, Eve thought, despite her and Justin not being on great terms right now. No wonder she was sore at Ashton if he'd really planted that underwear.

Leo had started drawing already. Eve went to fetch more coffee from the pot, and paused to admire his work. That took her round to the far side of the kitchen table, and there, she caught sight of a pile of printouts on the countertop, sitting on a presentation folder, with the Ingram's Designs logo on it.

They looked like part of a pitch for new work. The business name, Outside In, was represented in clean, crisp blues and greens. There were a number of alternative designs for what was clearly Justin's idea of how the company's artwork should look.

But Eve had seen Outside In's branding. It was on the brochure that Marina Shaw had brought round. Their existing logo was like a traditional illustration. The style reminded Eve of Arthur Rackham; it had a fairy tale, dream-like quality. It was slightly spooky in fact – a little unsettling – but most certainly memorable in a way that Justin's design wasn't.

At that moment, Amber appeared at her elbow. 'Justin was just messing around, his version of doodling. Outside In already has a designer.'

'You didn't show these to Ashton? I suppose he might have been interested in exploring a new look?' Maybe that's what Justin had hoped.

Amber shook her head. 'Oh no. It was just a bit of fun.' She led her over to a kitchen island, away from the printouts and Leo.

'So, you want people's memories of Ashton when he was younger? We were in the same class at school, so I might be more help than Justin.' She sounded bitter.

Eve nodded, and took her notepad from her bag.

'He always liked to stand out: to be the most daring, that kind of thing. I honestly wonder if that's why he got into trouble. People paid him attention when he played up, and the further he went, the more he got. He loved to be in the spotlight.' Her eyes hardened. 'Only somewhere along the line I guess he realised there was a lot of money to make if you're prepared to break the law.'

'It must have been a challenge to turn his back on that life and start afresh as an adult.'

Amber sipped her coffee. 'I guess he saw other ways to make his living, and better ways to get himself in the public eye. I don't believe his character ever changed. He always saw himself as invincible, whatever his current scheme was. There was no reasoning with him.'

Eve strove to see what was behind her words. 'He shared his latest project with you?' She wasn't even sure what she was asking; she was just poking about in the dark. She wasn't surprised when Amber's face turned blank.

'He told me a bit about his work for Billy Tozer,' she said at last.

'Various people in the village have mentioned how you used to run around together as kids,' Eve said. Instinct told her to stick with their personal relationship for now.

Amber shook her head. 'He talked me into doing a few things I regretted. He had a way with him.' She still sounded angry, but there was a sadness there too, behind her eyes. 'I shouldn't have been so weak, but I'm stronger now.' Her look was uncertain, but then she nodded. 'I am.'

Something told Eve there was a whole hidden story behind her words and actions. She took a deep breath and turned her thoughts back to the obituary. 'How did Ashton assess your home for the Outside In makeover?'

'He went through every room in the house, taking photos, getting a feel for the place. I left him to it after a while, which was obviously a mistake. He said our high white walls were perfect; they'd allow for indoor climbers, and be a great backdrop for shrubs and small trees.'

Eve glanced at the walls, which were currently covered in Justin's prints. It didn't sound as though they'd have survived the makeover. 'I suppose it isn't everyone who'd want their home transformed like that. All the watering and maintenance must take a lot of effort.'

Amber chewed her lip. 'A few people have said I didn't look that pleased when I won the prize,' she said after a moment. 'I was just surprised, that's all. I'd only bought a handful of tickets at Justin's insistence, and to be honest, I didn't relish the upheaval it would bring if we won the full makeover. But I was perfectly happy to take part. I never guessed Ashton would muck us around like he did. I kind of assumed he'd grown up.'

'I understand.' But Eve thought back to the way the woman had reacted that night. She hadn't been surprised, she'd been upset. And scared.

As for Justin, could he really have been the person who'd supplied Ashton with the cannabis he'd sold? And if so, and he'd frightened Ashton into keeping quiet about him at the time, was he so confident he still had him under control that he didn't mind having him in his house? Even to the extent that a business deal for his design firm was the first thing on his mind? It made no sense. But then Russell Rathbone had only been making guesses, based on what Ashton had said.

She thought again of Amber's reaction to her win. What did she know about Ashton and Justin's history? And if she was worried, why buy raffle tickets at all?

So many questions.

*

Back at Elizabeth's Cottage, Eve put her sodden umbrella to drip dry in the bath as Gus pottered around her feet. 'I don't know what's going on,' she said to him, 'but I'm keeping Justin Ingram in mind. He might have killed Ashton out of jealousy and hurt pride, even if there's nothing in the drugs link.' She sighed. 'But despite my mission, no one so far looks as suspicious as the eminently respectable Howard Green.'

A moment later she sat down at her laptop and emailed Betty Foley. Maybe Ashton had confided in her about Justin. She was keen to prompt an exchange with the woman too. She wanted to know if Howard had been in touch, and most especially, what he might have told her.

The thought made her feel queasy.

CHAPTER TWENTY

It was late morning when Eve finished her email to Betty Foley, and the rain had finally stopped. She went upstairs to swap her interview dress for her jeans and a black polo neck, then went down to the coat stand near the front door for her mac.

'Walk, Gus?' she said, pulling on her black ankle boots, but as he bounded towards her, ears flapping, her mobile rang.

She answered, tucking the phone between her ear and shoulder as she reached for Gus's leash. Maybe she could keep him sweet by walking and talking at the same time.

'*It's Detective Inspector Palmer speaking.*'

Perhaps not then. She didn't bother suppressing her sigh. If he was going to ask about her relationship with Ashton again, she'd rather not answer in public, despite having nothing to hide. She stepped away from Gus's leash and bent to stroke his head in response to his injured look.

'Inspector. How can I help?' Getting rid of him as quickly as possible was her sole desire.

'*I'm calling because I'm concerned I didn't make myself plain when I visited you.*' He cleared his phlegmy throat. '*For the avoidance of doubt, if I find you're guilty of going beyond your remit as an obituary writer, I shall be forced to request an order forbidding you to contact Ashton Foley's friends and family.*'

His words and tone sent her heart rate soaring; he was talking to her as though she was a criminal. Had Howard Green made a complaint? Told Palmer about her visit to Apple Tree Cottage? But surely he'd avoid admitting he'd been hanging around the house too? Either way, she wasn't going to mention her visit unless Palmer did. She'd been there with Betty Foley's permission, after all, and the police had done with the place.

'May I ask what makes you think I've overstepped the mark?' She managed to control her voice, but she could feel her body quivering from the effort.

He let out a dismissive laugh. *'I'm quite sure you don't really expect me to answer that.'*

He was right; she knew him too well anticipate common decency. 'If someone's reported me, I'd say it says more about the secrets they're hiding than my methods.'

'On the contrary, I imagine their complaint had everything to do with your pushy attitude. I've warned every witness I've interviewed that you'll probably be in touch with them too,' Palmer went on. She could hear the relish in his voice. *'And I've specifically asked them to let me know if you ask about matters that don't concern you. Do I make myself clear?'*

He wouldn't ring off until she'd confirmed, in so many words, that she understood. After he'd finally left her in peace she had to fight to contain the fury that was swelling in her chest. She bent to attach Gus's leash.

'The man is such a jerk,' she said to him, ruffling his fur and giving him a hug. 'Thank goodness you're here to redress the balance.'

She'd have to be careful, but if she managed to hand any useful information to the police it would be a double victory: she'd be using her skills in the pursuit of justice – an added bonus to the profession she loved – and she'd irritate the heck out of Palmer into the bargain. It was something to hold onto.

It was only after they left the cottage, and her stress levels reduced, that another thought occurred to her. Was it possible that she'd already interviewed Ashton's murderer, and they had reported her to the police?

As she and Gus made their way around the village green, both appreciating the break in the rain, she bumped into Simon. It was the first time in a while that she'd come face to face with him without Polly Cartwright on his arm. Her attempt at dignity – a warm, friendly yet unconcerned smile, while moving swiftly on – was ruined by Gus, who saw no reason for reticence. He took one look at Simon, did a giddy skip sideways and rolled onto his back, ready for a tickle on the tummy. Talk about shameless.

Simon laughed, crouched down and obliged, while Gus looked ecstatic. He'd fallen for Viv's brother's charms right from the word go. Eve herself had found them quite potent too, but unlike Gus, she had her head screwed on. She and Simon were just too different.

'How're things?' Simon said, his laughing brown eyes on hers. 'Gus has made me feel better, but I'm still reeling after the appalling news about Ashton.'

'Did you know him, back when he was a child?' Simon was younger than Viv, but still a lot older than the dead man.

'Hardly at all. Just had a vague impression of him as a tearaway. No one was surprised when he ended up in the young offenders' place, to be honest. His shift to successful local hero was much more of a shock.'

'I've agreed to write his obituary.'

'Wow.' His eyes were serious now, and he stood up. 'After what happened last time, that's a brave decision.'

'I'll be on my guard.'

'Good.' His eyes were on hers.

'How are things going with Polly?'

She was rewarded with a blush. 'Well, you know, it's early days.'

Eve smiled. She felt better now they were talking about it. And it gave her the chance to be gracious. 'You look good together. And

I saw her out with you the other day. She's at ease on horseback.'
Simon owned a stables. He'd invited Eve to ride with him when
they'd been seeing each other. The thought had filled her with
horror; why would you sit on something with a will of its own, that
far off the ground? And every horse she'd met had been hell-bent
on humiliating her; there were times when it was best not to push
these things.

'Turns out she used to ride as a child.'

She would. 'Lovely.' Eve could tell the conversation was about
to become stilted, but Howard Green flashed through her mind.
He was a local businessman, just like Simon. It was possible they
might know each other, and Eve needed to dig to find out more
about the man; she mustn't let personal feelings get in the way.
She asked the question.

Simon frowned. 'I know him a bit. Do you fancy a quick drink
in the Cross Keys? I can fill you in.'

Eve wondered where Polly was. People might talk. But maybe
she was being silly; Simon wasn't worried. And he might have more
information on her other interviewees too. 'All right. Thanks.'

Five minutes later they were sitting at a table Eve had selected,
well in the eye of the public bar, each nursing a glass of Toby's 'spring
cup' – a warming spiced apple juice, perfect to offset the chill of a
damp April day, as Toby had rightly said. They'd lit the fire again;
it crackled over to Eve's left. The room smelled of woodsmoke,
spices and rich food. Gus had gone over to say hello to Hetty, so
he was happy. So long as they didn't get overexcited, Eve would
have time to focus.

'You've interviewed Howard then?' Simon asked, his voice low.

She shook her head, thinking of her alarming encounter with
the man the evening before. 'We've exchanged a few words, but
I had the urge to find out more about him before I went in with
questions.'

Simon nodded.

'So far the only official interviews I've done have been with Ashton's business manager, Marina Shaw, his old lawyer, Russell Rathbone, and the Ingrams.'

Simon glanced over his shoulder before he spoke, just like she and Viv always did. 'Justin Ingram approached me with ideas for branding for the riding stables,' he said. 'It was a while back, before Ingram's Designs had really taken off. I wouldn't think he'd bother with me nowadays, but at the time he gave me the hard sell. He quoted crazy prices and I found him a bit obnoxious, to be honest. Too pushy. In the end I managed to source someone who did a decent job for half the money.'

Eve nodded. She'd felt just the same about the man, but it would be unprofessional to commit herself.

'As for Howard Green, we've chatted occasionally. Although our business interests are entirely different, some of the headaches we face overlap.' He nodded towards the bar. 'We've shared our woes and triumphs over the odd pint in here. Nothing prearranged – just when we've met by chance.'

'You get on?'

Simon took a deep breath. 'Well, I suppose I wouldn't have put it quite like that. He's so stiff and formal I never feel I can relax, and his outlook's very old-fashioned. But he's always been perfectly civil, and in a village this size it makes sense to rub along with people.

'He sought me out recently, as a matter of fact. He knows I dabble a bit more widely in business than he does, and he'd found what he thought was a prime investment opportunity in a housing development for wealthy senior citizens. It was called something really corny. Oh yes, I remember, Golden Vistas.'

Eve knew Simon had invested in property before too.

He shook his head. 'The deal he'd spotted was way too good to be true, and I told him so. I'm afraid he had that hungry look in his eye. I suspect he'd had the hope of a massive pay-off dangled in front of him.' His eyes were far away for a moment. 'There are two sorts of people who fall for that type of scam: ones who are greedy, and ones who are desperate. It made me wonder if things weren't going too well with his antiques outfit. He looked dangerously like a man who might clutch at straws, and I strongly advised him to get independent advice before going ahead.'

Eve remembered Moira had the impression Green's business was in trouble too. 'Do you know what he did?'

Simon shook his head. 'He just thanked me, but in that way a person does when they've decided they're wasting their time talking to you. I hadn't told him what he wanted to hear. Hopefully he got the same answer if he went for a second opinion. I kept an eye on the deal he'd mentioned, just to check I can still spot a racket.' He grinned. 'And I can. The bottom fell out of that scheme. Anyone who invested would have lost a packet.'

They sipped their drinks, but Eve was no longer focused on the sweet spiced apple. Simon's words danced in her head.

'After that, I didn't like to ask Howard what he'd done,' Simon said. 'If he'd found the money to invest, then gone against my advice and lost out, I guessed it would be a topic best avoided.'

'Thanks, Simon.'

'Think it's relevant? I gather the police are very interested in Howard.'

'I'd heard that too. And I don't know, but it's useful to have every bit of information going. Please don't report me to Palmer, will you? He's out to pounce if I ask any questions that don't relate directly to Ashton's life story.'

Simon's eyebrows shot up. 'The evil—' He stopped himself. 'Your secret's safe with me, Eve.' He bent down to make a fuss of Gus, who'd appeared by her side, clearly sensing that their chat was drawing to close.

*

Eve was sitting at the kitchen table in Elizabeth's Cottage, finishing a cup of tea, when a text came in. Viv.

Sit rep? Word has it you were drinking in the Cross Keys with Simon earlier!

Eve would have to take to wearing a false nose and wide-brimmed hat if this carried on.

I was interviewing him for the case. We didn't have anything stronger than warm, spiced apple juice.

Viv's reply came a second later.

That's what they all say…

She might have felt more irked at the teasing if she wasn't so taken up with what Simon had said. The rain had started again, and she sat listening to the gentle sound of water dripping off the ends of the reeds of her thatched roof. It was a soothing backdrop to the disturbing thoughts going around in her head.

Gus glanced up and she bent to stroke his head and long ears. 'None of what Simon said makes me any happier,' she told him. 'Both he and Moira think Howard's antiques business is probably in trouble, and Simon guesses he wanted to put money into this property development, presumably to try to recoup his losses. The question is, what funds did he have to invest, if he was down on his luck?'

Gus's brown eyes were on hers, as though he was trying to think of a good answer.

'He might have remortgaged his own house, of course,' Eve said to him, 'if he hadn't done that already. But after my visit to Apple Tree Cottage last night, I know he had access to another large sum of money: the funds that Betty Foley asked him to invest for her in that rental property.'

She closed her eyes. Betty clearly knew all the details. She had the email from Howard in her files, explaining exactly what the arrangements were. Some of the rental income would go straight to her, and some to the bank, to pay off the mortgage on the property. Presumably the money had been going into Betty's account, just as it ought to, but she could hardly ask… She shouldn't really have looked at the woman's private papers at all – most certainly wouldn't have, if she weren't in such a morally conflicted situation. She hoped her doubts about Howard were enough to justify her actions.

The thought persisted. Howard, a man who'd fallen on hard times had then – maybe – sunk more money into a scheme that had ruined him. While at the same time, he'd had access to Betty Foley's funds, in an irregular way. Although Betty had an email, setting out the details, Eve was sure as heck that didn't count as a proper legal arrangement. She guessed it would be good evidence in court, if she and Howard had a dispute, but things hadn't been done by the book.

Her mind ran back to Russell Rathbone. Property wasn't his area of the law, but maybe he'd be able to offer some advice on the paperwork Howard and Betty ought to have had in place. She sighed. She could ask him without mentioning any names: pretend she was putting the query for herself or a friend maybe. He'd seemed the sort who'd be happy to help.

What if Howard had somehow managed to siphon off money from the pot Betty had given him, and used it for his own ends? How would that fit with Ashton's death? But there was no hint of anything like that in Betty's files; nothing incriminating for Ashton to find that might have led him to confront Howard. And Eve was sure there never had been. Howard wouldn't have let Betty see anything that might give him away.

She couldn't work it out, but when a person found themselves in extreme circumstances, they sometimes crossed lines they never would normally. And Howard Green was probably no exception. His old-fashioned manners and outlook would make it even more likely; he'd hate to lose face in the village. What might he have done to avoid that?

CHAPTER TWENTY-ONE

After she'd put her teacup in the dishwasher, Eve sat on one of the couches in the living room, with Gus snuggled against her toes, and checked her emails. Betty Foley had replied. She must be sleeping badly – not that that was any surprise.

Dear Eve,

Yes, Ashton did mention Justin Ingram to me. All I know is that he hated him. If ever his name came up, all hell let loose. He never mentioned him in connection with his arrest though. As I said, Ashton always maintained he didn't know the true identity of the person who involved him in dealing.

She wrote as though Ashton had played no part in the matter.

But I sometimes wondered if he kept information back to protect me, and if Justin was involved it would fit with Ashton's feelings towards him.

Howard has been in touch to say he bumped into you leaving Apple Tree Cottage.

Not how Eve would have put it. She felt a wave of heat at the memory, and at what he might have told Mrs Foley.

Thank you for not giving me away. I didn't explain what I'd asked you to do as I knew it would hurt his pride to have a stranger

fighting his corner. When he challenged me, I told him I'd asked
you to look round the house so that you could describe it in your
obituary. I'm so sorry to have put you in an awkward position.
Yours, Betty

Eve breathed a sigh of relief. She seemed to have gotten away
with it – at least as far as Betty was concerned. What Howard Green
thought, and what his plans were, was more worrying. And what
was he doing 'challenging' Betty over her decision to let Eve in? It
was her house, after all. Viv had described him as protective – but
taken too far, that could be a form of control.

Eve had just composed a polite reply, her mind full of doubts
about Howard, when she heard a text come in. She pulled her
mobile out of her bag.

Robin Yardley. Loner. Gardener to almost all the villagers in
Saxford St Peter. A man with a secret past who was intent on
keeping it that way.

She caught her breath. What was on his mind?

The text said simply:

Are you around? Meet me by the old mooring block on the
estuary path? R.

She texted back, promising to be there in half an hour. By the
time she was ready to leave, the sky was clearing.

'Walk, Gus?'

He leaped up and went to stand next to the hooks by the front
door, his tail wagging on overdrive.

As she strode up Haunted Lane, towards Elizabeth's Walk, she
thought of Robin and everything she'd found out about him, the
summer before when she'd first visited Saxford. A series of lucky
breaks meant she'd guessed some of the truth about his past.

Only she – and, she suspected, the vicar – knew part of the story. And perhaps no one had the full version of events. Robin had once been a police detective, but Eve still had a lot of questions. What had caused him to leave his former job? And why was he so determined to cover up his past? He'd even changed his name. As far as Google was concerned, this particular 'Robin Yardley' hadn't existed until ten years ago. Secrecy mattered to him. You only had to look at how cautious he was about meeting Eve to see that. He'd chosen one of the loneliest locations in the area.

Eve had reached the end of Elizabeth's Walk now and turned to join the track that ran alongside the water, towards the sea. She scanned the path ahead, bordered by reeds on one side and a ditch and fields on the other. If anyone else was out walking, it would trash her chances of getting information out of Robin. Suddenly, they'd just be two villagers who'd happened to run into one another. But the estuary path seemed deserted, except for the wildlife. To her right, towards the village, the rooks cawed as they flapped round the nests they'd built, ready for the first eggs to be laid.

Off to her left, over Saxford Water, where the river widened and ran into reed beds, a marsh harrier swooped, hunting for prey. Gus had paused now, alert to the weird sound of a bittern's boom. It reminded Eve of a low monotone wind instrument.

She glanced at her dachshund. 'You'll have to find your sport some other way, Gus. I don't think you could catch a bird anyway, and if you could, I'm afraid I'd stop you! C'mon!'

Gus looked wounded, as though the very thought of him victimising his fellow creatures was a grave insult. But he still cocked his ear at the sound, Eve noticed.

The recent rain had left the path muddy. Eve was wearing thick-soled boots that kept the bottom of her jeans above the level of the dirt, but Gus would need some sorting out when they got home. Hunkering down to listen to the bittern hadn't helped. Now, a low shaft of sunlight reached down from between two dark clouds and lit the water. All around her were the dramatic greys, greens, blues and purples of a changeable day in a waterlogged land.

They were getting nearer to the old mooring block now – a chunk of concrete buried in silt.

A second later the cop-turned-gardener appeared from somewhere beyond the high reeds and grinned.

'Sorry about all the cloak-and-dagger stuff. Based on the gossip I've picked up from my clients since the weekend, I felt it was better if we weren't seen chatting in public.'

She could understand his reluctance. The entire village must know she was focused on Ashton's death. If Robin was seen with her, huddled in conversation, or visiting without his gardening kit, people would start asking questions. And sooner or later someone would probably tell Palmer too, which would be a serious problem. Robin's past was a secret from almost all of the local force.

'I know, for instance,' Robin went on, 'that you've been asked to write Ashton Foley's obituary, and that you've already spoken to Moira, Marina Shaw, the Ingrams, and Russell Rathbone.'

'How the heck did anyone know about the lawyer?'

Robin smiled. 'One of the office clerks at Rathbone's is the elder daughter of Julia Grant, the churchwarden at St Peter's. I do Julia's garden.'

She'd known from the moment she'd moved to Saxford that she'd have no secrets. And although Robin was smiling, she'd seen him glance over his shoulder as he spoke.

His blue-grey eyes turned serious for a moment, as though he was reassessing his previous impressions of her. 'I've got information. I don't want to hold out on you – not if you might come face to face with a murderer again – but my contact on the local force would be on a disciplinary if Palmer found out he was leaking details.'

'I understand,' Eve said, but she didn't entirely. What made DS Boles so forthcoming? And why did Robin hide his past from the other local officers? 'It won't go any further. I didn't think I'd find myself in this situation again.' Gus was getting muddier as they spoke, sliding down a bank in pursuit of something down in the ditch.

Robin nodded. 'Places like Saxford are odd. You get extremes. People look out for each other in a way you don't get in the city, but knowing quite so much about your neighbours can be oppressive. There's always a chance you'll discover something that puts a relationship under tension. Everyone gets set in their ways, too. And then along comes someone like Ashton, who's part outsider, part not, and the usual course of events gets thrown out of kilter. It wouldn't normally result in murder, but Ashton was no ordinary villager.'

'You're not kidding.'

He nodded, and suddenly the hint of humour was back in his eyes. 'So, I know you're a fast worker. What are your thoughts so far?'

She smiled herself. 'You miss your old job, right?'

He raised his eyes to heaven. 'I like my current one all right. But yes, okay, you've got me. So, if you're happy to share…'

Eve explained Betty Foley's plea for help, and everything she'd uncovered about Howard Green to date. 'So my mission is proving problematic. Nothing I've found makes him seem innocent. But a second person's come to the fore.'

She relayed her visit to the Ingrams, and all the information she'd picked up so far, from the hints Russell Rathbone felt Ashton had given about Justin, to the low-down on the 'prank' the dead man had played on him. 'All the same,' she finished, 'the evidence against him doesn't quite hang together. I get the feeling I'm missing something, though I don't know what it is. Whereas everything I hear points to Howard Green.'

Robin glanced over his shoulder again, and beyond her too, then moved slightly closer to where she stood, in amongst the reeds. 'The police are pretty interested in him. When they asked him what he was doing outside Betty Foley's cottage, he claimed he'd knocked because he wanted to talk to Ashton. Said he'd brought a bottle of whisky as a peace offering. Man-to-man thing.'

Eve thought back. 'I didn't see him carrying anything.'

Robin nodded. 'The police noticed he had a yellowing bruise. Howard told them he'd got it pulling up suddenly in his car, but they don't believe a word he's said. All the same, they can't prove he was letting himself out of the cottage when you saw him. And as he had a key, any evidence they find of his presence won't help. He's been inside lots of times before, for legitimate reasons.'

Robin frowned. 'On the subject of prints, there weren't any on Ashton's wallet, so it looks as though that was wiped, even though his cards were still present, together with a small amount of cash. There was nothing else obviously missing: his keys and phone were both on him.'

'Do you know if the police have identified any suspects who aren't on my list?' If they had, she should probably interview them for Ashton's obituary too. 'I'm already planning on speaking with his old teachers, the Adcocks.'

But Robin shook his head. 'No one else yet. I'll keep you updated, assuming I get more details.'

Eve guessed he would. For whatever reason, DS Boles seemed to share a lot. 'And any unshakeable alibis amongst the group?'

'Not by my book. The Adcocks are of interest, I gather, because of the very public way Ashton referred to some cruel words of Carl's at the prize draw. You and Viv were catering, weren't you, so I guess you heard him?'

Eve nodded.

'I wish I hadn't missed the event now. The police are keeping an open mind about an ongoing feud.'

It made sense. 'Ashton said he'd like to "pay them back". He claimed Carl had helped him find new drive and purpose, but I thought his choice of words was interesting.'

Robin's gaze sharpened. 'I agree. Carl and Tina alibi each other but my contact said they looked shifty when they were giving their stories. Meanwhile, Marina Shaw was staying at the pub. Guests can come and go as they please so it's not impossible that she went and returned without being noticed.'

'But?' It came to her just as he started to speak. 'Oh, of course. Hetty.'

He nodded. 'If Marina was careful she might have managed to return to the pub in the middle of the night without setting her barking, but it would have been a challenge. Toby Falconer's confirmed she was there at breakfast time. He didn't notice anything unusual.'

'What about Justin and Amber Ingram? Are they under suspicion?'

Robin gave her a look. 'The police are keeping Justin in mind, especially after Russell Rathbone got in touch to relay the conversation he had with Ashton. Incidentally, Amber's brother's a vet, so he owns a handgun, for putting down sick animals when the need arises.'

Eve felt the cool breeze in her short hair, followed by goosebumps tracing their way up her arms. 'I didn't know vets were allowed to keep that kind of weapon. Can the police examine it?'

'So long as Amber's brother gives them permission – they've got no excuse to request a warrant, given the lack of evidence. It would be stretching a point to put Amber in the frame at all at the moment, never mind connect her to a gun that's likely kept in a locked safe at her brother's surgery,' Robin said. 'And they haven't found the bullet or the casing, so that will hamper ballistics.' He sighed. 'Still, I guess the brother will play ball if they do ask. It'll look pretty suspicious if he doesn't.

'Anyway, I wouldn't set too much store by potential access to a weapon. Handguns are the most common type of firearm used to commit offences, despite them being banned for almost everyone in the country. Decommissioned guns can be reactivated, and blank-firing weapons can be converted. Whoever committed this crime probably wouldn't have relied on stealing from a local vet.'

'Betty Foley said the police were interested in the possibility of Howard having acquired a weapon through his business.'

Robin nodded. 'That's right. The use of antique guns in crime is on the rise as modern weapons get harder to source. People make homemade bullets for them because the original ammunition is obsolete.'

'Would Howard know how?'

He looked grim. 'Thanks to online videos detailing the process, anyone could find out.'

So he or Amber could have managed to sort out a gun with a bit of forward planning. 'It would be interesting to know where the investigation went, back when Ashton landed himself in the young offenders' institute. I presume the police tried to find out who supplied him.'

Robin's blue-grey eyes met hers. 'I've already asked the question. I'll let you know if my contact finds something he can pass on.'

She'd be curious to see if Justin's name appeared anywhere. 'Do the Ingrams have alibis?'

'Like the Adcocks, they alibi each other, but they admitted they were sound asleep all night. I wouldn't set any store by what they say. I'd watch your back when you're interviewing each and every one of them. Don't take any risks, Eve. We might be in a backwater, and Ashton's old contact could only be a small-time crook, but if they've already killed to keep their secret, they're out of control now.'

She caught her breath. 'I understand. I'll keep you updated.'

He gave her the smallest flicker of a smile. 'Thanks. And I'll keep passing on anything that might be useful. I hope Gus doesn't get this muddy every time!' His eyes turned serious. 'Eve, my contact told me someone made a complaint against you; they said you seemed to be investigating more than just Ashton Foley's life story.'

Eve sighed. 'I guessed they must have. Palmer warned me off.'

He took a deep breath. 'My mate says the call was anonymous. Palmer's done nothing to investigate who's gunning for you, but he looked into it. The informant used the phone box outside Moira and Paul's store. There's no CCTV.'

'A villager then.'

He nodded. 'It's possible. It might not be the killer; plenty of locals have other secrets. But watch your back, even when you're with people you trust.'

'You don't happen to know who told the police Ashton and I might be in a relationship, I suppose?' She felt a blush rise to her cheeks as Robin's eyes widened. 'We weren't, of course. I just want to know so I can strike them off my Christmas card list.'

He grinned for a moment.

'Joking apart, I suppose it's possible the anonymous complaint came from the same person.'

'Maybe. I'll see if I can find out. Stay safe, Eve.'

She shivered as she watched Robin walk off up the estuary path towards the coast. She wouldn't rest easy until Ashton's killer had been caught. The thought of one of her neighbours monitoring her every move, waiting to see if she got too close to the truth, set her hairs on end.

CHAPTER TWENTY-TWO

Back at home, Eve settled down to some more fact-checking. She wanted to dig into the matter of Betty's unofficial loan to Howard Green. The internet had some pointers, but she needed to make sure she understood the ramifications. With no expertise in the law, she might miss something important.

Five minutes later, she was on the phone to Russell Rathbone. 'I'm sorry to bother you again.' She pictured him in his swanky office.

'*Nonsense!*' She could hear the smile in his voice. '*It isn't any bother at all. How may I help?*'

Eve took a deep breath. If she managed the conversation carefully, she needn't relate it to Ashton's death. DI Palmer's threat was high in her mind.

'I wondered if I could ask your advice on a hypothetical situation. It might take time to answer, and I know your hours are precious. I can book an appointment if that would be better.'

He laughed. '*It would be a poor show if I couldn't give you a quick bit of help over the phone without charging you.*'

But in Eve's experience, lawyers usually billed for every five minutes of their time. Russell Rathbone was being generous.

'*So, what is this "hypothetical" situation?*'

It was clear he'd guessed it was far from being that.

'I was wondering, if someone wanted to invest in a property, but couldn't do it personally, what would they need to protect their interests, if someone else acted on their behalf?'

There was a long pause on the end of the line. '*It's interesting you should ask. Ashton came to me with that very same question. He also said he spoke hypothetically.*'

There was an awkward silence. Ashton must have seen what she'd seen. She had good reason for not going into details, but why hadn't *he* told Russell Rathbone more? After all, the lawyer was a long-term ally of the family.

'*A lawyer would normally draw up official paperwork, to make the arrangement clear, and send a copy to the Land Registry,*' Rathbone said. '*Without that, the person whose money was used could be kept in the dark about any further dealings relating to the property.*'

'That sounds hazardous.'

'*Indeed. For instance, the person who made the purchase – whose name would appear on the title deed – could then access the money entrusted to them, by taking out or extending a mortgage on the property. No one would ask the unnamed funder's permission; the bank wouldn't even know they existed.*'

Eve felt a wave of heat rush over her. She was beginning to see how Howard Green might have gotten himself into very deep trouble. 'It would be a way of stealing the true owner's money, effectively.'

'*It would.*'

And she knew Betty Foley had had £200,000 to invest. Potentially, Howard Green could have siphoned off almost all of that for his own use.

'If the person who'd put forward the funds for the property was receiving regular income from the tenants who were occupying it, I guess they'd notice a change. I mean, if the mortgage had been increased, and more of that income had to go back to the bank instead, to pay off the loan.'

Rathbone sighed. '*I'm afraid that's not necessarily the case. It would depend on how the repayments to the bank were set up. High payments*

on a small loan could be the same as low payments on a much larger
sum. The unnamed funder wouldn't necessarily see a change.'

Eve could hardly believe it. Was this what had happened? Had
Howard taken money from Betty to invest in the doomed property
venture Simon had mentioned? If so, it sounded as though he'd
lost the lot. Maybe he'd hoped he could make a fortune, plug the
financial holes in his business and repay the mortgage on Betty's
property without her ever finding out. And all the while she'd
trusted him so implicitly and he'd play-acted as her protector. His
selfish, cavalier attitude set Eve's adrenaline going.

'Do you mind me asking, did you go into all these details with
Ashton too?'

'*I did.*' He sighed. '*It's all right. You don't need to tell me more, or
break any confidences. It's not my specific area of law, but I would be
more than happy to advise Mrs Foley when she returns.*'

There was no point in pretending he'd got it wrong. And some
good advice from a sympathetic family contact would be just what
she'd need.

'Thank you.'

She hung up, took a deep breath, and sat at the dining room
table, thinking. How had it played out? Ashton had likely gone
through his mother's files out of nosiness, to find out if she'd done
anything without his knowledge. He'd found the information on
the bequest that Betty had received and the property Howard had
bought on her behalf. He might have been hurt and she bet he'd
been angry. Like her, he'd gone to his old friend and mentor, Russell
Rathbone, and asked for advice. And he'd had it confirmed that
Howard had far too much control over funds that were rightfully
his mother's.

What had he done then? Had he spoken with Betty about the
situation? On balance, Eve thought not. When she'd asked the
woman if she could think of any reason why Ashton and Howard

might have quarrelled, she'd taken time to ponder the question. Her reaction would have been different if Ashton had already challenged her.

But Eve guessed he'd faced Howard Green with his knowledge. He might not have known of the investment opportunity Simon mentioned, or that Howard's business was in trouble, but he would have wanted him to put the proper paperwork in place. After all, it was clear he'd hated the man, and although he'd been thoughtless when it came to Betty's feelings, Eve couldn't imagine he'd take kindly to Howard lying to her.

Maybe he'd threatened to speak with Betty when she got home unless Howard sorted the matter out himself. And of course, that put Howard in a very difficult position, if he'd really siphoned money from the mortgage.

He couldn't put the proper paperwork in place without Betty knowing he'd robbed her. Their relationship would have been over and Howard would have found himself in court. How was that for a motive for murder?

Gus had entered the room and was walking round the dining table as though checking the overall situation.

'It still doesn't make sense,' Eve said to him. He looked at her with questioning eyes. 'Howard could have gotten hold of a gun through his antiques business, so long as he'd acted quickly. But if all this is true, and he killed Ashton before Ashton could give him away, then why did Howard go to Apple Tree Cottage afterwards? It's not as though destroying the paperwork about the house would have helped. Betty already had those details and went into the arrangement knowingly.' She assumed the police wouldn't check Betty's files, given it was Ashton's murder they were investigating. 'And then why did Howard search Ashton's wallet but then leave it in place? Robin says it was wiped. What was he hoping to find?' She bent down to fuss her dachshund. 'I need to think of a way forward. This is all speculation. How can I expect Palmer to take me seriously if I pass it on? And how can I look Betty Foley in the eye if I hand the police more evidence against Howard Green without getting my facts straight first?'

She felt close to the truth now; it was time for an extra push. A plan was forming in her head, but it was risky. Gus seemed to sense her anxiety and put a wet nose against her hand. He was so reassuring. After staring into space for five minutes, an idea came to her. She could ask Robin for help – but he wouldn't like it. A moment later, she texted him. He called her back immediately. She was right; he didn't.

'The trouble is, I've reached an impasse.' She explained her worries about going straight to the police.

After five minutes, at her most persuasive, he sighed. '*I can't believe I'm agreeing to this, but all right.*'

'You see my point?'

'*I do.*'

It helped that he knew what Palmer was like.

Five minutes later, she typed the note she'd been composing mentally, and a short while after that, she and Gus walked across the village green to the top of Dark Lane, where Howard Green lived. She put the envelope through his letter box.

She'd seen movement inside. She knew he was home. His antique store must have closed for the day. She could only hope her message would lure him out into the open. She retreated again, her throat feeling tight. She'd made up her mind to tackle him somewhere public, for safety, and Robin would be there to look out for her, but her mouth still felt as dry as sand. Howard might not take her bait, and if he decided to tackle her on his own terms she could be in trouble.

He knew where to find her, and she knew how frightening he could be.

CHAPTER TWENTY-THREE

Eve took Gus with her to the beach. It wasn't like being accompanied by a Dobermann, but he gave her confidence and he might diffuse the tension. The weather had cleared completely now and the schools were on Easter vacation, so people weren't rushing home early. If Howard Green came to meet her, they wouldn't be the only ones on the beach. All the same, she was glad she'd asked Robin to be in the vicinity. If Howard brought a gun he could isolate her quite easily unless they were amongst crowds.

She and Gus approached the shore via the woods and the heath, past a Dartford warbler. She tried to focus on it, bobbing between the gorse bushes, singing its scratchy song, but her heart rate ramped up all the same. What if this all went wrong? What if Robin got delayed?

A second later, she caught her breath, her stomach muscles clenching. Just beyond the sand dunes, up the coast and away from civilisation, Eve could see Howard Green's gaunt figure: hands thrust into his trouser pockets, hair blown back by the wind, his jacket hanging loosely off this angular frame. He was further from the village than she'd suggested. At that distance he could hold a gun under his jacket and threaten her into going with him, with no one any the wiser.

She glanced around her. Where was Robin? A text came in.

I'm in the trees nearest the heath, just south of where Green's standing. Once you reach him, I'll start to walk north up the beach. He'll know I'm there, and I'll be ready to intervene; just ignore me.

Swallowing, she strode towards Howard. At last, she and Gus were just behind him and she called out to warn him of her approach, her words snatched away by the sea breeze. He must have caught something though. He turned, his eyes unfriendly.

'I can't help what I've found out in the course of my work,' Eve said. She was being economical with the truth, but Howard Green didn't deserve any better. 'It would help me a lot if you could explain what happened between you and Ashton in the run-up to his death.' She thought of Palmer. He'd get that order to stop her work if Green reported her. This was make or break. 'Your relationship is key to the obituary I'll write.' She didn't expect him to believe that was her real reason for asking, but at least she could argue the point if Palmer found out about their meeting. Her legs felt like jelly, but Green would hardly confess to murder, even if he were guilty. For a second, she thought of Robin. Was he somewhere behind her now, walking up the beach? She took a deep breath.

'The things I mentioned in my note are bound to come out.' She'd assumed a lot in her letter, to try to draw him out. She'd told him she knew about the house he'd bought with Mrs Foley's money, and how he'd siphoned off funds without her permission. His anger at finding her at Apple Tree Cottage fitted in with her guesses. If he was innocent he ought to be mystified, but there was no confusion in his eyes. 'Although your actions were dishonest, they're nothing compared with murder. I'd like to know what really happened.'

She'd done her best to defuse his anger. She was furious with him for what he'd done to Betty Foley, but he'd never play along unless she stayed calm. And if she pushed him too far, who knew what he might do? His eyes told her she'd have to tread very carefully indeed. If Robin was close by, she was guessing Howard had yet to spot him. He was entirely focused on her. She held her breath. She was sure DI Palmer would jump to the conclusion that Howard had killed Ashton if he had the same details she did. She guessed Howard knew that too. And he might well have done it; everything pointed to him. Depending on how this conversation went, Eve would need to catch Robin's eye, then call the police. She knew he wouldn't let her down, but she wished she could see him.

Green's eyes were on hers, and she felt her insides quiver. Gus's reaction wasn't helping. Despite being off the leash, the sea a few feet away, he'd stopped, stock-still, at her feet, his gaze fixed on the man, a low growl in his throat.

'You and Ashton fought. I understand your relationship was never easy, but this was something new. Something particular.' She paused. 'He'd seen Mrs Foley's file. He knew you'd bought the property and that you hadn't set up the proper paperwork for it.' When the man still didn't speak, she added: 'I know that much. He asked a lawyer for advice, to find out what should have been done.'

Howard Green swore sharply and Gus stood tall – well, as tall as he could – and snarled.

'He confronted you, I guess, and you fought.' She turned subtly as she spoke to see more of the beach. Way off, to the south of the village, more than one family walked along the shore, and out of the corner of her eye she caught movement closer at hand. Robin? But she needed to focus. He'd said to ignore him.

Green followed her gaze with angry eyes. 'All right. Yes.'

'I imagine he wanted you to sort out the paperwork, but you couldn't. Not without revealing that you'd stolen money by extending the mortgage. And of course you wouldn't want to risk your relationship with Mrs Foley.'

He had a cast-iron reason for killing Ashton, a young man who'd been a thorn in his side for years. All that pent-up anger, just waiting for some release… Eve's chest felt tight.

'I intended to pay it all back – with interest too. Betty would never have known. I'd have saved my business and done her a good turn too.'

'Except the investment you wanted the cash for was too good to be true.' She remembered Simon's words. He had his head screwed on straight.

'I was promised a lot, but I lost everything.'

'Presumably Ashton got angry when you refused to make things right. Did you admit what you'd done after he hit you?'

It took Howard Green a long time, but at last he shook his head. 'He hit me afterwards. He lost control.'

It all explained why Howard hadn't risen when Ashton had knocked into him so deliberately in the village store. He knew he was on thin ice. Ashton was in a position to ruin his life if Howard made one false move.

'So he planned to tell his mother.'

Howard Green let out a hollow laugh. 'Yes. He wanted to wait until she came home again so he could tell her in person. He probably knew he could demolish her opinion of me more completely if he could influence her face to face.' He spat the words out.

Howard had had time to act, then. He'd have known he had a few days' grace at the very least. Eve felt sick, but Gus seemed to have calmed down now that she and Howard were conversing. He was giving her sidelong glances, no doubt wondering why they were spending beach time with this aggressive individual.

'You thought there was a chance she might forgive you?' Eve couldn't keep the incredulity out of her voice. If she were in Betty's position, whether she'd heard the truth face to face, over the phone or by carrier pigeon, Howard would have been instant history.

Green's hard eyes met hers. 'You don't understand, but I could have made Betty see. My business is on the rocks, my house is on the point of being repossessed. I've barely got enough to live on.

I'll have to let Amber go. I can't afford an employee. I've held out until the last minute, trying to find a way through. And along comes Ashton, able to shower Betty with expensive presents and flash his cash around when I can't even afford to buy a round at the Cross Keys.' Eve remembered his half-hearted offer to cover the bill when she'd seen him in there with Betty and Ashton. 'Can you imagine how that made me feel? I borrowed Betty's money for her sake. I wanted to invest it, make a good return, and get to the point where I could take care of her.'

Eve's heart rate was going through the roof. Take care of her? Betty could have afforded to take care of herself if he hadn't defrauded her. She'd got plans in place to provide an income for her retirement, and Howard had stolen her money so he could boost his own ego and keep himself in a position of power.

'I planned to take her on cruises – away for weekends – all the things she deserved.' He looked uncomprehendingly into her eyes. He could see she didn't sympathise, clearly, but he didn't get why. 'She'd had a hard life!' He stepped forward and Eve shrank back. She could feel Gus up against her legs again. 'I needed to make things right for her. Ashton had no room to criticise; he was careless of her feelings. He'd pick her up when he felt like it, and then drop her without warning as soon as he got bored. It was up to me to look out for her happiness.'

Eve shivered. The gloss he'd put on his reasons for stealing Betty's money was completely abhorrent, and she had a feeling he believed his own lies, too. As for his motive for murdering Ashton, it was looking stronger than ever.

'I didn't kill him.' It was as though the man had read her mind.

Just beyond them now, Eve could see Robin, ambling along slowly, hands in his pockets. He paused to look at his phone.

It gave her the courage to push Howard. 'That's easily said. But he was in a position to ruin your life. And you let yourself into

Apple Tree Cottage, the morning after he was murdered.' She was sure of it now. He'd looked so shifty when he'd stood there on the front path.

He threw up his hands, making her jump. 'I hadn't been sleeping well, what with the money worries! I was up early, *yet again*, and I went for a walk, out on the heath, to try to think. That's when I came across Ashton's body! I didn't murder him!' He was looking at her as though the very suggestion was crazy.

'What time was it, when you found him?'

He shrugged. 'I wasn't checking my watch! Seven thirty maybe? He was already stiff and cool when I touched him.'

'Why did you touch him?'

Green looked down at the pebble-strewn sand. 'I checked his wallet for cash. I've already told you how desperate things are.' He laughed. He sounded as wild as the wind. 'I hoped he'd have plenty on him. He always seemed to be flashing it about. But his wallet was empty except for some credit cards – which would be too traceable – and some small change.'

The mist was clearing now. 'So then you went to Apple Tree Cottage?'

He nodded. 'I thought he'd have money or valuables there that I could take. I didn't feel guilty. Ashton made his profits through crime once. Maybe he still does. And I don't count filling the houses of celebrities with plants as honest work, anyway.'

His tone was heavy with derision. Eve wasn't sure why dealing in antiques was any better. Both businesses were based on selling something that gave people pleasure.

'I didn't dare take too long about it,' Green went on. 'Once Ashton's body was found I guessed it wouldn't be long before the police arrived at Betty's cottage. But it was still relatively early on a Sunday morning, so I took my chances and kept an eye out. In the end I didn't find much, though I delayed longer than I meant. I know from the police that I was seen on the doorstep by a witness. And if you know that as well, then I assume that witness was you.'

He loomed over her, and she swallowed.

She'd been aware of Robin, walking a little further up the coast. At that moment he turned side on to them, alert, and she realised he must have been paying closer attention than she'd thought. She bet he'd been a good detective.

For a moment it seemed as though Howard might let his anger get the better of him, but then his shoulders went down. 'And now you'll tell them what I've said.'

'It would be better if you told them yourself.' The police would need his statement – and Palmer would probably sit on anything she said, feeling irritated for several hours before he acted.

'I don't imagine they'll believe me.' His jaw was taut.

'Why did you go back to Apple Tree Cottage, the evening you caught me coming out?'

'I was desperate. I wanted to search more carefully for anything that might help me raise some funds.' His eyes were down on the sand and pebbles again. 'I still hoped to find something of Ashton's he'd left about the place: electronics or a showy watch maybe.' He hung his head. 'But in the end I took a pair of candlesticks. A bequest from the same relative who left Betty the money for the rental property. I could have taken them before, but I held back.'

Hmm. Noble.

His gaze drifted out towards the waves. 'I was going to pawn them. I needed enough cash to apply to declare myself bankrupt.'

Everything Howard Green said made her loath him, but she found she believed his version of events. It explained why someone had wiped Ashton's wallet of fingerprints, then put it back, and also why Howard had let himself into Apple Tree Cottage. If he'd killed Ashton, he'd still want money of course, but his pathetically injured and defensive tone was convincing, and he'd given her a lot of detail.

'I think someone had been in Apple Tree Cottage before me, the morning Ashton died.' Green spoke suddenly, putting a claw-like hand on her arm.

She stepped back a little, her skin crawling. 'What makes you say that?'

He let her go, but his eyes were both desperate and angry. 'A faint smell. An aftershave, maybe. Musky.' He shook his head. 'I couldn't place it.'

'You should definitely go to the police. It might help them trace the killer. Will you do that?'

At last he nodded. 'I'll go to the station now.'

But would he? He was in such a precarious position and there were no good options for him. She'd give him a couple of hours to act on his own, then send her own report to Palmer. She'd have to word it carefully, and even then, she wasn't sure he'd believe she'd come across all of the information in the course of her work. But if he banned her from approaching Ashton's contacts she'd have to put up with it. This was far too important to keep to herself.

'Was there anything else you noticed?'

Howard Green let out a sharp sigh. 'One thing. When I searched Ashton's pockets for his wallet, I noticed his house keys were missing. But the newspaper reports said nothing had been stolen. I wonder if the killer used them and then put them back.'

So whoever took the keys – presumably the killer – must have replaced them early that Sunday morning then: after Howard found Ashton's body – at around seven thirty – but before Jo Falconer did. They'd clearly wanted access to Apple Tree Cottage, just like Howard, and their presence fitted with the smell the antiques dealer claimed he'd noticed in the house.

She glanced at her watch. It was just after 7 p.m. 'You'll go now then, to tell DI Palmer – or whoever's on duty?'

He nodded.

But as he walked away, back towards the village, she was torn inside.

'Gut instinct tells me his story's true, Gus,' she said. 'But as for going to the police, I just don't trust him on that.'

She turned to glance around her before making her own way back. Robin was well up the beach now, but when she looked in his direction, he seemed to sense it, glanced over his shoulder and raised his hand in a mock salute. It was subtle, and no one was watching. She smiled to herself. She'd have to thank him by text later.

She and Gus followed the same route Howard Green had taken, and watched him cross the heath, towards Smugglers' Lane. Eve felt as though she should do more, but tailing him all the way to the police station wasn't really an option. He walked towards the village and his home, passing Billy Tozer's place, where Marina was just leaving, striding out with an 'I'm-so-in-demand-I've-simply-no-time' look in her eye.

She'd give Howard until nine at the latest; at that point she'd send a message through to the station.

As Gus relaxed at last and paused to sniff a gatepost, thoughts of Betty Foley's desperate pleas circled in Eve's head. But she couldn't hold back to spare her feelings. How would she cope when she found out her boyfriend had defrauded her?

Eve didn't sleep well that night. She'd sent her email to the police by eight fifteen in the end. If Howard was going to keep his promise he'd have had time to reach them, and she was too anxious to wait any longer. She'd called their incident line just after, to alert them to the message's contents. By that stage her anxiety had built up; she'd spent some time emphasising how his evidence might lead them towards the real killer. The email contained the exact same information she'd sent to Robin, with her thanks, as soon as she'd returned home. It would be good to get his take on it.

After she'd contacted the police, she'd emailed Betty Foley to warn her that Howard had mentioned going to the authorities with new information, though it didn't relate directly to Ashton's murder. She couldn't bring herself not to sound a note of warning. She'd wondered whether to give her the full story, but she guessed Howard would have to contact her to confess, and it would be even more painful for Betty to hear the truth from a third party.

The following morning dawned clear and bright. She wrapped up warm against the stiff breeze that whipped down Haunted Lane, and headed off with Gus for a soothing walk to try to clear her foggy head. She kept to the main routes, not knowing where Howard might be that day. As they strolled down Love Lane she could see Jo Falconer opening the curtains in the cottage next door to the Cross Keys, where she and Matt lived. Toby had a flat above the pub, alongside the paying guests. Jo raised a hand and Eve responded in kind. Even at that distance, Gus spotted the woman and scampered a little closer to Eve's ankles.

They headed on down Heath Lane, towards the woods, the heath and the coast. Other than the estuary path, it was their quickest route to the sea. The third alternative across the village green and down Dark Lane would take them straight past Howard Green's house, and she didn't fancy that.

They were just approaching Apple Tree Cottage on the right when Gus halted. He had many forms of halting. There were the sort where he just wanted to pause a moment and sniff something interesting, the sort where he wanted to chase something (involving a sudden sharp tug on his leash as he followed his instincts) and the 'this is serious' sort. When it was one of these last, Eve found it very hard to shift him until he'd investigated whatever it was that had caught his attention. This time, he didn't pull Eve towards the woods like he had the morning after Ashton had been killed, he just halted and stared.

'C'mon, Gus. Let's get down to the beach!' The area already made her uneasy after recent events.

But Gus remained rooted to the spot, and then, as she watched, he seemed to shrink back and a whine rose in his throat.

Eve felt a prickling sensation run over her skin. She stared into the trees, trying to see what Gus had seen – or sensed. There was no movement she could discern at his eye level, so she raised her gaze upward and tried to focus through the undergrowth.

At last she saw it. Movement between the trees. A very slight shifting of shadows, of light and dark. It coincided with each new strong gust of wind. When the trees bent to its force, the darker patch of shadow did too.

Whatever it was, it was raised off the ground. Swinging.

Eve put her hand over her mouth, her stomach turning as she realised what she was seeing.

She found herself in the middle of Blind Eye Wood without being conscious of having gotten there. Her extremities felt numb. Gus was cowering close to her side, the whine in his throat rising again. Up ahead of her, hanging from a noose, secured to the branch of a pine tree, was Howard Green.

She tugged her phone from her jeans pocket, gulping for breath, and called the police.

CHAPTER TWENTY-FOUR

'Interesting that he was in the woods, just like Foley.' DI Palmer was looking at Eve like he was convinced she was personally responsible for what had happened. Deep down, she was worried she was, too. The thought of Howard's painfully thin, limp body filled her mind. She should have handled things differently – somehow. She'd contacted the police with her information, but she'd guessed Palmer would be slow to respond unless Howard had kept his promise and gone to them in person. The detective inspector had probably thought the matter could wait until morning, or that Eve was deluded. And so Howard Green had never told his tale.

'At least it wraps up the case,' Palmer went on. He sat back on her couch and laced his fingers over his stomach. 'It's clear Green shot Ashton Foley, spun you a line and then went off into the woods to end it all. He had no future. He'd stolen his girlfriend's money, ruined himself financially and then crossed the final line when he stooped to murder.'

Eve's mind spun. 'Why would he go to the woods to kill himself? He lived alone. Surely it would have made more sense to do it at home?'

Palmer's look was superior. 'I imagine it was symbolic. He returned to the same spot where he'd killed Ashton Foley – near enough.'

'And why choose hanging when he had a gun?' Eve couldn't stop herself.

The DI gave a deliberate sigh. 'Howard Green wouldn't be the first murderer to dispose of his weapon after committing a crime. He'll have got rid of the gun immediately after shooting Foley and no doubt regretted the fact last night. But the rope did for him just as surely.'

'It must have been hard for him to climb up, out there in the woods.'

'Didn't you see the log to one side of where he was hanging?'

Palmer sounded judgemental, but Eve hadn't. She'd been staring at Howard's body. Everything else had been a blur.

'We think he mounted that, then kicked it aside.'

Eve thought again, her mind on the missing murder weapon now. 'I didn't see Howard Green carrying anything when I spotted him on the doorstep of Apple Tree Cottage. If he'd gone straight there from the crime scene, he ought to have been carrying the gun.'

Palmer looked as though he could barely be bothered to answer. 'He would have known he might bump into someone. He probably hid it somewhere, then went back to retrieve it and dispose of it later.'

He had an answer for everything, and it was hard to argue against what he said, yet still Eve felt uneasy. Howard Green's story had rung true. He'd been guilty of a lot but, she felt sure, after her talk with him, not of murder. It was an ironic turnaround in her thoughts.

'You should have come straight to us instead of approaching Mr Green directly.'

'I didn't have any hard facts, just what I'd heard around the village.' She hadn't admitted to what she'd found in Apple Tree Cottage, nor been specific about where she'd gotten her information in the note she'd written, thankfully. The police would find it now, of course. 'It made me curious about Ashton's relationship with Mr Green, so naturally I requested an interview. As soon as he confirmed my suspicions I asked him to go straight to you and he promised he would. But as you know, I got in touch too, just to make sure you knew everything I'd found out.' She felt sick at heart; she was trying to justify herself, just as Howard Green had the day before.

'We can only assume your report contains all the information he would have passed on to us. It's a shame we couldn't question him further.'

Eve was mad at Palmer as well as at herself. They could have spoken with him, if they'd acted as soon as they'd received her message. She guessed he knew that. It explained why he wasn't being more confrontational. If he complained, so could she. Plus, she'd handed him a bunch of useful leads on a plate. But guilt was still gnawing at her insides. If she'd gone straight to the authorities with her piecemeal evidence and hunches, without waiting to speak with Howard, would they have taken her seriously? Could she somehow have saved his life?

'What will happen with Mrs Foley?'

'We've made contact with the police locally to where she's staying. They'll break the news while we check out the financial records relating to the house Green allegedly bought with her money. Sooner or later she'll have to know what he did, of course – assuming you're right. We'll check for any paperwork there might be inside her house.'

Poor Betty.

CHAPTER TWENTY-FIVE

Soon after Palmer left Elizabeth's Cottage, Robin texted.

Just heard about Howard. I'll find out what I can. Contact says no note found as yet, but most of team agree he might not have written one. Possibly felt he couldn't explain himself.

Even that sounded plausible. Eve sat staring into space, feeling powerless. And what if she was wrong? What made her so convinced Howard had been murdered, when yesterday afternoon she'd thought he was guilty? It was weird that she'd confirmed how very flawed his character was the day before, but also crossed him off her list of suspects. Her mind moved on to Robin, and what he might think of her. He hadn't wanted her to tackle Howard on the beach. If she'd taken his advice and gone straight to the police, might he still be alive? She'd only managed to talk Robin round because he knew how slow and blinkered Palmer could be, and how much she wanted to spare Betty Foley pain.

She tried to switch off her guilt and turned back to the questions she'd put to Palmer. Okay, she could see Howard might have disposed of the gun if he'd been the murderer, but she still didn't buy the DI's reasoning for him killing himself in the woods. Why would he do that when he might be disturbed? It would have taken time to tie up the rope and whatever Palmer said about the log that had been kicked over, it all sounded awkward. It would make more sense if Ashton's real killer had set it all up to look like suicide, using the gun to force Howard to comply.

She texted Robin with her thoughts. He was back in touch in under a minute.

I agree; it's odd. Palmer will never buy it though. At least he'll be off your back, now he thinks the case is closed, but if you're right this killer's both skilled and ruthless. Take every precaution, Eve. I bet they reported you to Palmer in the first place. If so, they're on to you. They won't relax just because he has.

Robin's text left Eve's nerves jangling. She was on high alert, listening out for any odd sounds outside the cottage. Gus seemed calm, which helped soothe her at last. She was glad she was doing an early shift at Monty's. A chat with Viv was just what she needed. Thoughts about Howard Green's death and what it might mean were teeming in her head. Sharing them would provide some relief and maybe some clarity. They ought to have time for a proper talk. Sometimes things in the teashop were just too busy, but Angie was going to help induct a new waitress that morning, and Viv and Eve were planning to act as customers, to put her through her paces.

Eve received an email from Betty Foley before she left for the teashop.

Please don't give up on trying to prove Howard's innocence. He wouldn't have killed Ashton.

The situation was horrendous. How could one person have to deal with so much? She sent a message back immediately, expressing her profound sympathy and assuring her she believed her and would carry on her work. But although Eve was convinced Howard was innocent of murder now, the thought of all he'd done, and the hard truth Betty would have to face, bore down on her. Proving he hadn't killed Ashton wouldn't be enough to ease her pain, but it would drive Eve on. And whatever she thought of Howard Green, Palmer's conviction that he was guilty would compel her to keep going too. Eve's whole job was about revealing the truth, good and bad, about the dead.

Fifteen minutes later she was outside the teashop with Viv, waiting to go in and play-act as a customer.

'You've heard about Howard?' Eve asked.

'And that you found him.' Her friend put a hand on her arm and gave it a squeeze. 'Awful. I can't believe he killed himself.'

'If he did.'

Viv gave her a sharp look. 'I can see we need to talk. Let's just get sorted and then you can fill me in.'

'So who's the new waitress?' Eve asked as they entered Monty's, setting the bell over the door jangling.

'A friend of Angie's from college called Tammy.' Viv spoke in an undertone. 'Apparently she's very sweet but rather shy.' There was a gleam of mischief in her eyes.

'Well, we could do with an extra student or two to take on some shift work. You will be nice to her, won't you?'

Viv opened her clear blue eyes wide. 'Of course! I remember what it was like when I first started out. I'll be very well behaved. We can sit down and enjoy being waited on.' Her face clouded suddenly. 'And then you'd better tell me the latest on the murder enquiry.'

She marched up to the counter, where Angie nudged a dark-haired girl in front of her and grinned. The new girl went red, which Eve could well understand. She had no problem interacting with people in normal situations, but role-playing was her pet hate. She didn't mind asking questions undercover but it was just plain embarrassing if everyone concerned was in the know, and going along with the charade. They'd done it once in a training session on how to deal with aggressive parents at the state school where she'd worked. Dreadful.

'This is Tammy,' Angie said.

'Thank you. We'd love a table overlooking the village green!' Viv said.

Tammy blanched. All the seats at the front of the teashop were taken.

Eve gave her friend a look and stepped forward. 'If you get awkward customers, it's best to divert them. In this case, you could direct us to a table looking out over the back lawn instead. It's a much better view. Or, if those were taken, you could recommend an alternative that you thought would be nice and cosy, or near to the counter for quick service.'

'I was waiting to see if she'd work that out for herself!' Viv hissed, as soon as Tammy had gotten them settled and dashed back to the desk for a menu.

'Sorry. I just couldn't bear to watch her squirm. Don't you think she'll get the knack more quickly if you give her a few pointers?'

Viv grinned. 'So much less fun though!'

Their table looked out over Monty's garden and the River Sax. Across the water, Eve could see a collection of avocets, wading in the shallows. They dipped their long upcurved bills into the river, then preened their feathers, while others glided overhead, then swooped down to join them on the sun-dappled water.

Viv followed her gaze. 'Pleased you moved here? In spite of everything, I mean? I never dreamed you'd have to write about a second murder victim.'

'Nor me. But yes. I wouldn't swap my life here for the world.' She felt grounded and her own person, something she hadn't enjoyed for years.

'Here are your menus.' Tammy had returned, her blush deepening.

'So,' Viv scanned her own wares, 'please may we have… Eve – any thoughts? Trying day so far? The chocolate medley and a pot of Assam suit you?'

'Perfect.' Eve just wanted to let the poor girl get on with it.

Tammy scribbled on her notepad and retreated to where Angie stood by the counter with its appetising display of cupcakes and tarts.

'So, you don't buy the police's conclusions about Howard Green's death then?' Viv said. 'I'm confused. Getting caught outside Apple Tree Cottage always made it look as though he *might* be guilty. His suicide would fit right in with that.'

They were well away from the other customers, but Eve lowered her voice and checked over her shoulder. 'I'd honestly started to think that he was, but all that changed yesterday evening. I'm pretty sure I was wrong now.' She relayed all the recent developments in the case, and in particular, her visit to Apple Tree Cottage, Simon's information and her talk with Green the day before. 'His explanation included incidental details that wouldn't have helped prove his innocence. So why give me them unless they were true? I've spent years interviewing people with all kinds of hidden agendas, and reasons for covering up small-scale stuff. I've gotten used to the signs that someone's lying. My gut instinct is that Howard Green was finally being honest. He was guilty of a lot of things, clearly, but I don't think he was a killer.'

'Wow.'

At that moment, Angie and Tammy appeared with a tray and Tammy started to unload it, rattling the cups and saucers.

Eve could hardly bear to look.

'Beautifully done,' Viv said, with a rather fixed smile. One of the chocolate heart cakes had tipped onto its side. 'You'll be fine once the nerves have worn off.'

The girl blushed some more and scuttled away as Viv leaned forward to pour the tea. 'See. I'm not that scary, am I?'

'You look like a woman who takes cake delivery very seriously, and you're Tammy's prospective boss. Your forced grin didn't entirely take away from that.'

Viv rolled her eyes. 'So, if you're right about Howard Green, what does it mean?'

Eve picked up a chocolate raspberry cake – her favourite. 'Well, an outside possibility is that we have a single killer who wanted both Ashton Foley and Howard Green dead from the start. They did have one thing in common: Betty Foley loved them.'

'Misguidedly, from what I can see.'

Eve nodded. 'Poor Betty. Still, if someone really wanted to hurt her, or even to protect her maybe, they might kill both the men in her life. But I can't see it. If hurting her was the motive, Ashton and Howard were doing that already. Ashton was thoughtless and hardly ever came home – and it sounds as though he had some murky plans on this trip – and Howard was robbing her blind.'

Viv sighed. 'True.'

'And killing them both to protect her seems far-fetched. That would imply someone who's fixated on Betty, with a totally skewed view of reality. I guess if they existed, the whole village would be aware.' She paused and sipped her tea. 'Then, Ashton and Howard could have been killed by two separate people for unrelated reasons.'

'Very methodical of you to mention it, but you don't believe that, surely?'

Eve shook her head. 'Way too much of a coincidence.'

Viv nodded.

'So we're left with the most likely scenario, as far as I can see: Howard knew something crucial about Ashton's murder and he was killed before he could talk. My guess is the real killer only just found that out, hence the timing.'

Viv swallowed the rest of her chocolate heart. 'That makes sense.'

'So there must have been some kind of development, probably sometime yesterday.'

'What do you think it could have been?'

As usual, Eve found Viv's cakes were helping her think. The tang of the raspberry tingled her palate. 'Maybe something he told me suddenly gave him an idea; he made some link that he hadn't seen previously.'

'Sounds possible. But if so, why didn't he go and tell the police about it?'

Eve took a sip of the Assam. 'Maybe he doubted they'd believe him. Even I was scared about their reaction when he promised to go and tell them the truth. You know what Palmer's like. If he's got a fixed idea in his head he's not keen to let it go, and he's been convinced of Howard's guilt from the get-go. But I can think of another reason.' She leaned forward. 'Howard was on the point of total collapse, financially and in his relationship with Betty. He told me he wanted to find any money or valuables Ashton had left at Apple Tree Cottage so he could afford to apply for bankruptcy. Maybe, if he suddenly realised the truth, he saw one final opportunity to haul himself out of the mess he'd gotten into.'

'Blackmail?' Viv breathed the word. 'He risked going to meet the killer to try to get money out of them?'

'It seems possible.' Howard hadn't been a perceptive man. She could imagine his desperation clouding his judgement enough that he'd take the risk. 'It would explain how he ended up in the woods. It was a good venue for a secret, late-night meeting. And if the real killer still has the gun, they could have forced him to follow their instructions and make the whole thing look like suicide.'

'Wouldn't he have refused?'

Eve sipped her tea. 'I believe, if you're faced with death, you keep opting for the choice that might give you one more chance.

If he thought he might be shot instantly, but could buy himself another minute by complying with the killer's instructions, I think he'd have gone for it. After all, during that time there was a chance some passer-by might arrive on the scene.'

Viv gazed at her. 'What a thought. But yes, it makes sense.'

'On the night of the original murder, I'd guess the killer entered Apple Tree Cottage shortly after they'd shot Ashton. Then, early the following morning, after they'd left, but not long after, Howard let himself in. He noticed that the door keys were missing from Ashton's pocket when he searched him. If he'd been less shocked or less desperate he might have hesitated to let himself in with his own set. The killer could still have been there. As it was, they didn't actually cross paths, but it must have been close. The killer could have replaced the keys in Ashton's pocket as Howard was going into Betty's house, or just a bit later. Either way, by the time the CSIs searched Ashton's body the keys were back. All the reports say none of the standard stuff was missing. My bet is that they were replaced sooner rather than later. The more the morning wore on, the greater the chance of Ashton's body being discovered.'

'It was still a risk, going to put them back.' Viv sipped her tea.

'Yes. It must have been important to them to hide the fact that they'd been inside Apple Tree Cottage. I'd guess they had some specific motive for entering the place, which would help identify them, if it was discovered.'

'So they weren't just thieves, for instance, after Ashton's valuables.'

'Exactly. And if the timing was as tight as I think, it's possible the killer saw Howard go into the house as they were leaving. Or that Howard saw something he later realised was significant.'

'Do you think the killer went into the house to remove something that might have given them away?'

Eve frowned. 'Maybe, but not something straightforward. When Palmer interviewed me about Ashton's death, he asked where I was between ten on Saturday night and two on Sunday morning. If the killer hadn't put the keys back on Ashton's body by the time Howard searched his pockets, it looks like they hung around at Apple Tree Cottage for some time. If it had been a case of removing a glass they'd drunk out of, or picking up a scarf they'd dropped, for instance, that ought to have been a quick in-and-out operation.' She ate the last of her chocolate raspberry cake. 'But I wonder if they were searching for something. Something Ashton had and they wanted, but he'd hidden it well. Maybe an item that would provide a clue to their identity. The question is, did they find it, or did they give up because it was simply too risky to stay any longer?'

A short while later, Tammy had practised making up their bill, and been offered some more paid try-out sessions the following week. Viv and Eve were back in Monty's kitchen when Eve noticed a stray receipt that had fallen to the floor.

'What's this?' She held it up.

Viv frowned. 'Must have dropped it. You're not going to tell me off for overspending at the village store, are you?'

Eve raised an eyebrow. 'It's what's written on the back that concerns me.'

Viv frowned. 'I don't remem—' And then a look of realisation flooded across her face, together with a pink flush Eve felt she had every reason to display. 'Right, right. Erm.'

Eve looked at the scribbled notes on the reverse side of the tiny receipt. They were only semi-legible. 'Choc h. Lem CC? Min. something – looks like treacle? For twenty? With a day – Sat. But no apparent date…'

'Ah, yes. I was going to copy all that into the reservations book.'

'Had you set yourself any particular deadline?'

A desperate look came into Viv's eye. 'While I could still remember what they'd asked me for, obviously. Only I must have got distracted.' She hung her head.

'It's no use you trying to get round me by looking pitiful. I'm meant to be organising your business. It won't work if I keep letting you off the hook.'

'Oh, you!' Viv laughed.

Eve picked up the receipt again. 'Phone number? Contact name? Time of booking?'

'Well, the receipt was a bit small and I ran out of room, but I did take them down.'

'Please tell me it wasn't on the back of your hand.' Viv might be disorganised, but she was fiercely hygienic.

'I grabbed something.' Viv was in the office doorway now, looking to left and right, scanning the kitchen. 'No wait. I've got it.' She went to one of the cupboards and pulled out a mammoth paper bag of plain flour. Eve could see she'd written on it, near the top where it was folded over.

'All sorted,' Viv said brightly.

'Do you know which Saturday they're coming?'

'Let's just say it's really good news that I took their number down. I'll call them today and then put all the details in the book.'

'Any special reason you didn't do that in the first place?'

'Ah, well, I couldn't lay my hands on it when the phone rang.'

Eve gave her a tired look.

'I know, I know! I remember what you said. Always put it back in the top drawer by the oven so it'll be handy whether I'm baking or doing the prep and I'll never lose it again. Has anyone told you that being extremely organised can be a tiny bit wearing for other people?'

'Many times. You'll thank me when twenty picky customers march through your door and have somewhere to sit and the food that they ordered.'

Viv laughed. 'I hate it when you make sense.' But after a moment her look turned serious. 'Eve, what are your plans? About investigating the murders, I mean? If you're right, then whoever's doing this is completely ruthless. I know Betty put her trust in you, but it feels like a different ball game now. If she was on the spot, I'm sure she'd realise what she's asking, and tell you to stop.'

Eve took a deep breath and thought of Robin's warning. He was concerned for her too, though he knew she wouldn't give up. The idea of accepting the official verdict on Howard's death was so tempting in some ways, but it would be utterly wrong to let this go. 'I know. And I think you're right; Betty's a thoughtful person. But honestly, Viv, after seeing Howard's body hanging there, so spent and defenceless, I can't turn my back on this. He did some abhorrent things, but does that mean it's okay to let everyone think he was a murderer? And to relax about the fact that the real killer is still out there? They could do it again, and if I sit back then I'd bear some responsibility for that. It would be different if the police were digging for more information, but Palmer's ready to close the case.'

Viv sighed. 'I see your point, but please be careful. I don't like this.'

'I will be. At least you know how sensible I am.' It was time to lighten the mood.

Her friend managed a smile. 'About teashop bookings, yes, but you did go off on your own to talk to Howard Green.'

Eve hadn't told her about Robin's presence, of course; she'd have a million and one questions if his involvement got out. 'I stayed close to the crowds.'

'You have an answer for everything. So, if you're going ahead, who will you focus on now?'

It was a good question. 'With Howard out of the picture, I guess Justin has to come top of my list of suspects.'

'You don't sound too convinced.'

She sighed. 'I'm not. Ashton hated *him* – and that's according to his mom, Rathbone and Marina. And after Justin found the underpants Ashton planted, we saw he was really mad. But enough to kill, over twenty-four hours after he spotted them, when Amber had no doubt told him it was just Ashton's idea of a joke?'

'Hmm. Put like that, it does sound questionable.'

'And then Rathbone had the impression Justin could have been the one who supplied Ashton with cannabis, back when he was a teenager. But it sounds as though he was reading between the lines, and none of what I've seen makes it seem likely.'

Viv chewed her lip. 'True. The underpants prank was hardly an act of gangland revenge. And Justin was certainly keen to have Ashton at his home.'

Eve nodded. 'But I can't write him off altogether. I was scared for Amber when he came and frogmarched her out of here.'

'So more work to do?'

She nodded. 'I feel as though I've only just scratched the surface. I've got an appointment to talk to Tina and Carl Adcock later this afternoon.' She pictured the guarded look on Carl's face at the prize draw, and Tina's world-weary expression. 'I just have to keep on digging, so I can see what's going on underneath the veneer everyone's presenting in public.'

Viv frowned suddenly. 'Something was tugging the edge of my memory about the Adcocks. I'm sure it was in a text...' She'd been weighing out flour from the annotated bag, ready to start baking, but now she paused and took out her mobile. 'Just a minute. If I scroll back it'll take me hours, but I should be able to search...

'Here,' she said, after a few moments scrutinising her screen, 'a message Sam sent about Carl Adcock, when he was on school camp a couple of years back.'

Eve had been on her way to help Angie, but she stopped to look. It hadn't occurred to her that Viv's son would also have been taught by the guy.

Adcock's being a disgusting flirt as usual. Going into people's tents when there's no excuse. Gross – though one or two people seem keen.

He'd added a throwing-up emoji.

That was interesting. Was there any possibility that Ashton had seen Carl Adcock behave inappropriately with the students back when he was in school? If so, Carl's comments on Ashton's worthlessness would have seemed all the more hypocritical. Obtaining proof would be a fine way of getting his revenge. Maybe he'd hoped to find something in their house that would work as evidence – photographs perhaps?

'I texted back of course.' Viv peered at her phone again, pulled a face and showed Eve the screen.

That's terrible. We should report it.

And then came Sam's response.

No one's feeling threatened, Mum. Chill out!

'None of my children take me seriously,' Viv said. 'Want me to message Sam and Kirsty and see if they know anything more about Carl? We might have to wait a while for a response, I'm afraid. They're off the grid in Bhutan at the moment, but they're bound to find an internet café sooner or later.'

Eve's mind was still working. 'That'd be great. Thanks.'

CHAPTER TWENTY-SIX

Eve had finished her shift at Monty's and still had a couple of hours before she was due to meet the Adcocks. She needed to switch focus. The background to the two deaths was uppermost in her mind, but *Icon*'s deadline for the obituary copy was on the horizon too. She sat at the dining room table in Elizabeth's Cottage and forced herself to concentrate. So far, she had the material for a good essay on which of Ashton Foley's contacts might have killed him – currently thrown into disarray by Howard Green's death – but his life story was still looking a little patchy.

She'd covered his childhood to some degree, and the interview with his old schoolteachers ought to improve her knowledge. Then Russell Rathbone had helped when it came to his chequered teenage years, and Marina Shaw had covered his move into business. Now she wanted to speak with his Outside In clients to make the last section more rounded. She'd emailed Billy Tozer's publicist, and the woman said she'd passed on her message, but even if he agreed to see her, she wouldn't get the full picture; his time working with Ashton had been cut short.

The list of clients Marina Shaw had provided was a good starting point. She wasn't intending to drive around the country to talk to them all, but one or two personal visits might be useful.

Choosing who to target involved some background research on the names Marina had listed. If she was thorough at this stage it would pay dividends later. At last, she settled on a celebrity client down in London, the model Heaven Jones. She was a household name (in fairness, who would forget a moniker like that?) and came across as warm and open in her previous interviews. She'd be a good balance for Billy Tozer, and similarly high-profile. Eve called her agent to ask if he might broker a meeting, and then set about contacting others on Marina's list. She could get quotes from them over the phone, then decide what to include once she'd amassed a decent number.

She was curious about what each of them had been trying to achieve when they'd hired Outside In, and how much difference the makeovers had made to their lives.

She took her phone from her pocket as Gus trotted past, on his way to the kitchen, and dialled the first number on Marina's list. A moment later a maid was telling her the family were away in Portugal. Of course, it was the Easter vacation. She left her number and email address, in case they had the chance to contact her before her deadline.

The next people on the list – a couple – didn't answer the mobile number she'd been given, so she left a message. On to number three…

Marina had given her six contacts in total, in addition to Heaven Jones. Five of the six had mobile numbers, but not one of them was available. She scanned the web, looking for other Outside In clients who'd given the company public endorsements in the past. At last she found a handful that Marina hadn't mentioned and set herself the challenge of tracking down their contact numbers. If they'd spoken to journalists previously and recommended the company, they probably wouldn't object to her calling.

She drew a blank with two of the named contacts, but the third and fourth were professionals with business numbers. Their makeovers each went back a long way, so they'd be able to tell her how the arrangements had worked out as their plants matured.

One of the two picked up, and Eve explained her mission. 'As I say, I'm sorry to call out of the blue. I'm just keen to get a little more variety, and I noticed you'd spoken to the press before. I know it's a long while back now, but the pictures of your house in the *Sunday Times* looked spectacular, I was wondering if you could tell me—'

'*I hadn't heard that he was dead.*' The guy on the line cut across her. '*I've been out of the country.*'

'I'm sorry to be the one to tell you; it's shocking news. And I guess all Outside In's clients must have gotten to know him to some degree.'

There was a long pause. '*Oh yes, we got to know him all right. One of the first things he explained was the need to understand us, in order to shape the designs he and his partner created. They were in and out for weeks.*'

'I'm interested in that process. I wonder if you'd mind telling me a little more about how it worked for you, and how long it took for the ideas to take shape.'

'*I'm sorry, but no.*'

Eve never took someone's agreement for granted, but the reply was pretty abrupt.

'If it's not a good time, I could—'

'*I don't want to give an interview, full stop. I have to go now.*'

He hung up.

Eve followed Gus through to the kitchen. 'You know what's weird, Gus?' He looked up from his water bowl. 'Well, I know what you think. People are weird, right? In the dog world, I'm guessing behaviour's a little more rational. But in fact, people are normally pretty predictable. That guy I just spoke to runs his own architecture practice. He was perfectly happy to talk to the press about Ashton Foley and Marina Shaw's work when it was first done. He sang their praises, couldn't recommend them highly enough. And his firm got a nice bit of publicity out of the feature he did. Now, here I am offering him more of the same. Okay, so maybe not on the same scale…' Gus had pottered back through to the sitting room. She followed. 'Not on the same scale. But in a big glossy monthly with a massive circulation. And suddenly he's not interested. Not only not interested, but dismissive and unfriendly.'

She flopped down on one of the couches, comforted by its welcoming softness. 'That is simply not usual. When a person's just died, people are normally more generous about spending a few moments to comment on them, not less.'

The guy hadn't been a fan of Ashton's personally. His tone had told her that much.

So why had he been so gushing in that other feature?

CHAPTER TWENTY-SEVEN

With the phone call still turning over in her head, Eve took Gus out for a quick walk along the estuary before giving him his supper. Half an hour after that, when she was already hungry herself, Eve was standing in an empty secondary school a short way outside Saxford. It was where all the children from nearby villages got bussed in to complete their studies. The sun was already low in the sky, and as it was the Easter vacation the building's heating was off. Eve stood there in her cool-weather uniform (tweed trousers, ankle boots, a chocolate-coloured cable-knit sweater and her fawn overcoat). It had been Tina Adcock's suggestion to meet there. Apparently she and Carl had spent the afternoon at the school, finishing off some paperwork and planning for the coming term. Eve was happy to go where the woman wanted, in exchange for a word with her and her husband. Talking to Ashton's old schoolteachers ought to add a lot to her article. All the same, staring at the empty desks, she decided she could have imagined the place without needing to experience it. Even the display boards on the walls were empty; there were bits of torn paper still attached in places, trapped under large staples. Was there some reason why Tina hadn't wanted a home visit?

'I taught him in this room,' the woman said, sashaying up to the teacher's desk. Eve suspected she was always conscious of how she looked to others. She was wearing a tan leather jacket, a low-cut top, tight-fitting pencil skirt and high boots. Her make-up was noticeable but also immaculate. Carl Adcock hadn't joined them yet.

'What's your subject?'

'English.' She gave Eve a wry look. 'Ashton would have called it torture. I tried, but he was never interested. School wasn't exciting enough.'

'He played up?'

Tina nodded. 'He wasn't the only one. I'd say I usually have the goodwill of around half my class.'

Eve couldn't imagine anything worse than standing in front of a critical mass of students who were set on making your life hell. Back in London, she'd hated her job as a school administrator, but at least she'd never been on the front line.

'It sounds like a challenge. So Ashton didn't stand out, especially, then?'

'Oh no, I wouldn't say that.' For just a second a slight smile crossed her lips, but then her look hardened. 'No. I'm afraid to say he led me a dance in a way I'm not likely to forget.' She paused. 'I suppose I shouldn't offload when you're writing his obituary though.'

It was common for interviewees to slam the brakes on like that. She couldn't blame them. They always seemed to imagine she was hoping to do a hatchet job, but all she wanted was an honest and engaging article. She'd have to make her comments about his school days rather generalised. 'I understand. There's no pressure, but if you have a specific anecdote you'd like to share that would be great. You could always come back to me with it.'

She nodded. 'I will.'

'Do you have any fond memories of him, despite what he put you through?' It was weird, but the question often got to the heart of the more negative feelings a person had, too. If an interviewee had to get creative in order to reply, that spoke volumes.

Eve caught the faraway look in the woman's eye, but it was only a second before her hard, direct stare returned. 'No.'

There weren't many people who'd admit as much. It said a lot about her, as well as about him. 'I noticed you spoke up for Ashton when he ended up in the youth court.'

Tina tucked her blonde wavy hair behind her ear. 'I felt guilty. I saw a guy come into school here and leave an envelope on Ashton's desk just before class. When he got into trouble, I realised I should have reported it at the time. It couldn't have been a one-off; I saw that later. How would he have known which desk Ashton sat at unless he'd watched through the window, or been in to meet him before?' She shrugged. 'Security's way different these days. If you're not a student or a member of staff you'd find it hard to get inside, but back then it was easy. And the guy who delivered the envelope looked out of place: too old to be a student, but too young to be a member of staff.'

'And you'd have recognised him, anyway, I guess, if he'd belonged here?'

'Probably. Though we often have supply teachers in.' She pulled a face. 'We're all exhausted. If a virus goes round, I guess it's no wonder it takes the place by storm.

'Anyway, I spoke up in court, partly to help the police, and yes, partly because I thought Ashton was being controlled by an older "friend". But it was just the moral thing to do. I can't honestly say that I felt much sympathy for him.' She put her shoulders back. 'I'm horrified that he's dead though. And after he'd finally made such a success of himself. It's what every teacher hopes for their students: that somewhere deep down you're making them feel it's worth working and achieving something for themselves.'

They sounded like lines she'd rehearsed for a parents' evening. 'And you supported him by buying raffle tickets.' Eve was still slightly surprised by that. In Tina's position she'd have been glad that Ashton had found his vocation too, but she wouldn't have wanted to risk him landing up inside her home, potentially for many weeks if she'd been picked to appear on his TV programme.

Tina Adcock frowned. 'I felt, as his old teacher, the least I could do was buy a few. And of course, I support Jim Thackeray's fundraising efforts too.'

But she could have just made a donation. Eve had seen the raffle tickets around the village. Some had been left with honesty boxes next to them, together with places to post the stubs of the tickets you'd bought. It would be easy enough to put a contribution into the box without actually taking any numbers.

At that moment, Carl Adcock appeared, in casual trousers, an open-necked white shirt and a black jacket. He gave her a quick smile and she suppressed a shudder as she thought of Sam's message to Viv, about his inappropriate behaviour with his female students.

'Come and see the drama studio. That's where I had the challenge of coaching Ashton.'

Eve and Tina followed him down a corridor and into a large space with huge windows, edged with floor-to-ceiling blackout curtains.

'He had talent,' Carl said, 'but I couldn't see him using it for anything honest at the time. When I said he'd never make anything of himself, it seemed like a dead cert.' He shook his head. 'I lost my temper that day and came out with an overused cliché.'

Perhaps he wished he'd been more original, now he'd had his words quoted back at him in public.

'Will you write what Ashton said, about it helping him to come to his senses when he was detained?'

People often wanted to know the content of an obit in advance, to see how it would reflect on their loved one or – just as commonly – themselves. In this case the answer wasn't straightforward. She hadn't believed Ashton when he'd said it, but it was a direct quote. As for the readers of *Icon*, their reaction might depend on how she couched the words.

'I haven't decided what content to use yet.' It was quite true. 'I still have a couple more people to interview before I start to draft anything.'

'I don't suppose the school will like having that sort of quote flying around. Though I imagine it will be overshadowed now by the news that he was killed by his mother's boyfriend.'

Eve watched his eyes. Did he really believe that version of events? Or could he be guilty of the murders himself? If Ashton had proof of his criminal behaviour with teenage girls, Carl Adcock would have had a lot to lose.

'How did the session go, when he visited you for the Outside In consultation?'

Eve was grateful for her training. An old mentor had told her to watch first, take notes later. If she'd been glancing down at her pad she would have missed the look between husband and wife. It was over in a microsecond, but it gave away a dynamic that set Eve thinking.

There was anger there – a confrontation between them – and alongside that, a short, sharp injection of fear.

'I was glad he'd made good,' Carl Adcock said, 'but his business, and his ideas to bring nature into our home?' He gave a quick shake of his head. 'I could have come up with all that myself. I was teaching when he came to do our consultation; Tina held the fort as she had free periods. He couldn't make this week, when we'd both have been around, but Tina told me all about it. If you ask me, with Outside In, it's a case of the emperor's new clothes.'

As Eve manoeuvred her Mini Clubman out of the school car park, she glanced up and caught a face at the window of the room she'd just left. Tina Adcock was watching her leave. The teacher raised a hand when she realised she'd been seen. Outwardly, she was all poise and control, but Eve had a feeling there was a lot going on under the surface. And she and Carl were the second couple who'd won raffle tickets despite having reasons to avoid Ashton.

It was another thing she needed to investigate.

CHAPTER TWENTY-EIGHT

'Thanks for letting me in.' Eve stepped through the door into the church hall early on Thursday morning. The large airy room was bathed in watery spring sunlight. Dust motes drifted in the air, stirred up by her and the Reverend Jim Thackeray's entrance. Jim in particular set a lot of them shifting; he was a great bear of a man, with thick grey hair, and eyes that were kind yet knowing.

'No trouble at all. There once was a time when we didn't have to lock up, but those days are gone, sadly.'

The room looked tidy compared with when she'd last seen it; you'd never know so many people had thronged there to watch Ashton pick the Outside In prize winners. It was weird to be back after his death. She could still see him, standing on the stage in his black top hat. It was almost impossible to accept that he'd gone; he'd been larger than life.

'I've been in touch with Betty Foley, poor woman,' the vicar said. 'What she must be going through, I can't begin to think. I hoped it might help to talk.'

That was like him. Eve was glad Mrs Foley had someone looking out for her.

'I hear you'll be writing Ashton's obituary?' Jim Thackeray went on.

'That's right. I've spoken to his mom too. She wanted to talk to me about the job.' Eve glanced at him sideways, wondering what Mrs Foley might have said about Howard's death. 'If you have any memories you'd like to share, I'd love to include them.'

A brief smile crossed the vicar's face. 'You might want to hear what they are first.'

She laughed. 'We obituary writers don't baulk at the truth. Though if you've got any positive comments for balance that would be great.'

'Well, he helped me raise nearly a thousand pounds for the church roof.' The man smiled. 'And he was a live wire. Life in Saxford was never dull when he was around. He had a great deal of charisma. I didn't officiate here when he was a child, but I remember a couple of his visits to the village, after he'd left to live in London. One was just an overnight job. It stuck in my mind because Betty told me all about it; she was very emotional and excited.' He shook his head. Eve had the impression he'd felt a great deal of sympathy for her back then, too.

'Prior to that,' the vicar went on, 'his last trip home was at least a decade ago, I believe. He was here for longer then, and everyone was well aware of it. His parties were the talk of Saxford. The villagers either lapped it up or responded angrily, depending on their age group.' He paused, a slight twinkle in his eye. 'And a variety of other factors. I rather think some people found the whiff of scandal he exuded compelling.'

Eve stood up and pulled her notebook from her bag. Ashton had been controversial, but popular in some quarters, even if it had been for the wrong reasons.

'It was rare for him to see his mother, then?'

Jim Thackeray sighed. 'I believe that's true, though I do remember Betty travelling down to London to visit him once. She was full of smiles when she came home: he'd bought her a new outfit at Harrods, then taken her to eat at some exclusive club he'd joined, before whisking her off to a West End show.'

Eve could imagine what a treat that must have been, though it sounded as though Betty Foley had had to suffer a lot in return.

'Wonderful.' She met his look. 'She hadn't had much fun over the years, maybe?'

'Perhaps not.'

And then Eve started to imagine Betty Foley telling Howard Green all about her son's lavish lifestyle and the expensive presents he'd been able to shower her with. Even if she'd been too tactful to share the information with him directly, he'd probably heard about it on the grapevine. He'd have seen her new clothes and the spring in her step. Had Ashton really minded about his mom? Or had it all been point scoring?

When she met the vicar's eyes again his look was knowing. She bet he'd followed her thoughts precisely.

'I did see him and Betty having a proper talk during this most recent visit home,' he said.

She nodded, thinking of the time she'd seen them walking on the beach. 'So did I.' And there'd been a closeness there. It might be a memory Betty could hang on to in future.

'Did Mrs Foley happen to mention the extra task she's given me?'

The vicar raised his eyebrows. 'She did not.'

Eve wasn't surprised. She hadn't wanted Howard to know; maybe Eve was the only person she'd confided in. But prior to her next request, she'd really have to share her mission.

'In confidence, although the police suspect Howard Green murdered Ashton before killing himself, she's convinced he'd never have done it. She'd already asked me to help prove his innocence. I failed to do that before he died, but I did find out enough to convince me she's right. And I've promised I'll keep looking for evidence that might help clear his name.'

He nodded. 'I'm glad you've told me. I found it hard to believe Howard would kill Ashton too. He'd set himself up as Betty's protector – it was part of his identity – and he of all people saw how dearly she loved her son.'

Of course, the vicar didn't know how much Howard had had to lose. The details of his fraudulent activity hadn't been publicised yet, but still it made sense. And thinking back, she thought Howard had enjoyed seeing himself as occupying the moral high ground too. Each time Ashton had behaved thoughtlessly – disappearing off with his friends, or mucking up Betty's plans to get to the airport – there was Howard, ready to stand in or stand down, and show himself in a good light. Ashton's continued existence helped him with that. It was still shocking that behind that loyal and stoical facade, Howard had stolen her money.

'And I can understand Betty asking you to help,' Jim Thackeray went on. 'Your reputation precedes you. So, you're here because you've had a hunch?'

'It's just an anomaly. I don't suppose you still have the raffle ticket counterfoils – the ones that were put into the box for Ashton to draw from?'

Jim Thackeray's brow furrowed and his intelligent eyes met hers. 'Follow me.' He took her through to the kitchen. They looked at the immaculately wiped stainless steel surfaces. The smell of bleach hung in the air. On the windowsill, Eve could see the ring holder Sylvia had mentioned. 'Mrs Crocket the cleaner is very thorough,' the vicar said, 'but you're in luck. The paper recycling isn't collected until later this week.'

He pointed to the bins behind the door: one for general waste, and three others for various categories of recycling. One was still full of raffle tickets – a mass of folded pink, blue and yellow paper.

The vicar followed her eyes. 'It was a popular draw. I wonder what will happen now – for the prize winners I mean.'

It was a good point; Eve hadn't heard whether the television series would go ahead, which could affect the prize for the overall winner. To be fair though, that was only to be awarded at Ashton's discretion, if any of them proved suitable. She assumed Marina

Shaw would finish the promised initial consultations, if there was more work to do.

But her mind was preoccupied with the draw itself. Amber hadn't wanted to win, but said she'd taken part at Justin's request, and certainly on the night of the draw, he'd seemed delighted with the result. Meanwhile, the Adcocks had bought tickets, even though Carl had clearly despised Ashton. And something about their old pupil had made them anxious; she'd seen it in their eyes.

'Jim, would you mind if I had a look at the raffle slips?'

The vicar shook his head. 'The draw was a strange event. I thought I knew Ashton's game when it began, but by the end I felt I'd missed something. I've no doubt you're working in a good cause. And although I've had the new data protection laws driven home very forcefully by the chairman of the parish council – as well as the local diocese – names written on the back of raffle tickets weren't covered. A terrible oversight. Perhaps I should leave you to it. If you would be so kind as to lock up and return the key to the vicarage when you've finished?'

She nodded. 'Thank you.' Hooray for Jim Thackeray. She pulled the bin into the middle of the room and started to go through the tickets systematically.

The project took a while, but it was worth it.

Moira Squires had bought a crazy number. Oh boy, had she been keen to win! Sitting as she did at the centre of village life, she'd probably hated the thought of having to listen to other people popping in to tell her just how wonderfully Ashton was going to transform their houses. Much better to make sure she had every chance of winning herself, so she could be the one to relay exciting snippets of news.

Viv's in-laws had also bought a large number, despite being absent from the draw itself. Viv said when they heard they hadn't won they'd debated simply paying to get Ashton in, more to flaunt their wealth, Viv reckoned, than for any other reason.

But it was Eve's results for Tina Adcock and Amber Ingram that really made her think. She found not one ticket stub in either of their names, or the names of their husbands.

Of course, the tickets Ashton had actually pulled from the box would probably be elsewhere. Eve imagined he'd have stuffed them into his jeans pocket or something. But the fact remained: either Tina Adcock and Amber Ingram had bought only one ticket each... or they'd bought no tickets at all, and Ashton Foley had rigged the draw.

CHAPTER TWENTY-NINE

'Guess who I've been to see?' It was early afternoon and Eve was taking off her navy puffer jacket in the office at Monty's. She'd had further excitement between raiding the vicar's recycling collection and reaching the teashop.

'Who?' Viv put her head on one side. 'No – wait! You haven't finally had an appointment with Billy Tozer?'

'Correct. I was starting to worry that he'd never invite me, but apparently when the muse takes him, he doesn't check his messages. He finally called out of the blue late this morning and asked me to go straight over.' He'd said Ashton's death had filled him with raw emotion that he needed to express artistically. It might have come across as pretentious, had the guy not had tears in his eyes.

'So what was the house like? Did you take photos?' Viv's daffodil hair was dancing, her tone breathless.

Eve shook her head. 'Photography's not really my area; I wouldn't have done the job justice.'

Viv gave her a severe look. 'This isn't just about professionalism, Eve!'

'You'll have to be patient, like everyone else! I got his permission for *Icon*'s photographer to go in and get some decent shots. They'll be worth waiting for.'

She sighed. 'You're so disciplined. Tell me all about it instead then.'

Eve hung her jacket on the hook on the back of the office door. 'I'm sure a psychologist would have a field day. There was a lot of phallic cacti and other spiky stuff. Of course, it was Marina and Ashton who'd designed the scheme for him, but working with his input. He's got passion flowers trained over a frame in his bedroom.'

'He took you to his bedroom!'

'It was all entirely innocent and professional. He was the perfect gentleman.'

'What else?'

'They've made him a "quiet room". It's full of mosses and ferns, all chosen because they're some of the oldest plants on earth. He can sit in the middle of them and feel centred "in a space of historic botanical interest".'

'But not as centred as if he came in here to feast on a chocolate raspberry cake.' Viv had one eyebrow raised in a challenging way.

It was true that her confections had a sustaining hit like no other Eve had known. And besides, she was loyal. 'Naturally not. Though I must admit, I quite liked the moss and fern room.'

'Don't tell me you're going to ask Marina for a consultation!'

'I thought I might limit myself to buying a few geraniums. The trouble is the atmosphere has to be controlled to suit the plants.'

'And you're not sure you and ferns have the same needs?'

'Maybe not – at least, not 24/7.'

'Thank goodness! I thought I'd lost you for a second. Anything else you liked?'

'The orange trees in his sitting room were nice.'

'Why are you blushing?'

'They were set into beds of earth sunk into the floors. It helps them feel integral to the room if they're not in a pot, apparently.'

Viv nodded. 'I guess I can see that.'

'Gus peed on one of them.'

'No!'

Eve could see sympathy in Viv's expression, but glee came topmost by some margin.

'Billy was very nice about it. He likes dogs, thankfully. He's got a Great Dane called Thor – size of a small horse.'

'Blimey.'

'Turns out he's a softie, like his owner. He ran away when Gus pottered into the room. I suppose it's a bit like someone my size being scared of spiders. Billy gave me Earl Grey tea and some chocolate chip cookies out of a packet.'

Viv pulled a face. 'Eww to the cookies.'

'I told him about your wares. He's considering putting in a regular order.'

She opened her eyes wide. 'Fantastic! Well done! D'you think I can put "By appointment to Billy Tozer, rapper" in the window here? We could probably get coverage in the papers!'

'Let's wait until we get the order in first. He made encouraging noises *before* Gus drenched his orange tree. Still, he seems like a nice guy, not like he's portrayed in the press. I'd guess he works hard at his bad-boy image, then goes home and brews up a cocoa.'

'Anything useful on the murder?'

'Just one oddity. He told me his house was down to feature in a one-off television special about Outside In. He had no idea there was anything else planned.'

'But didn't Ashton say one of the prize draw winners might be picked to feature on TV, as part of a whole series?'

'Uh-huh. So that made me curious. I called the production company who are doing the documentary on Tozer's place, and they don't know anything about an ongoing series either.'

Viv's mouth formed an O. 'You think Ashton made it up, just to make the prize sound more enticing?'

'And maybe to tempt in someone like Justin Ingram, who's hungry for publicity?' And who clearly thought his wife had bought plenty of tickets. 'Yes, perhaps. I just asked Marina about it. Apparently Ashton told her he'd mooted the idea with someone from the production team. But I can't find any evidence of that.'

'Ah, so you saw Marina on your way in, I take it?'

'Yes.' She was sitting in the teashop as they spoke, opposite a man with model-standard good looks: high cheekbones to match hers, silky dark hair and deep brown eyes. 'Who's the guy? Do you know? I caught Marina on the way back from the bathroom, so we weren't introduced.'

They both went over to the doorway to the teashop, so they could peer at the couple.

'No idea,' Viv hissed, 'but they're just about ready for some staff intervention, if you want to get in there before Angie does.'

Angie was on duty again; her college was closed for Easter so she was putting in extra hours.

Eve slipped through the teashop, past Angie (who looked slightly startled at her sudden appearance) and up to Marina's table.

'Hello again! I wondered if you'd like a second pot of tea, or some more cake?'

Marina gave her an unfriendly look, but there was something extra in her eyes as she glanced at the man opposite her. Pride.

'We need to get going,' she said. 'Lots to do. I can't neglect Billy, despite Ashton's death. We need to get out of his way. He's about to start work on his new album.'

The dark-haired guy stretched in his chair, and sighed as though moving didn't appeal. He reached to touch Marina's hand as he turned to Eve.

'I'd love to have stayed longer. Marina and I don't get much time together, what with our careers; they're so full on. This is a lovely place to relax. Are you the owner?'

He probably guessed she might be, because she was so much older than Angie. 'Just a hanger-on. Viv, with the yellow hair, is the mastermind behind Monty's.'

He grinned. 'I'm a restaurateur by trade: I launched the MacAskill bistro chain.'

'Oh wow!' Eve hadn't heard of it.

'This is Eve's day job,' Marina said. 'She's the one I told you about, who dabbles in obituary writing too.'

Eve took a deep breath.

'Of course!' The man let Marina's hand go and held his out to shake Eve's. 'I'm Zach Campbell, Marina's partner. I wanted to come as soon as I heard about Ashton, but I had operational commitments I couldn't get out of. As it is I have to leave again shortly. I'm due back in London by five. There's just no rest when you're in hospitality, is there?'

Eve shook hands, catching a slight eyeroll from Marina, who no doubt regarded Monty's as very low key.

'Still,' he glanced sideways at his girlfriend, 'at least I'm not always off on tour like Jack.' Eve wasn't surprised to find the woman had some rock-star ex. What with Outside In's work for celebrities, she was probably tripping over them: witness Billy Tozer.

'I feel a good deal more relaxed about leaving now that Ashton's murderer's dead.' Zach Campbell leaned back in his chair. 'Anyway, it's been good to meet you.'

'You too. I hope you've managed to enjoy the village a little, despite the awful circumstances.'

He smiled. 'I have. And everyone's been very welcoming.' He nodded over his shoulder, towards the front of the teashop and the village green. 'That Matt Falconer from the pub is a character, isn't he?'

Eve smiled and nodded. She was embarrassed to admit she'd had Matt down as a beer-swilling freeloader to begin with, enjoying life while his wife and brother got on with all the work. But he was excellent with customers; he always knew how to make them feel better.

'He took us out in his boat. A small thing really – no cabin, and with a dinky little outboard motor – but he said being out on the open water would do us the world of good, and it did.'

Marina's look was sour. Matt's dinghy had clearly fallen well below expectations as far as she was concerned.

Eve glanced back to Zach Campbell. His existence, and that of an ex before him, made the idea of any ongoing relationship between Marina and Ashton a lot less likely. She could see how pleased Marina was to be at Zach's side.

'So just the bill, thanks,' Marina said, with a slight edge to her voice.

'Of course.'

Eve went off to prepare it. For all the woman's scratchiness, she cared about her business. She wasn't going to let personal feelings stop her from completing the jobs she'd got on. It was in character for her to have quarrelled with Ashton over the silly prank he'd played on the Ingrams – and for her to avoid a relationship with her co-worker too.

Five minutes later, Eve was back in the kitchen. She was on scone detail, while Viv prepared honey and raspberry cakes and Angie did battle front of house.

'So, update me then,' Viv said.

Eve told her about the hour and a half she'd spent going through the raffle tickets in the church hall recycling.

'I can't believe you did that.'

'It's hard to get the big picture without checking small details.'

Despite extensive practice, Eve still hadn't mastered the art of making scones without getting sticky dough between her fingers. She eased it off with the back of a knife.

'So you reckon Amber and Tina never really bought tickets at all?'

Eve put more flour on the work surface. She'd gotten the mix too wet, that was the trouble. 'That would be my guess. Who buys just one raffle ticket? It's not impossible, but they weren't expensive. Limiting yourself to an outlay of a pound would seem a bit mean.'

Viv was measuring out raspberries without using anything as conventional as scales – she did it by eye. 'I thought Amber looked pretty shocked when Ashton read her name out.'

'And now we know why. Tina managed better. I wonder if she noticed Amber's reaction and put two and two together when he called her name too.'

'Or if she's just a cool customer.'

The scone dough was behaving itself now. Eve breathed a sigh of relief and reached for a rolling pin. 'She does seem to be. My mind's been running through what it tells us.'

'Go on,' Viv said. 'You're good at this. I can teach you to bake and you can teach me sleuthcraft.'

'Well, Ashton clearly selected Amber and Tina specifically, and both women must have wanted to keep the fact a secret. They could have spoken up at the draw itself, but they didn't. At first, I thought Amber might have kept quiet because Justin had asked her to buy a whole bunch of tickets and she'd ignored him.'

'Lazy so and so,' Viv said, gently folding her ingredients together. 'Like he couldn't have bought them himself if he was so bothered.'

'Quite. Anyway, I'm not sure I was right. She lied to me about buying the tickets too, and she looked upset when Ashton told her she'd won. I think the reason she didn't buy a ticket – and the reason she's keeping it a secret – add up to something significant. And the same for Tina Adcock. Yet it looks as though it was their husbands who had quarrels with Ashton.'

Eve relayed what had happened when she'd met Tina and Carl the previous day.

'When I asked about Ashton's visit, they caught each other's eyes for a moment before they answered and they looked weird – sort of angry with each other, but almost scared, too.'

'Strange. Want the scone cutter?' She held it out.

'Thanks. And the other thing is, Ashton must have been pretty sure they wouldn't give him away when he called out their names. I'd guess he had some kind of hold over each of them, even if it was only by extension, and they kept quiet to protect their husbands. I assume they decided to wait and see what he had to say in private.'

'That makes sense. So the Adcocks and the Ingrams are all on your list of murder suspects now then?'

Even though Eve had them down on her spreadsheet, it felt weird when Viv said it aloud. 'I guess so.' She worked to cut the scones as neatly as possible.

Viv's eyes were round when she glanced up. 'And if Ashton's motive in rigging the raffle was to settle old scores...'

'Then he might have targeted Carl Adcock for telling him he'd never amount to anything, Justin because he hated him – though I'm still not convinced I understand why – and Moira because she'd bad-mouthed him as a child.' She paused with her work. 'Though Moira's win was probably genuine; she'd bought half the tickets on offer. It all adds to the picture I'm building, but I'm missing something. Nothing I've found so far explains why any of them would react by killing Ashton.'

'So what next?'

Eve sighed. 'I want to talk to everyone again. But I can't interview them all twice.'

'At least there's the celebration launch of the church roof repairs coming up,' Viv said. 'The whole village will probably be at that, knowing Jim's ability to twist people's arms.' She laughed.

It was true. The vicar had been planning for the event when she went to return the church hall key. He'd said he'd decided to go ahead with it, despite Ashton and Howard's deaths, as it would provide an opportunity for the villagers to come together. But then he'd looked at her from under his bushy grey eyebrows with a twinkle in his eye and added, 'Also, we need the money.'

The do was another fundraiser. There would be drinks and nibbles this time, all paid for by Billy Tozer, with the church taking donations in return.

Eve would be ready to make small talk and keep her ear to the ground.

At that moment, a bleep sounded from Viv's pocket. 'Message notification. It'll be one of the kids; no one else contacts me that way.'

She went to wash her hands, then pulled the instrument from her pocket and unlocked it, her brow furrowing as she read the message.

'Everything all right?' Eve said.

Viv looked up and met her eyes. 'I've been guilty of sexism.'

'What?'

'It's from Sam. You know I asked him for more details when I found his message about Carl Adcock making up to the female students at school camp?'

Eve nodded.

'Well, it wasn't Carl, and it wasn't female students.' She shook her head and fiddled with her phone. 'He's right. He never said it was. "*Adcock's being a disgusting flirt as usual. Going into people's tents when there's no excuse. Gross – though one or two people seem keen.*"' She shook her head. 'I can't believe I was that blinkered. It just never occurred to me. Sam says Tina's renowned for flirting with the seniors at school, but he remembers her being quite fresh with some of the fifteen-year-olds too.'

CHAPTER THIRTY

Eve was down to travel to London that evening, to speak with Heaven Jones about her dealings with Ashton and Outside In. As soon as she'd finished at Monty's she went to fetch Gus to let him run off steam before she got going.

He dashed along the beach, the fur on his stomach barely clearing the pebble-strewn sand. His healthy wet black nose was pointed into the wind and his ears were flung back. Seeing him made her feel embarrassingly emotional; Eve wasn't the only one who'd benefitted from the move to the coast. As usual, he treated the sea as an entertainment that had been laid on especially for him, dashing in and out of the waves as they broke on the shore, getting the ocean foam on his chin hairs.

Eve strode along, slightly higher up the beach. The breeze worked its way underneath her thin draped sweater, through to her skin, but it felt bracing rather than unpleasant.

It was good just to smell the saltwater and feel the wind in her pixie-cropped hair. She let her mind freewheel, and thought about Tina Adcock.

It was still possible Ashton had rigged the raffle to get back at Carl, but by the look of it not with the hope of finding evidence of wrongdoing against *him*. Could Ashton have once been close to Tina, and now realised how unforgivable it was for her to take advantage of her position like that?

Eve remembered her conversation with the woman the previous day. 'So Ashton didn't stand out, especially, then?' she'd asked. 'Oh no, I wouldn't say that,' Tina had replied. And for just a second a secret smile had crossed her lips. Eve had it all down in her notebook, and she'd typed it up afterwards too. It meant the details had stuck in her mind. And then after that smile, Eve remembered, the woman's look had hardened. It was as though once-fond memories had been buried by more negative feelings.

If Ashton and Tina had once been in a relationship, had he wanted to expose her? Tina had looked scared when Eve had asked about Ashton's visit. And she'd spoken up for him in court; that might fit if they'd once been close.

Eve took a deep breath of sea air. 'It clears up another query too,' she said to Gus. 'I'd been wondering how Ashton managed to arrange to visit Tina when Carl wasn't home. He could hardly ask to come when he was out if he was after dirt on Carl, and Tina knew nothing about it. But if Tina had something to hide – a good reason to speak with Ashton in private – then she'd be just as keen as he was to sort out a time when Carl was out of the house.'

Her mind skipped back to Justin and Amber. Ashton had visited them when Justin was out too. How had he arranged that?

Justin still seemed like a possible suspect, but Tina Adcock was also looking interesting. Ashton might have had all the information he needed to ruin her career. Had he worked his way into her home to gather hard evidence? Or simply to make her squirm – to hold out the threat of what he might do? Or was Eve on the wrong track? Had Ashton still been fond of Tina? But that seemed unlikely. They'd been out of touch for years as far as Eve could tell.

It was like trying to grasp at smoke. She felt her heart rate ramp up. She could only hope she found something concrete that would change the minds of the police and give Betty Foley a small sliver of comfort.

She checked the time on her phone. She needed to leave for London in the next half hour.

'Sorry to desert you this evening, Gus,' she said as they made their way up the beach, 'but guess who's coming round to look in on you? Angie! Yes, she is!'

Angie had stepped into the breach before, and Gus appeared to appreciate the student's attentions just as much as Eve's. It was slightly hurtful, but obviously very handy.

Heaven Jones had offered Eve a tour round her nature-enhanced home. As one of Ashton's first clients, her Outside In makeover had taken place ten years earlier, so Eve would get to see an established treatment.

'What do you think, Gus?' she said, as they neared Elizabeth's Cottage. 'Will it be like a scene from *Sleeping Beauty* by now? Maybe Heaven has to hack her way through the undergrowth to reach the front door…'

She couldn't wait to get down there to find out, and to see what kind of person Heaven was. As an early adopter of Outside In, she might also be one of the people who'd bought drugs from Ashton after he'd moved to London, if the rumour of him dealing down there was true. It could be an interesting evening…

Heaven Jones's house was huge, detached and set well back from the road in leafy Hampstead – a far cry from the narrow terraced place Eve had once owned in the capital. She'd put on a smart fitted dress and jacket for the occasion. The dress was burnt orange and the most high-end item of clothing she owned. She tended to dress well for interviews, but in this case, she was especially conscious of Heaven Jones's profession. Though presumably models got used to everyone else looking a bit shabby.

Eve walked the five steps up to the glossy white front door and rang the bell. A moment later (so presumably no hacking with a sword involved) a woman answered. Her face was familiar from the photographs Eve had seen. She was around six feet tall, skinny and angular, with features that made her look like an elf from *The Lord of the Rings*. Her silvery hair and pale blue eyes accentuated the impression. She seemed to be dressed in a very large pillowcase, with head, arm and leg holes, and wore silver sandals and silver polish on both finger- and toenails.

'Eve? Welcome!' Her voice was deep and melodic.

'Thank you for seeing me.'

This was not a person who'd let plants grow untamed through her home, Eve guessed. Everything about her and the outside of her house was immaculate. Her hallway was beautiful: wide, with a high ceiling. The backdrop was brilliant white, but someone had fitted a sage-green painted wooden frame partway along its length. You could walk under the archway it made, and also see through parts of it to the rest of the hall beyond, but round it trailed some kind of climber, with lush green leaves. Beyond it, at the end of the corridor, Eve could see huge glass doors, the height and width of the hall, leading onto Heaven Jones's back garden. Smaller plants sat on narrow wooden tables running along the hall walls, giving the space splashes of colour. Although evening was drawing on, low beams of light still filled the space.

'Your hallway's beautiful, Ms Jones. And this was all part of what Outside In did?'

She nodded and smiled. 'Please, call me Heaven.' Eve would do her best. 'It's surprising, isn't it? It makes the place feel so tranquil, and I find I really need that. My work's very pressured.'

It was interesting. Eve knew Outside In's treatments were crazily expensive, and that some people might commission them purely to keep up with the latest trend, but walking into Heaven's home, she felt the impact of the firm's work. The stress of the drive down to London faded as the scent of leaves and earth reached her.

'Do come through.' She led Eve into a spacious kitchen. 'What can I get you to drink? I was about to have a kale smoothie.'

'That sounds interesting, and, er, nice. I'll try one too. Thank you.' Eve hoped it wouldn't have ill effects on her journey home.

'This was another of Ashton and Marina's interventions,' Heaven said, waving an elegant arm behind her. 'A herb wall. I like it because it makes the room smell so nice, as well as looking green. And it's a practical touch I hadn't thought of.'

A panel above one of her kitchen counters held a number of rustic-looking wooden planters containing basil, sage, rosemary, oregano and thyme.

Eve watched as Heaven whizzed up kale, avocado, blueberries, lime and ginger in a blender.

'Here.' She poured out two glassfuls. 'Let's take these through to the dining room.'

It was a lovely, light space with what Eve imagined Marina Shaw might call a statement tree that stood in a huge pot in one corner of the room, on top of the wooden floorboards. Visiting dogs would not be a danger here, unless they were very tall. The tree's glossy leaves contrasted with the white wall behind. Once again, Eve could see the skill behind Ashton and Marina's showy outfit. In good weather, the sun would create shadow patterns on the wall that would change as the hours wore on. She liked the idea of that.

'It's a ficus,' Heaven said. 'Ashton, Marina and I decided not to go overboard in any one room. All the plants need a certain amount of care, but they're well worth it. And that tree is especially tolerant. It actually likes several days of dry soil.' She dropped gracefully onto a transparent plastic dining chair and motioned for Eve to do the same. 'So' – she sighed – 'I was very sorry to hear about Ashton.' She shook her head. 'I'd heard he enjoyed living dangerously of course, back when he was at school. He was still a party animal when I met him, but he was driven too. I can't believe he was involved in anything criminal by that stage.'

That was interesting, given the rumours she'd heard about his dealing down in London. She mentioned the gossip, and Heaven grimaced.

'That's the press for you, they invent drama if they can't find any. I remember reading something like that in one of those anonymous gossip columns, now you mention it, but I'm sure I'd have known if it were true.' She leaned forward, placing her chin on one upturned hand, her brow furrowing. 'I had a wild boyfriend back then who was a drug user. If Ashton had still been involved in that world, my guy would have been asking him about his prices and making deals on the side.' She smiled ruefully. 'Plenty of that went on, but not with Ashton.'

Eve readjusted, mentally. Maybe he really had left all of that behind then.

'So, tell me what you'd like to know for your article,' Heaven said.

'We could maybe start with how you and Ashton met. Or was it Marina you were connected with?'

She shook her head. 'No, it was Ashton – indirectly, through the ill-advised boyfriend I mentioned, in fact. He was mad, bad and exciting to know! Ronnie Randall.'

Another rock star, like Billy Tozer. Heaven said Randall's name as though Eve might not have heard of him.

'Ashton was one of Ronnie's roadies for a while.' Heaven sipped her drink. 'They went their separate ways, but when Outside In was born, Ronnie saw an article about the company and pointed it out to me. He knew I wanted to do stuff to this house, and that I needed something that would make me feel grounded. And he was intrigued to know about the gardening business too. It was so quirky. But then so was Ashton. It was one of the things I liked about him. He often surprised me.'

Eve took a tiny sip of her smoothie and found it was unexpectedly drinkable. She was glad Heaven hadn't been too pure to add the blueberries. 'That's interesting. Would you mind giving me some examples?' It sounded as though Heaven had seen a different side of Ashton, and her reminiscences would add colour to Eve's piece.

'Well, I don't think he'd have minded me saying he had a playboy reputation. He was charming, and I suspect he broke a lot of hearts. But one day when he was round here, he admitted he'd been on a secret visit to a childhood sweetheart, during a recent trip back to Suffolk.' Heaven gave a delicate sigh. 'Someone he'd been at school with, apparently. It was a Romeo and Juliet type of thing, from what he said. Or at least, her parents wouldn't have approved.'

Eve held her breath and the model went on.

'Who could blame them, really? It sounds as though he was a total tearaway as a teenager. They weren't to know he'd turn his life around. And although I had a lot of time for him, even as an adult, I couldn't call him steady.' She gave a sad smile. 'And steadiness is what parents want for their children, right?'

Eve couldn't deny it. When her twins chose partners, she fervently hoped they'd be down to earth, law-abiding and constant in their affections.

'Ashton said he and this girl had always kept the romantic side of their relationship secret. I wonder what happened to her? It sounded as though she was already involved with another man by the time he went back to visit. I think Ashton went to try to patch things up – talk her into seeing him again. I overheard him telling Ronnie they'd had a moment of passion, and he'd thought he might win the day, but she ended up opting for the other guy. Ashton was very down on *him*, whoever he was. He sounded very conventional. The sort that could be relied on to pay the mortgage and be home in time for tea.' She took a deep breath. 'It's a while ago now, but I imagine the girl's hurting after his death.' Her eyes met Eve's. 'If she and Ashton couldn't resist each other when they were back in contact, even if she broke it off, she must have felt pretty strongly about him, deep down.'

Eve felt goosebumps rise on her arms as realisation flooded through her. 'Was she called Amber, by any chance?'

Heaven nodded and smiled sadly. 'You know her? Yes – I'd forgotten the name, but that was it.'

Eve remembered Amber's taut jaw as she'd talked about Ashton. He'd sneaked back into her life on his latest visit home, but now it was clear that hadn't been a first. He'd plunged her into confusion all those years ago, just when she was settling down with a new man. Justin, probably. The old spark between them had reignited when Ashton had tried to get her back. But it sounded as though Amber had regretted it afterwards. Maybe she'd been angry with Ashton for reappearing and throwing her out of kilter. Either way, she'd rejected him, and gone on to marry Justin instead. Leo's arrival three years later would have further cemented their relationship. How had that left Ashton feeling? Angry with the pair of them? Out for revenge?

And if he had evidence that Amber had cheated on Justin with him, it might be Amber who'd wanted to keep him quiet.

CHAPTER THIRTY-ONE

'It's looking good,' Robin Yardley said. 'It just needs some regular effort to keep on top of it.'

'That's where I might run into trouble.' What with her obituaries, caring for Gus, and her shifts at Monty's, she didn't have a lot of free time.

He laughed. 'Just remember that even the most relaxed gardens only look that way because someone's loving and caring for them, week in, week out. Once that stops, things get out of control and a garden that once made you feel serene leaves you stressed and guilty.'

'Wise words.' Eve hated feeling out of control.

Robin was standing in the garden of Elizabeth's Cottage, surveying the state of the plan he'd originally designed for Viv and Simon's parents. The garden was currently decorated with a range of plants providing some spring colour. Hardy pale-pink geraniums and some subtly coloured hellebores nestled together in the flowerbed to her left, while an indigo clematis sprawled over the worn red-brick garden wall, and a white magnolia tree's delicate petals shifted in the mild breeze. The apple tree was coming on too, its buds still mostly closed, but promising glorious pink blossom within days. Gus rushed around the various beds, periodically stopping to look up eagerly at Robin, as though seeking his approval for what the dachshund clearly regarded as his own personal territory.

'I could come in once a month, to keep on top of the most essential jobs.'

She could see he couldn't switch off making professional assessments in relation to his current work, any more than he could if a new police case erupted in the village. Eve was the same. She was always analysing the people she met, trying to see beyond the surface.

But right now, horticulture wasn't the main issue. The garden was a useful decoy. Robin had news on Ashton and Howard's deaths from his contact on the local police force. Either they had to keep finding clandestine locations in which to 'bump into each other', or they needed another solution that could be explained away. If word got out that Robin knew more about the case than he should, it would land him and his contact in hot water with DI Palmer. Still, her garden was an ongoing issue; it had been on her mind.

'That would be good, thanks.' She'd sneaked a look at the prices on his website since they'd spoken last, and it was doable. She loved the relaxed layout of the garden, but she didn't want a jungle. Some degree of order calmed her.

Robin glanced over his shoulder, past the apple tree, where there was a direct line of sight towards Haunted Lane. Daphne and Sylvia were the only other residents, but the locals used the byway to access the estuary path to the beach. He caught Eve's eye and walked into the lee of the house where they wouldn't be seen.

Eve would definitely have to find out more about his past; she respected his privacy, but if the information was out there, somewhere in the public domain, it was fair to make use of it.

'It's warm enough to sit at the table.' It was a decorative ironwork affair that sat on the grass – another item she'd bought with the house. 'Can I fix you a coffee?'

'That'd be great. Thanks.'

A few minutes later she rejoined him, with the drinks on a tray, and her notebook and pen as well.

'Thanks again for watching my back on the beach.' She still felt awful about the way things had turned out.

He leaned towards her. 'You couldn't have predicted what would happen.'

She stared into her coffee for a moment and took a deep breath. 'So, you've got updates?' she said.

'A couple that might lead somewhere. But before we start, I've got one that doesn't.'

What was coming?

'You asked me to find out who told the police you and Ashton might have been in a relationship. My contact was more reluctant to give me that information than anything else. I had to promise him you weren't the sort to go and yell at her. Apparently it was a woman called Gwen Harris, who lives on Heath Lane. She heard it from April Davies.'

Moira's sister.

'Who heard it from…'

'Moira.' She'd probably seen Ashton chatting to her in the store and at the prize draw and become overexcited.

'You got it. Shop gossip that found its way to the police. Gwen's the sort who bustles around the village, talking about civic duty. I don't think she's our killer somehow. I do her garden though – I can deadhead her roses as soon as they come into bloom if you like.'

'Much appreciated. Please bring photos.'

He grinned. 'So, where are we at with everything else?'

'I still don't believe Howard Green's death was suicide, and everywhere I look the whole set-up gets more complicated. I'd like to get it all in order.' Everything had come at Eve at high speed so far, and all the disparate facts felt like a horrible jumble of paint spatters over a white wall. If she got everything lined up neatly, a proper picture might emerge.

Robin nodded and relaxed back in his chair. 'Let's go back to the beginning and recap. We can slot the new information in as it becomes relevant, so we don't take anything in isolation. You start.'

She took a deep breath. 'Okay. So, we have Ashton, who comes back to his childhood home, having been asked to work on Billy Tozer's house with his business partner, Marina Shaw. Ashton stays with his mother, and Marina stays at the Cross Keys. They get on with the job for Tozer, but Ashton involves himself in village affairs too. He catches up with old friends, and suggests a raffle to help raise funds for the church roof. Only now it seems the top prize – the appearance on TV for one winner – was actually invented by him.'

Robin's eyes widened.

'I can't find any evidence the TV company had agreed to it. Then he picks three winners, live on stage, but it looks as though the draw was rigged – at least partly. Moira Squires bought a whole bunch of tickets, but there were no other tickets at all in Amber Ingram's name, nor in Tina Adcock's – I checked the recycling bin at the church hall.'

'Wow – nice work. I agree, it would be quite a coincidence if they'd each bought just one ticket. It has to be more likely they bought none. Yet they didn't say anything when their names were called?' He hadn't been at the draw.

'No. Amber looked upset. He called her name out second, after Moira Squires. And then Tina came third. She looked – I don't know – sort of wary, but hardened too. But when I talked to them neither of them admitted they hadn't bought tickets. Amber said she was surprised she'd won because she only purchased "a few". And Tina went on about wanting to support St Peter's.'

'Okay. So they both had some kind of reason for not wanting to tell. What are your thoughts on that?'

Eve explained what Heaven Jones had said about Ashton and Amber's Romeo-and-Juliet love affair – and how they might have had one last fling after Amber and Justin got together. 'My guess is that Ashton still threw her feelings into confusion, and she didn't want him in their house. She might have been scared he'd try to get back with her, or that he intended to make trouble to get his revenge. But admitting she was upset over winning, or querying the result, would have made people ask questions – including Justin – so she couldn't risk it.

'Maybe she felt it was safer to sound Ashton out in private. It would explain how he was able to arrange to visit her when Justin was out. He had information that could damage her relationship with her husband, and they've got a young son too, of course. No wonder she didn't want him around when they met.'

'So Ashton was a threat to Amber. And of course Justin would have all the more reason to hate Ashton too, if he found out he'd slept with his girlfriend while they were an item. It's not impossible that it came out as a result of the row they had over the planted underpants. Assuming they were planted.'

Eve nodded. 'And I believe they were. Amber looked so perplexed when Justin stormed into the teashop after he'd found them. There was no guilt in her expression at all: just anxiety and confusion.'

'On the subject of Amber, I've got information from my police contact.'

He still wasn't referring to Greg Boles by name. Eve wondered if he'd prefer her not to have too many details, for whatever reason. She raised a questioning eyebrow.

'It was Amber Ingram who informed on Ashton Foley when he was a teenager.'

'What?' Eve sat back in her chair, trying to take it in.

'Following her tip-off, which the police agreed to treat as anonymous, they caught him with drugs on his person – too much for individual use – and started a full investigation.'

It took Eve a moment to lean forward again and sip her coffee. She opened her notebook and added this new fact to a timeline she'd been drafting. 'If Ashton was aware of that, he'd probably be all the keener to get his revenge on her and see her suffer.' Amber's feelings towards Ashton must have been so confused. It sounded as though there'd been a powerful chemistry between them, but that she hadn't liked his tactics or – perhaps – his involvement with drugs. But she'd known about it. How mixed up in the business had she been? It was another fact she'd be desperate to keep from Justin. Eve thought again of Leo, and the tight hug Amber had given him in her perfectly ordered, clinical kitchen. She'd have known her secure life was under threat.

'So, now we come to the question of why Ashton wanted access to the houses of each of the prize-winners, I presume?' Robin's blue-grey eyes were on hers.

She nodded, as she made notes to remind her of her thoughts, then looked up. 'I think maybe Moira was the decoy – the one genuine winner of the three. It's fair to say she was ecstatic when her ticket was drawn and although it sounds like she needled Ashton when he was little for running riot in her store, I haven't found any more concrete reason for him to target her. On top of that, she seemed relaxed when I asked about his visit. If he tried to take revenge for past wrongs it looks like she didn't notice.' That would be just like her. She benefitted from a thick skin.

'Okay.'

'But for Amber Ingram, maybe it was related to his old relationship with her, his consequent hatred of Justin and his anger at Amber for reporting him to the police, if he'd somehow found out. That reasoning fits well with the prank Ashton played. It's the type of stunt a guy might pull after having his ego dented.'

'True.' Robin leaned back in his chair. 'So Amber had a motive. Just because he was playing jokes, doesn't mean Ashton had finished with her. And she'd already shown some ruthlessness by reporting him secretly to the police. Maybe she wanted to make sure he was out of the picture for good this time.'

It sounded possible. She remembered the pride she'd seen in Amber's eyes as she'd talked about Justin's design skills. She was pleased to be with him, even if Eve found that slightly hard to understand. And if they split up she'd have to share custody of Leo and her whole life would change.

'Did her brother ever let the police look at his gun?'

Robin nodded. 'It was a dead end. Hadn't been fired recently. But she could still have got hold of a weapon through the antiques business.'

'But would Justin alibi Amber if she was guilty?' Eve said at last. He was pretty angry with her right now; anyone could see that.

'Well, he said he slept soundly the night Ashton died. It's possible she could have sneaked out without him knowing. And given they had a blazing row after Justin found the underpants, maybe they weren't even sleeping in the same room at that point. It's the kind of thing a man like him might decide not to mention, out of pride.'

'True.'

'What about Justin being Ashton's cannabis supplier?' Robin said.

'It's still possible that the guy Tina Adcock saw leaving a package on Ashton's school desk was Justin. Though it's pretty thin. And Justin clearly didn't see any danger when he asked Amber to buy a whole bunch of raffle tickets.'

Eve was scribbling in her notebook again. She felt as though she could see bits of clarity in the jigsaw puzzle she was assembling, but trying to visualise the whole picture still left her with a fog.

'I'm starting to wonder if Justin should come off the list,' she said. 'The way he's acted simply doesn't fit with him having a guilty conscience. It was always Amber who looked scared.'

Robin nodded. 'I think you might be right. But Justin could still have killed Ashton out of jealousy.'

'He could. Especially if he had an inkling Amber still felt something for him, even if it was a love–hate dynamic.'

'But—' They both spoke at once.

'You go,' said Eve.

'Whoever killed Ashton went to search Apple Tree Cottage afterwards, and that doesn't fit with the jealousy motive. It's more as though the killer knew Ashton had information that could damage them.'

She nodded. She'd been about to say the same thing. Justin Ingram was out of it, as far as she was concerned. On reflection, she couldn't see him sacrificing his hairdo in pursuit of an enemy, anyway.

'But that would still fit with Amber.' A tiny thrill went through her. 'She knew enough about Ashton's drug dealing to report him. She might have just been an onlooker, but if she was directly involved, maybe he had proof of that. Or evidence that she'd slept with him after she'd started going out with Justin – a letter from her that referred to it, perhaps. Ashton could have told her he had something with him that he could show to Justin whenever he wanted.' What might she have done to get her hands on it?

Robin's eyes were serious as he sipped his coffee. 'I agree. She had a lot to lose, potentially. What about the Adcocks? Any idea why Ashton wanted to access their house?'

'I initially guessed at something small, like wanting revenge on Carl for dissing him, back when he was at school, or a simple chance to crow, even. But I now know that Tina had a thing for her male students.' Eve felt a burst of satisfaction at having the information. She really must keep a hold of herself. Everyone knew pride came before a fall.

Robin whistled, which buoyed her up still further. 'O-kay. Any firm evidence?'

'Anecdotal, but I'd imagine there are plenty of witnesses.'

'Good.'

'So my thinking evolved. Maybe Tina tried it on with Ashton when he was young, and he only realised how wrong that was once he'd left school. Perhaps he wanted to see if he could find hard evidence against her. Or maybe try to drive a wedge between her and Carl, just to get his own back. After all, he had a grudge against him too. If my guesses are right, he had a hold over Tina, so he could push her into seeing him alone.'

Her notes were all over the place: a jumble of arrows, asterisks and insertions. She'd have to lick them into shape.

'So Tina had a potential motive for his murder, if she wanted to save her name and her career.'

'And again, she and Carl alibi each other, right?'

Robin nodded and she remembered the look she'd seen the couple exchange when she'd interviewed them at Ashton's old school. That spark of fear. Had Tina asked Carl to lie for her?

'I guess the police haven't bothered checking alibis for Howard Green's death, given Palmer's convinced it was suicide?'

Robin's eyes met hers. 'They haven't. *Yet.*'

She raised her eyebrows.

'I've been saving the biggest and best news until last. One of the CSIs has put a spanner in the works of Palmer's case for the death being suicide.'

Eve held her breath.

'They noticed that although everything in Howard Green's house was tidy on the surface, the contents of several of his drawers were jumbled – notably, those where things might be hidden – clothes drawers and the like. The ones in his kitchen containing things like string and cooking utensils were all meticulously tidy, as were all other areas of his house. Thankfully, it made the CSI look further. She noticed that most of the books on his shelf were alphabetised but a few were out of order. After that the team found tiny fragments of glass on the floor, as though someone had tidied up in a hurry after breaking something.'

'Someone had been in there after Howard died? They disturbed stuff? Searched the place?'

Robin took a breath. 'Palmer's not convinced yet but the latest is that my contact on the force called in Howard Green's old cleaner. He let her go a while back – couldn't afford her any more – but she confirmed he'd never have left his drawers like that. And that there's a vase missing that used to sit next to the books. It was made from pale green glass, which matches the fragments that were found. It looks as though someone went in and tried to cover their tracks but time was short, and they slipped up.' His eyes met hers. 'Getting Palmer to face facts will be the difficult part.'

'But for our purposes, it looks like the killer searched Apple Tree Cottage after Ashton's death, didn't find what they were looking for, and concluded Howard might have taken it?'

Robin nodded. 'I'd say so.'

CHAPTER THIRTY-TWO

'So it looks as though the murderer knew Howard had been in Apple Tree Cottage after them,' Eve said to Gus. 'Maybe they saw him, or perhaps he gave himself away when he confronted them. I guess they murdered him chiefly because he could give them away, but also because they wanted to search his home.'

Gus looked up at her thoughtfully from under his long eyebrows.

She'd finished lunch and stood up, ready to take him for a walk along the estuary path. He dashed towards his leash.

'So what could Ashton have hidden, that the killer wanted so badly? Evidence that proved Tina had affairs with high school students? It would cost her her job, her reputation and probably her marriage. And depending on the age of the students, she might go to court too. Or something that proved Amber had two-timed her husband or been involved in dealing as a teenager maybe?'

Her mind drifted for a moment to the other contacts she'd interviewed, then came to a sudden halt as she recalled the former Outside In client. The man she'd spoken to had sung Ashton's praises years back, but was no longer willing to do so.

What had changed?

Could it be that Ashton had had damaging information about him too? Something the client hadn't known about when he'd given that first interview, just after his makeover was complete, but which Ashton faced him with a little later? He must have found out a lot about his clients by occupying their houses for weeks on end. He'd have had plenty of chances to stumble across damaging secrets.

An icy chill ran over her. Had he been a serial blackmailer, with all those former contacts in his pocket?

She ought to contact more of Outside In's clients as soon as she had time. If her guess was right, the man she'd spoken to might not be the only one affected.

Her mind was racing. Ashton had been very wealthy when he died, but it must have taken time for the firm to turn a profit. And even if he'd wanted for nothing lately, he'd had old scores to settle. Maybe it was a sport to him. And as a teenager he'd made money wherever he could: from trying to steal Daphne's ring to selling drugs. Why wouldn't he use blackmail as part of his portfolio? She remembered Sylvia's words. It was always about the money, and always about himself.

She thought of Amber again. She couldn't believe Ashton had wanted her back; he hadn't visited her in years. This whole project – revenge on his neighbours – had only come together when the opportunity presented itself: in the form of the invitation to come and work for Billy Tozer. He'd had his ego dented, and he'd fancied paying the Ingrams and the Adcocks back. It looked as though his actions had been driven by spite, not love.

'I'm not sure this makes things any clearer,' she said. 'But I've seen families torn apart by both those things in the past. Spiteful wills leading to pain and discord, and blind love for one person leading to the neglect of other family members.'

She frowned as she attached Gus's leash to his collar. Eve didn't want it to be Amber. The thought of Leo finding out his mother was a double murderer was appalling. But she'd had the means to get hold of a gun. And what about the woman's temperament? Forcing Howard Green to take his own life was a horrific crime, but if Amber was guilty, letting him live would have meant sacrificing everything. And of course she'd worked with him, and ultimately

Eve had found out what an unpleasant and immoral man he was. He might have treated her badly for years.

She sighed. But the killer was a smooth and ruthless operator. They'd almost managed to pass Howard's death off as suicide. She might be barking up the wrong tree. She clung onto the thought that Ashton's old cannabis supplier – whoever they were – might yet be the guilty party. He could have been blackmailing them too. And surely someone with criminal connections was more likely than your average villager?

Gus was tugging her along Haunted Lane, towards Elizabeth's Walk and the marshes. Seabirds swooped overhead and there were enticing rustles in the gorse bushes ahead of them. Some devoted dog time was called for, but on her return she needed to sit down at her computer and research the heck out of this. It was the only way she knew.

With Gus settled at her feet, underneath the dining room table, and the spring sunlight lancing in through the casement window, Eve got to work, focusing on the drugs angle. If Ashton's supplier was still operating, they must be leaving clues all the time – and although Palmer and his crew had never caught them, that didn't mean there'd been no drug-related incidents since Ashton was prosecuted. She started researching every relevant news item meticulously, including the most minor mentions of youths caught in possession of illegal substances.

It was slow work, focusing on years of news stories. After an hour she'd gotten the beginnings of a list. There were reports of a series of minor drug offences locally.

She broke off to make a drink, and gave Viv a quick ring to update her on the latest developments and offload her woes. She knew there were two people covering the counter that day, thanks to her weekly plan for Monty's. All the same, she felt guilty calling during work hours.

Viv snorted when Eve asked if she had time to talk. '*I've got time. I've been waiting for your latest.*'

It took her a while to complete her update.

'*What will you do now?*'

Eve sighed. 'I just need to keep going with the drug-related research I've been doing. I really hope it leads me in a new direction, for Leo's sake.'

'*Let me know how you get on. And don't take any risks!*'

She went back to googling local news stories and added two more arrests for possession to her notes: in Darringham and Roxford. She'd gotten a decent list now. It was time to see if there was any pattern. She printed out a map of the local area, then entered the place names into Google Maps one by one and marked each of the locations on her printout.

There was definitely a cluster locally. Was any of this related to Ashton's particular supplier though? It seemed possible. Probable, even. She imagined dealers had their own patch, and weren't keen to share.

She stared at the annotated paper map again, and then at the same area on-screen, zooming in, looking at the other hamlets and villages in the vicinity.

It was then that she saw it: sitting there in the middle of the cluster. A youth club in a place called Little Mill Marsh. Within a second she'd opened a second browser tab and googled the village, together with the words 'youth club'.

There it was. The Drop In.

It was the same club that Ashton had attended after he'd been in trouble for shoplifting, before he'd gotten involved in drugs. Could there be a connection? Was it possible that the very idea Russell

Rathbone had suggested, to try to keep Ashton out of trouble, meant he ended up at a young offenders' institute?

According to the website, the club was currently running extra sessions, thanks to the school vacation. She needed to get a closer look at the place. Without evidence there was no way she could influence the police's thinking. And she couldn't cut corners. If she didn't pursue this, Howard's name might never be cleared, and Betty would have to live with the whispers and the uncertainty forever.

Gus looked up hopefully as Eve shifted in her seat.

'Maybe not this time, buddy.' She bent down to fuss him. 'You are the most excellent companion, but you do attract attention by being one hundred per cent adorable. I'll take you out as soon as I get back. Deal?'

His look had turned disdainful.

'I know, I know. I won't be long!'

Little Mill Marsh was a large village that looked down-at-heel. It was full of narrow terraced houses with peeling paintwork and untidy front gardens, the grass too long, the flowerbeds unkempt. Of a row of five stores, two were boarded up, one was a betting shop, one a grubby-looking Chinese takeaway and the fifth a small store with a 'Bargain Booze' poster in the window and dog mess on the pavement outside.

Eve found the youth club and parked up the road. Her car was a much-loved but rather battered old thing, which was just as well. She already felt she stuck out.

According to the website, the vacation session was due to start in ten minutes. She got out of the car and walked up and down a side road. She didn't want to sit tight; it might attract attention. She found a block she could walk round, which would take her a short way from the club's entrance; she could view the comings and goings from a distance. Then maybe she'd speak with someone who was attending – pretend she had a child that might be interested – get an idea of who went along and what they got out of it.

She was just on the home straight towards the club building when a woman emerged from the doorway. A familiar sardonic smile crossed her lips as she greeted a youth in a leather jacket, jeans and heavy boots.

It was Tina Adcock.

CHAPTER THIRTY-THREE

Eve took a sharp breath and turned back the way she'd come, grateful she'd decided to leave Gus at home. She missed him, but he marked her out, and he was none too keen on sudden changes in direction.

Eve's heart rate had ramped up. It had been a very narrow escape. Had Tina seen her? She risked a quick glance over her shoulder. The woman had disappeared inside the building. There was no way of knowing. She'd looked focused on the lad who'd just arrived. Perhaps Eve had been lucky. She walked back round the block towards her car, starting to think as she calmed down.

So, Tina Adcock ran the Drop In – the youth club Ashton used to attend. It wasn't so unexpected. It related to her job as a teacher, and maybe she was committed to helping young people. Or, after what Viv's son Sam had said, maybe she relished the opportunity to mix with a large group that probably included a number of strapping male youths. She shouldn't be allowed to continue if the rumours about her were true. But was there even more to this?

Eve went and sat in her Mini, staring at the youth club's exterior. Ashton hadn't been selling drugs when he'd first attended. And it was Tina who'd mentioned him getting drug-related deliveries at school. Had she made it up, to direct attention away from herself and the club she ran? Ashton hadn't pointed the finger at his teacher. Maybe because he knew the consequences if he spoke out. She'd been there at his trial, keeping her eye on how he behaved. And if it had been his word against hers, who would have believed him? But maybe he'd wanted to wait anyway: to take revenge in his own time, using his own methods, rather than handing the police the victory. She could imagine that: it fitted with his personality and with his life experience. She doubted he'd been a fan of the authorities. The interviews Ashton had given came back to her. When he'd referred to his troubled youth, he'd frequently mentioned Tina Adcock, and said he'd always remember 'her contribution'. At the time she'd thought he was grateful to her for speaking up in court, but if he'd known she was lying to save her skin, that put a whole new spin on things. Had he been issuing her with a veiled threat, each time he mentioned her name? Warning her he hadn't forgotten? Telling her it wasn't over?

She was holding up her phone and fiddling with it, hoping anyone who noticed her would think she was pausing to text, or check directions. Her head was running through all the implications when she noticed movement. She glanced up at the youth club. A guy who looked a little too old to attend had arrived on a pink bike that was too small for him.

Eve shrank down in her seat as the newcomer glanced briefly up the street. He was off his bike in an instant. He slung it, unlocked, outside the club and opened the zipper of his bomber jacket as he moved. As he walked in through the entrance, his hand was on a packet he'd had tucked under his outer layer.

Eve's skin prickled. She bet he wasn't there for table football, or whatever it was Tina used to keep her charges busy. And if that was his own bike, she was the Queen of Sheba.

He was out again in a couple of minutes.

Eve sat there, wondering what to do. The youth yanked the pink bike up from where it lay and set off, wobbling down the road, his knees reaching his elbows as he pedalled.

It was an opportunity she oughtn't to miss. She started her engine and manoeuvred slowly after him, waiting until he was well ahead of her before she made the same turn that he had.

After they'd travelled down a residential street, they headed out into the countryside, on a road bordered by a muddy field, home to pigs belonging to a local farm. Eve kept well back, driving way slower than she normally would. Luckily it wasn't uncommon to come across cars moving at a snail's pace along the country lanes. The guy ahead didn't seem to be aware of her or remotely bothered about his mission, whatever it was.

A short while later they entered Blyworth – the nearest local town. The guy on the pink bike led her to a street full of modern red-brick stores including a hair salon, a place selling wool and a café.

He swung across the road outside one of the units. Eve pulled up behind a VW van at a safe distance and got out.

Her legs felt a little shaky as she walked up the street on the same side as her quarry. She'd only been intending to look at the youth club out of curiosity. Now she was following a guy who might be involved in drug dealing, even if he was only a minion.

She walked slowly, uncertain of which shop the guy had entered. Keeping calm was important; she mustn't give herself away. But he had no prior knowledge of her. She was just another Suffolk resident, going about her business. The thought wasn't enough to calm her rapid breathing.

At last she drew level with a shop called Ticks the Boxes. The stolen bike guy was inside. He took out a key, walked straight up to one of the mailboxes that lined the walls – the sort you could hire – and then opened his jacket. As she walked slowly past, he put a smaller packet than the one she'd seen him carrying previously inside the mailbox and locked it again. The old guy behind the counter gave him a sideways glance, but then busied himself with some paperwork, hunching down over his desk.

Within a moment her quarry was outside the premises, back on his bike and away. She watched as he pedalled off up the road, a car honking as he wobbled into the driver's path.

She could watch and wait, but whoever had hired that box might not come for hours. And if Tina had seen her and sent a warning, whoever arrived might be primed and ready…

CHAPTER THIRTY-FOUR

Eve was with Gus, waiting amongst reeds that rustled in the gentle spring breeze, listening to the cry of a marsh harrier. Normally the sound would have brought her peace and joy, but today it reminded her of what the birds of prey that circled the heaths and wetlands were all about. They kept a sharp eye out for their victims, ready to swoop and pick them off with pinpoint accuracy.

'Eve.'

Robin. She'd asked for an extra meet-up. She wanted to explain everything, then see if he could get his contact on the local police force to take her seriously. Fear crawled around the pit of her stomach. What if Tina *had* seen her outside the youth club?

'Thanks for coming.' She still felt shaky as she explained what she'd witnessed that day. 'It's all circumstantial, but it looks as though the youth club is central to Tina's business. It's a convenient drop-off point, with few other adults around to see what goes on, and it explains why things got worse for Ashton when he started there, not better.'

Robin nodded. 'I'll get onto my contact straight away; he'll be interested. He might be able to arrange for someone to monitor the next few youth club sessions. Hopefully they'll pick up on the same activity you did. If so, they'll be in a position to start asking questions. Tina Adcock might talk if she thinks she can get off lightly by cooperating. It depends whether she's guilty of Ashton and Howard's murders too.'

Eve nodded. If she was, presumably she'd shut up like a clam. And what would happen then? Would there be enough evidence to convict her? Would Palmer even bother to search for it, if he was still wedded to the idea of Howard as the killer? The thought of leaving this unresolved was horrific.

Robin gave her a sympathetic look. 'The police can interview the mailbox company too; that might be enough to get Tina a conviction for the drug offences. And I'm sure they'll look at other people who attend the youth club, to see if there's a pattern. Beyond that, it's clear she had a motive to kill Ashton now. So long as Palmer accepts Howard was innocent, they ought to investigate fully.'

It felt as though everything hung by a thread.

Robin shook his head. 'Nice work, Eve. Nice, but dangerous.'

She swallowed. 'I had no idea what I was walking into when I decided to take a look at the club. I only hope Tina didn't spot me.'

Robin's eyes sharpened. 'You think she might have?'

'I can't be sure. I don't think so.'

'I'm going to follow you back now. I'll keep you posted, but please take care. There are two people dead already, and Tina's got a lot at stake.' He frowned. 'Get in touch immediately if you get any sense you might have been seen. But don't overlook Amber. She still has a strong motive for the murders too.'

'You don't have to tell me twice.' Either of them could be guilty. She didn't know where the threat was coming from.

Eve lived on the edge of her nerves for the rest of that day. Sleep was hard to come by at night, despite the soothing atmosphere of Elizabeth's old bedroom, with its encircling beams, and the quiet of the countryside outside.

After staring at the ceiling for hours on end, she'd gone downstairs briefly to browse the internet. Was there any way she could find out subtly if Amber had attended the Drop In youth club, just like Ashton had? She couldn't possibly ask her directly; if there was any chance she'd also been involved with the drugs racket, she'd guess Eve was onto her, and that she understood the role the club played too. The internet produced nothing. Moira Squires might know, but there was always the risk she'd tell half the village that Eve had been asking. At last, she gave up, and, back in bed, finally managed to drop off.

The following day she made herself focus on writing Ashton's obituary, with Gus sitting loyally at her feet, sensing her nervousness. It seemed to be contagious. Each time there was the slightest noise from outside the house he twitched when she did.

The obituary was tricky too. The thought of Betty Foley reading her article pained her. Eve was duty-bound to provide an honest account; what was the point of her profession otherwise? She couldn't gloss over Ashton's difficult past. She found herself feeling nervous on Betty's behalf about what might come out next. His possible role as a blackmailer? The fact that Ashton had searched his mother's private papers? If proof emerged, she'd have to at least reflect that side of his personality, or be guilty of airbrushing her account.

'I need to go through everything again,' she said to Gus, 'and make sure I've identified every positive comment about Ashton, for balance, and for Betty's sake.' Russell Rathbone's testimony was a godsend. He'd seen promise in Ashton, and refused to give up on him. There was Ashton's success in business too.

'And Heaven Jones liked him.' She scanned her notes from the interview with the model. 'His and Marina's work made a real difference to her.' Heaven's information on his visit home to see Amber Ingram made her pause. His childhood sweetheart, Heaven had called her. And she'd said he'd gone to see if he could patch things up with her. A last-ditch attempt before she settled down with Justin. She frowned. Heaven had actually portrayed Ashton's efforts as touching, and rather romantic. She'd thought of him as a diehard playboy, but that had changed her view.

'Heaven's report is one of the most complimentary, on a personal level,' Eve said to Gus. And she'd liked Heaven. She'd come across as sensible and perceptive. Eve got up and paced around the dining room. Of course, Amber had knocked Ashton back, but Heaven said it had been her boyfriend he'd hated, not her. It certainly didn't sound as though he'd known back then that it had been Amber who'd reported him to the police.

The thought stopped her in her tracks. If he hadn't known then, after he'd moved to London, wasn't it likely he'd never found out? Gus followed her with his eyes as she began walking round the dining room table again, and over to the casement window. She stared out for a moment. After all, Ashton's arrest happened years back, in Suffolk. How would he have found out, when the police local to Saxford were likely the only people who knew, and he'd been down in the capital, and out of touch?

She considered Ashton's actions in that light. If he hadn't been after revenge on Amber because she'd reported him, had he decided to blackmail her simply to pay her back for marrying another man? Yet by all accounts it had been Justin he'd hated – not her. She'd been his sweetheart. So why try to make her suffer in such a cruel way, using a method that didn't affect Justin at all? Planting the underpants made sense, if he'd wanted to get at her husband, but not blackmailing Amber. Even if his anger with her had gradually built up, it still seemed odd when Marina, Russell Rathbone and his mother all said it was Justin he couldn't abide.

She frowned. 'Does that really make sense, Gus?'

The more she thought about it, the more she knew she couldn't let it rest. There was something she wasn't getting and leaving a stone unturned left her feeling twitchy. A minute later she was dialling the Ingrams' number. And five minutes after that, she was in her Mini Clubman, driving towards the antiques' store Howard Green had owned. Amber was over there apparently, going through his books and stock at the request of his executors. Justin had said they were wasting no time, given the amount of debt he'd been in. He'd sounded disgusted.

Eve needed to face Amber with what she knew and see if she'd talk, but she hoped the executors were also on site. Although she'd found an anomaly, she still didn't know if she could trust her.

CHAPTER THIRTY-FIVE

'What do you want?' Amber's face was red. She'd been bending down and packing something into a box.

Eve had walked in through the open front door of the antiques and curiosities shop. It was clear people had been coming and going. She'd been glad to see a man in a suit in the car park, talking on a mobile phone, and she could see the shop's CCTV camera too, although there was no way of knowing if it was working. The presence of other people was reassuring, but it meant she'd have to try to get Amber to talk quickly, while there was no one else inside.

She walked across a room painted dark blue and crammed with objects that gave the place an eerie feel. There were old globes, side tables, walking sticks and jewellery, but oddities too, like an ancient diving helmet and some kind of nautical instrument she didn't recognise. The sense of the past and of lives that had gone before was heavy around them.

'Amber, I came because I need your help.' Maybe appealing to her was the only way. If she was innocent there was just a chance she might pass on the information Eve needed.

'I don't see how I can help anyone,' the woman said. She sounded hopeless and Eve wondered if Justin had forgiven her about the underpants yet.

'You can help Betty Foley.'

Amber looked up, her anxious questioning eyes on Eve's. 'What do you mean?'

'She's lost her son, and the police still believe her boyfriend killed him. She's in a state of utter misery and clearing Howard's name would provide her with a small crumb of comfort.'

Amber had picked up a paperweight and was turning it over in her hands. Eve couldn't help thinking how heavy it looked. But there was a man just outside. She stood her ground and spoke again.

'I don't understand what part you've played in all of this.'

'Part?' She put the paperweight down. Her lips were parted, her jaw slack.

'I know Ashton rigged the draw. You never bought a ticket.'

'It wasn't just me!' Amber folded her arms. 'Tina Adcock didn't buy one either.'

She knew about that? Eve tried to mesh the facts together. 'He targeted you both for the same reason?' Maybe Amber knew he'd intended to blackmail Tina too. Maybe she and Tina had compared notes.

'No. But it was related.'

'I need to know, Amber. I've got no hope of helping Betty otherwise, and unless you murdered Ashton and Howard—'

'Murdered?' She was genuinely shocked, Eve could see that.

'Unless you murdered them, then I should be able to keep what you tell me secret. It will just help me to know where to look.'

The woman was still staring at her.

'You had a motive. Hushing up your past affair with Ashton, and what he might have told Justin about your teenage years: the attempt to steal Daphne Lovatt's ring, for instance.'

She didn't want to mention Amber's knowledge of Ashton's drug dealing. It would make it clear the police had been leaking information.

'So why did Ashton want to visit you in private, when Justin wasn't around?'

Eve heard movement behind her and turned to see the man who'd been talking on his mobile had entered the store. He nodded at Eve and then spoke to Amber.

'I'm just going to nip back to the office to deal with a couple of things and then I'll return.'

'Okay.'

Eve waited with bated breath until he left, closing the door behind him.

'Amber?'

She'd been standing ramrod straight, but at last her shoulders slumped. 'All right. But if Justin finds out any of this, our marriage will be over, and who knows what will happen with Leo. This is on you.' Her eyes bored into Eve's. 'On your conscience. You have to protect me. And don't expect me to go to the police with any of this. I don't have concrete evidence, only my own story, and I doubt anyone would believe me.'

'Okay – I understand. And I'll do my very best to make sure what you tell me stays private.' She only hoped she could stick to that. The thought of Leo, drawing in the kitchen at the Ingrams' house, filled her mind.

'Ashton wanted my help.' She was twisting her hands. 'Back when he was a teenager, selling drugs, he tried to get me involved. At the time he thought it was fun and grown-up, even though I tried to warn him it came at a price.

'It wasn't long before he got found out.' She looked down at the floor. 'But before he did, I saw him taking a package from Tina Adcock. I knew she supplied him, down at the youth club.' She took a deep breath. 'He never forgave her for the way she treated him. He hated the time he spent in the young offenders' institute – that really wiped the scales from his eyes. It was tough. At first, he wanted revenge, but on his own terms; he wasn't going to pal up with the police after the way they treated him – and he doubted they'd take his word over hers, anyway. But as time went on, and he got some distance, he started to see the bigger picture. He told me he was sure Tina was still at it: recruiting kids, making up to them, paying them loads of attention and drawing them in. Grooming them and then making them do her dirty work. He'd been looking for his chance to bring her to justice.'

'Bring her to justice?'

Amber looked confused at her tone. 'Yes. He came to me because he wanted to persuade me to write up what I knew and sign it as a statement he could present to the police, together with any proof he could find inside Tina's house.'

Everything Eve had thought shifted inside her head.

'He didn't understand.' There were tears in Amber's eyes. 'It wasn't fair of him to expect me to do that. Justin's got no idea of the sort of circles I used to move in back then. We were already going through a rocky patch when Ashton showed up. If I'd done what he wanted, and my past had come out, it would have been over between us. I'd only see Leo part-time, and everything I have would be lost. I like my life. I just need to get back onto an even keel.'

But she felt guilty; Eve could see that.

'Do you think he found the proof he needed at Tina's house?'

Amber nodded. 'I'm sure that's why he's dead. He should have gone straight to the police with his own story; got them to watch her. I don't know! But he wouldn't. His relationship with the local cops was bad. He was determined to find evidence and hand it to them on a plate. He didn't trust them to do the job themselves, and he was sure they'd never believe him without a whole pack of evidence.'

Eve thought of Palmer for a moment, and couldn't help feeling Ashton had been right.

Amber looked up at Eve. 'If I'd helped him, he might not be dead. But I might also have lost my husband and my home, and had Leo growing up hating me for breaking up the family.' She ran her right hand up her left arm. 'I feel so guilty.' Her voice dropped to a whisper. 'I was the one who tipped the police off about Ashton. I was scared and it seemed like a way to make it all stop. I never knew how serious it would be for him.' Her hands were over her face now, and her next words came out muffled. 'And I was jealous of Tina Adcock. Ashton swore there was never anything between them, but Tina flirted with him like hell. The stupid, ironic thing is, that after he was caught, I offered to stand with him and tell the police about her. I thought if we both came out with the same story, they might believe us, but at *that* point he refused. He said she'd find a way to hurt me unless we had something concrete. This time his plan was only to go to the police when he had evidence she was active now. My statement would have helped prove it had been her back then too.'

The full awfulness of the timing washed over Eve.

'I thought Ashton would guess it was me who told on him, but he never did. He was always kind, right up until that last visit. He only lost his temper with me when I wouldn't do the right thing, and help stop Tina.'

'He left the underpants in your bedroom?'

She nodded. 'I didn't know what he'd done until Justin found them, but Ashton was furious and frustrated when he left the house. He told me to think of all the young lads Tina was grooming, and that it could be Leo, one day. And then he shouted at me for being too wedded to my middle-class values and security. I guess he decided I needed a shake-up.' She shook her head. 'He was always impetuous. Acting on the spur of the moment.'

Eve sat in her car, where she'd parked by the Saxford St Peter village green, and stared into space. How the heck had she been so wrong about Ashton? Thoughts of what she might have written in her obituary, and what she'd like to write now, flew through her head. Unless Tina Adcock was arrested and proof found, she wouldn't be able to write any of it, but inside her chest, a weight had lifted. Ashton hadn't been the amoral chancer she'd imagined. She reviewed what she knew of him, seeing everything in a new light. Yes, he'd been thoughtless and enjoyed point scoring. He'd needled Howard Green before he knew what he'd done. He'd also been a lothario. Perhaps he'd never stopped loving Amber, and no one else made him want to settle down. It was no excuse for leading women a dance, but at last she was starting to see him in the round.

He'd gone through his mother's files, which didn't look great, but he'd wanted Howard to be straight with Betty and put things right. And maybe that had been for Betty's sake after all, and not his own. Perhaps he'd only looked at her papers because he didn't trust Howard in the first place. She'd never know for sure, but she *had* thought how close Ashton and Betty looked that day on the beach. She should have given that more weight.

She sighed. He'd been like most people: a complex mix, but also unique. By turns thoughtless and loving, foolish but brave, and underneath it all, principled in a way she'd never have guessed.

She got out of her car. What did it mean for the case? Ashton's killer – Tina, she assumed, unless she had an accomplice – had searched Apple Tree Cottage, and Howard's house too, looking for the evidence Ashton had likely pinched at the Adcocks' house. Howard had known nothing about it, so there'd never been any chance of Tina finding it there. She could have returned to Apple Tree Cottage to search again, once she drew a blank at his place, but how would she have managed to get in? She'd returned Ashton's keys to his pocket, so she hadn't used those. And she couldn't know about the spare set – or she would have used them from the start. And there'd been no break-in reported at Mrs Foley's house. Eve guessed there was every chance Ashton's cache of evidence was still hidden somewhere, leaving Tina desperate.

And now the clock was ticking. Even if the police managed to charge her with drug dealing, that didn't mean they'd get her for the murders. And Amber Ingram had flat-out refused to talk to the authorities when Eve pressed her.

Nerves cramped her stomach. Was Tina onto her? It was likely. She'd been far too careless outside the youth club. If there was any chance the evidence against Tina was still out there, it was essential for Eve to find it before she did. It ought to be enough to convince the police she'd killed Ashton for it, and once she'd been charged, Eve would feel safe. But the task was daunting. She could risk searching Apple Tree Cottage a second time herself – that had to be the mostly likely hiding place – but what were her chances of success? Ashton's murderer had stayed all night, and still gone away empty-handed.

She glanced across the green towards St Peter's as she locked her car. The celebration launch of work on the church roof was the following day. The idea of standing around eating canapés and drinking sherry was so incongruous she almost laughed. It was a reaction against the fear that curled itself round her, tightening its grip. Tina Adcock was bound to be there. The desire to skip the event was strong, but if the teacher was still uncertain how much Eve knew, turning up and acting normally was her best move. If she hid away, people would comment on her absence and any suspicions Tina had would grow.

Eve was dreading meeting her eyes, and seeing a knowing look in return. One that told her she'd been spotted outside the youth club.

CHAPTER THIRTY-SIX

Jim Thackeray stood at a lectern at the front of St Peter's, and gave thanks for the generosity of the villagers which had enabled the church authorities to start work on the roof repairs. He also paid tribute to Ashton for his fundraising efforts. Eve wondered if Ashton would have suggested the draw if he hadn't wanted to search Tina Adcock's house. But in a way it didn't matter. He'd had good motives for what he'd done, and the church had benefitted too. She was pretty sure Jim would see it that way if he knew all the facts.

Eve tried to concentrate on the vicar's words, but she was distracted. Tina Adcock was in the row in front. They were bound to have to interact sooner or later. She knew she needed to act just as she normally would, but inside her heart was impersonating a drum being played by an irate toddler. Could you feel that tense inwardly and hide it from your face? Carl was next to Tina. She could see he was smiling. How much did he know about his wife's dealings? What might he do if he knew she was under threat?

Amber and Justin Ingram were just across the aisle. Justin was smiling and nodding, as though he was personally responsible for the money donated to the church. Of course, he had asked Amber to buy a lot of raffle tickets. She was standing next to him, her arm tight around Leo's shoulders.

Russell Rathbone was also across the aisle, a row in front of the Ingrams, smiling and nodding at the anecdote the vicar was telling. Up at the front, Marina Shaw sat next to Billy Tozer. Her restaurateur boyfriend had gone back to London, but she and

Tozer made a striking couple. He'd caused quite a stir when he'd entered, all six foot four of him, complete with arm muscles the size of ham hocks. Marina was in a well-cut trouser suit Eve guessed had a designer label. Tozer wore a black and white bandana, and though his outfit of choice was jeans and a hoodie, he didn't look any less striking than she did. For a second, Eve's eyes lit on Moira from the store, who was staring at Tozer, her mouth slightly open, until Paul nudged her and she snapped it shut.

'And last,' Jim Thackeray was saying, 'but most certainly not least, my thanks to the young people of the Drop In youth club, some of whom are here today serving the refreshments.'

In the pew in front of Eve, a man standing next to Tina Adcock turned to pat her shoulder, nod and give her a smile.

'That's the headmaster of the school where the Adcocks teach,' Viv said, under her breath.

Tina was gracefully accepting his acknowledgement of her efforts with the local youth, all the while knowing she was turning them into young criminals. Or some of them, anyway. Her gall and her perfect cover, as a respected local community figure, took Eve's breath away. And she'd made up to the young lads in her care too. Why hadn't the ones in school reported her inappropriate behaviour? But maybe they'd see that as grassing to the headteacher, and besides, they were young. They might not realise how wrong her actions were. She remembered the text Sam had sent Viv about her behaviour. *One or two people seem keen…*

Eve glanced around at the handful of teenagers who were gathered at the sides of the church, behind trestle tables that had been put out for the occasion, covered with white cloths and plates of canapés.

A moment later, her mind drifted back to the evidence Ashton must have found, proving Tina's guilt, but as the vicar wrapped up his address, she shifted her focus to the present.

'Good old Billy Tozer,' Viv said, as their row stood and began to shuffle towards the nave. 'I like the look of the drinks and nibbles he's laid on. Let's go and get stuck in!'

They were greeted by Sylvia and Daphne from Hope Cottage, who reached the snacks and drinks station at the same time they did, and were handed glasses of sherry by a young guy with pimples.

'Cheers,' Sylvia said, holding up her glass.

'Your good health.' Daphne's eyes were sad and anxious. 'I still don't feel comfortable celebrating the church roof after Ashton and Howard's deaths.' She was wearing a ring that glittered in the overhead lights. Eve wondered if it was the one that Ashton had tried to steal.

'Oh, you!' Sylvia said. 'If it makes you feel any better, it's continuing the work Ashton started, with that fundraising draw of his. And Billy Tozer seems to have very good taste in sherry. Something of a surprise really.'

Eve saw what she meant. Tozer didn't look like a sherry man, but now she'd met him, she knew he was thoughtful enough to have taken advice on what to buy.

'The drink's doing me good,' Sylvia went on. 'I need something to warm me up. The church might be heated, but the walk over in this stiff wind chilled me to the bone.'

Daphne sighed. 'It's blown our trellis over and broken the stems on the clematis. Just as it was about to flower too.'

Eve had noticed the destruction it had caused on her way over to St Peter's. An oak tree branch had come down on the village green.

Viv was asking Daphne about the new style of pots she was working on, and whether she'd be able to supply some for Monty's craft market. Meanwhile, Russell Rathbone had introduced himself to Sylvia.

Her mind wandered to the case again, but a moment later Moira Squires' voice broke into her thoughts. She was speaking (breathlessly and at high speed) with a woman whose name she didn't know.

'Well, yes, they do look like a very handsome couple, but in fact, I happen to know that Marina and Billy' – first names, Eve noted – 'aren't in a relationship.'

Her friend's eyes opened wider. 'I didn't realise you knew them personally.'

Moira's smile widened. 'Well, given my position in the village…' *Nice and economical with the truth.* 'I've met Marina's current partner, of course. The restaurateur, Zach Campbell, who runs the MacAskill bistro chain.'

The friend smiled hesitantly. She hadn't heard of it either, Eve guessed.

'Poor young things,' Moira went on, 'they have very little time together – what with them each being so successful. But they snatch their happiness when they can. And I do hear' – the friend leaned forward – 'that their relationship is a most positive turn of events for Marina. Dear Zach told me all about it in the store.' That could happen to the unwary. 'Marina's former boyfriend was an alcoholic, and *very* troubled, I gather.' She licked her lips. Other people's misery and drama was her meat and drink. 'The stresses and strains of his work—'

Fleetingly, Eve remembered the mention of some rock-star ex.

'Hello, Eve.' Russell Rathbone had arrived at her side. 'It's nice to see you here. And good for the village to come together over something positive.'

She nodded.

'I imagine everyone felt a bit calmer, though upset, when it became clear Howard killed Ashton.' He shook his head. 'Poor Betty.'

How long would it take before Palmer finally admitted Howard's death hadn't been suicide? Was he still denying the truth, or could the police be working secretly to find the real killer, knowing the guilty party would have been lulled into a false sense of security? She only wished she could believe it.

At that moment a woman in a beige suit bustled up to them and beamed at Russell Rathbone. 'Lovely to see you here! So good of you to always patronise these events.'

'I like to keep up with life in the local villages.'

The woman turned to Eve. 'Russell's been our family lawyer for years, but he's a local hero too!'

'Really,' Rathbone laughed, 'you're making me blush.'

'And look at all the lovely young people here from the Drop In.' She turned to Eve again. 'Russell sends a lot of teenagers their way – lost souls who've got into bad ways. And out they come the other side, with a real sense of responsibility.'

She clearly didn't know about the ones that didn't. Tina might well groom the youths Rathbone passed on specifically, knowing they'd already gotten into trouble and were likely susceptible to her offers of cash and excitement.

She glanced up and saw Rathbone was looking at her. Something in his eyes – a wariness – made her pause a moment. She felt the hairs rise on her arms. As a local lawyer, he'd probably know if a significant number of the kids he passed Tina's way ended up in trouble again. You'd think he'd have wondered about it, and whether the club wasn't quite the safe and improving environment he'd thought it was. Unless...

As the silence between them lengthened, a whole fresh wave of alarm flowed over her, like ice-cold water. She tried to shut down the thoughts coursing through her brain and the effect it might have on her expression, but something changed in the lawyer's eyes. Something that made her mouth go dry and her chest tighten.

'Excuse me,' she said, 'I must just go and catch my friend Viv. I think she said she needed to leave early.'

'Of course.' Rathbone was smiling, as smooth as ever, but his eyes were cold and knowing.

She'd thought him charming before, but charming people could be ruthless.

Instead of walking over to Viv, she made for the bathroom, just off the vestry. She caught Jim Thackeray's eye as she went, over the shoulder of one of the villagers, and saw the concern in his expression.

And then, just before she exited the room, she caught sight of Russell Rathbone and Tina Adcock in conversation. Their heads drawn together.

She locked herself in the bathroom and hoped no one else was in a hurry to go. She needed to text Robin, who was absent from the launch, just as he was from most village events.

Just spoken with Russell Rathbone. Odd look in his eye when someone mentioned the number of young offenders he sends to the Drop In youth club. Gut feeling is he's involved.

Her palms were clammy, her thoughts racing. She typed a follow-up message.

Rathbone said he thought Justin had been Ashton's dealer, but there's been no sign of that. Evidence points to Ashton hating Justin because he's a jerk and he won Amber's affection, not because of anything drug related. Could have been directing attention away from himself and Tina.

No wonder the way Ashton had behaved seemed so at odds with the story Rathbone had told. Why hadn't she thought of that before? It was the lawyer's evidence that had jarred.

Would have had ample opportunity to groom young kids at risk and send them to the youth club in return for a cut of Tina's profits.

She thought of the photograph on the lawyer's bookcase, showing his kids in posh school uniform. He probably had plenty of outgoings. The extra money from his sideline would come in handy. And of course, he'd told her himself that he'd gotten into trouble, back when he was at boarding school. Robin's reply came in seconds.

I'll notify my contact but without firm evidence he'll need Palmer's approval to dig. And a successful philanthropic lawyer will be the DI's least favourite type of suspect. Stay safe.

Eve had the urge to leave the event immediately. The idea of getting back to Elizabeth's Cottage and locking herself inside while everyone else was still at the church was appealing. She spoke briefly to Viv, saying she needed to get on with writing her article, and then slipped out and cut across the village green as quickly as she could, glancing over her shoulder at the church as she went. What could Robin's contact do, really? Would he take her accusation seriously? Even Robin probably thought she'd gotten ahead of herself. She had no proof. But Russell Rathbone had stuck to Ashton like glue. He'd gone above and beyond the call of duty – apparently because he was such a fine and upstanding man. Eve realised that she no longer believed in the guise he presented. Keeping in touch had allowed him to ask Ashton over and over again who had supplied him. Even though Ashton had clearly trusted the lawyer, Eve guessed he'd never once mentioned Tina, and had kept his plans for bringing her to justice to himself. If he'd let on to Rathbone, Eve was sure the lawyer would have sounded the alarm, and Ashton would have been killed even sooner.

The fact that Rathbone had instantly recognised the suspicion in her eyes made Eve think Tina *had* spotted her outside the Drop In. And that she'd told Rathbone that. He'd already been wary.

What were their plans for her? She might have to wait for days or weeks before the police got anything on them. They'd be extra careful now, their guard up. They'd have plenty of time to hunt her down.

She needed to get hold of proof herself. If she was right, she'd be in constant danger until she managed it.

The wind was still high as she walked, the oak branches thrashing angrily. The advertising board outside Monty's had been knocked flat too. Normally she'd have gone over to set it right, but she was too anxious to get home. It would only go over again anyway. It was the fold-out sort, and needed a sandbag over one of its struts to keep it anchored. That would look ugly though. If there was a way of hiding a weight—

Suddenly, Eve felt a tiny connection link up in her brain. A bag of gravel, stuffed up inside Betty Foley's cheap cast-iron owl in the garden. Eve had guessed it was to stop it blowing over in the wind.

She felt her cheeks go hot, and the hairs on the back of her neck rise. The owl was hollow – stuffed with weighty stones at its base, but what about above? And it wasn't the only ornament in the garden at Apple Tree Cottage. There'd been a hare too, and a duck. They were each quite large – big enough to hide a small cache of evidence, such as the one she assumed Ashton had collected.

In her experience, the people of Saxford St Peter were very fond of hiding things in their gardens…

She hesitated halfway across the green, her eyes back on the church. No one else had come out yet. Now was the perfect time to sneak into the garden of Apple Tree Cottage to examine those ornaments. Apart from Robin, everyone associated with the case was still inside St Peter's. She ought to be safe. If Rathbone or Tina went looking for her, they'd go to Elizabeth's Cottage, get no reply and know she'd gone out, but they'd have no reason to suppose she'd go to Ashton's childhood home. And if she was successful, she could cut this nightmare short. The thought of the relief she'd feel left her longing to get on with the job. And it would only take a minute to check.

She continued in the direction of her home, just in case anyone was watching, but after she'd crossed Love Lane she turned right towards Blind Eye Wood and the heath. She didn't dare go the hidden way, via the estuary. It was too lonely, and it would take too long. She wanted to finish the job before the fundraiser broke up.

She walked through the deserted village. Even the Cross Keys had a closed sign up. Jo, Matt and Toby were all at the church. ('It's important to give our support,' Jo had said. 'None of us actually wants that great roof falling down on our heads.')

The wind ripped through the trees, making their branches twist unnaturally. As she neared the woods the noise was impressive.

She reviewed everything she knew as she went, her mind poring over the details, tugging and pulling at them. Could Russell Rathbone be the killer, rather than Tina Adcock?

But it seemed unlikely. She didn't think Howard had met the lawyer, so the chances of guessing he'd been responsible were low. And if Howard had left the village to find Rathbone, why had Rathbone brought him back to Saxford to kill him? Besides, Eve couldn't imagine the lawyer getting his hands dirty. She guessed he kept himself at arm's length, happy to pass children Tina's way, take his cut and wash his hands of anything that happened afterwards. But now it was different. Now he could see how he was under threat too. She shivered and checked behind her again.

The lane was still deserted but she felt scared. She took out her phone and found she had coverage. In a second she was speed-dialling Robin's number.

It went to voicemail. Maybe he was busy. Or had no signal. The mobile network in Saxford was hopelessly patchy.

Her heart was thudding as she left a message. 'I'm trying the hollow garden ornaments at Apple Tree Cottage in case that's where Ashton hid the evidence his killer was after. Everyone else is still at the church roof fundraiser, and it'll be a quick job. I'll let you know how I get on.'

She felt better for having let him know where she was.

Looking over her shoulder, she cut across the front garden of Betty Foley's house and went to the side gate, leading round the back. She closed it again after her. The garden was lined with conifers, and what with the woods surrounding the house, it was no less noisy there than it had been in the lane.

Holding her breath, Eve crouched down next to the owl, flipped it onto its side, which revealed the spare key she'd used previously, and pulled out the bag of gravel. The ornament was entirely hollow apart from the owl's head, but she found nothing else inside.

She paused a moment, her thoughts back with Howard Green. What about that musky smell he'd mentioned, when he'd visited Apple Tree Cottage just after Ashton had died? Aftershave, he'd thought, though he'd sounded uncertain. Did that point away from Tina, towards a man after all? But she couldn't be sure. The smell seemed to have puzzled him.

Mechanically, she stuffed the bag back inside the owl's body and left it as she'd found it.

She'd just turned the hare onto its side – almost without seeing it – when a fresh thought struck her. Drugs. Could that have been what Howard had smelled? The pungent smell of cannabis?

But surely Tina wouldn't smoke when she was on such a serious mission? In fact, Eve couldn't imagine her taking drugs at all. She was far too controlled. She probably thought the people she sold to were suckers.

As Eve grappled with the question, memories filtered through her mind. Her thoughts drifted back to the evening she'd heard Marina and Ashton arguing, along the estuary path. She'd wondered if they'd been smoking something illegal. Ashton might not have sold cannabis these days, but that didn't mean he avoided the stuff altogether.

Her breath caught. A creeping feeling ran over her skin, moving up her neck and over her scalp, pricking her forearms.

Howard had walked right past Marina as he'd made his way back from the beach, that day she'd gotten him to confide in her. Might the woman have smelled of drugs then? She and Billy Tozer might have had a smoke together. Could it have reminded Howard of the odour he'd detected the morning after Ashton's murder?

She pulled herself up short. There was no reason to suppose it had actually been Marina who'd entered the cottage, or that she'd been the one to kill Ashton. Anyone could smell of cannabis.

Except... except that he'd walked right past her, and in the course of that evening he'd seemingly realised the truth, decided not to go to the police, and been murdered – possibly after a failed blackmail attempt, if her guess was right. Maybe chancing across Marina had sealed his fate.

But if that was true, why had she killed Ashton? What had he found and hidden that was such a danger to her?

Her heart beat faster. Whatever it was, searching Apple Tree Cottage had produced nothing, and scouring Howard's house would have been useless too.

And then suddenly Eve realised the danger she was in. Whoever was involved, they were almost certainly still looking. Trying to find a time when no one from the village would see them attempting to re-enter Ashton's old home.

Like while everyone else was at the fundraiser at the church...

Eve tensed and stood up, but a scraping sound stopped her in her tracks. Someone was raising the latch on the side gate.

There was no time. A small shrub stood between Eve and the house and she shrank behind it, crouching, her legs quivering.

Through the leaves of her hopelessly inadequate hiding place, she watched the gate to Betty Foley's back garden open.

Marina Shaw walked in, her eyes on the lane behind her.

CHAPTER THIRTY-SEVEN

Eve felt the air leave her lungs. Her mind was spinning. Where would Marina have gotten a gun?

And if she was armed now... Her leather jacket swung loose at her sides. It was impossible to know what she might have in her pockets from that angle. Eve held her breath as Marina edged across the garden, her eyes on the house. She could see her quite clearly through the shrub's foliage. If Marina once looked round...

A second later the woman took a key and placed it in the lock of the cottage's back door.

Eve switched her phone to silent. Robin might call her back, and she was desperate to avoid any possible sound that could give her away. Marina had the door open now. If she just went a little further – and didn't look properly as she closed it behind her...

But at that moment, a crow swooped over the garden, cawing suddenly, and Marina turned towards the noise.

Her focus was on the shrub in a microsecond. 'What are you doing here?'

Her eyes were like ice as Eve stood up, her legs still shaking.

'I've been in touch with Betty Foley over Ashton's obituary. She asked me to come by every so often to keep an eye on the place. I was just finding the spare key she keeps hidden in the garden. What about you?'

Marina held up the back-door key. 'Ashton mentioned there was a spare. Maybe this is the one you're looking for. I wanted to go inside and search for myself, to see if I could find any clues as to who killed him.' She looked down for a moment and sighed. 'He was my business partner for years. I've heard there are questions now over Howard Green having shot him. I mind that the police aren't making any headway.' But her attempts to look sad weren't working. And Betty Foley had never mentioned a second spare key – Marina seemed to have had it on her. She could have let herself into Apple Tree Cottage with Ashton's set after she'd killed him. She'd have wanted to replace them, to hide the fact that she'd accessed the house. But she could have taken a spare back-door key from a kitchen drawer or somewhere, and kept it, so she could carry on her search later. She'd have assumed she wouldn't be disturbed on the afternoon of the fundraiser.

'What kind of thing did you think you might find?' Eve said. Did she have the gun on her? Would Eve stay safe so long as she went along with her excuses?

But Marina moved towards her as she spoke, out beyond the shrub. Her gaze was on the cast-iron hare at her feet now. It was still on its side. She frowned and walked nearer still, until she was level with it. Her eyes opened wider as she saw the animal was hollow – its innards stuffed with a gravel bag.

'I'm not sure I believe you came here to keep an eye on the house, Eve. It's an odd time to choose.'

Their eyes met. Eve tried to hide her fear, but it wasn't easy. Marina's hand was edging towards the inner pocket of her leather jacket. And now she could see it looked bulky.

Marina smiled. 'As for me, I think you know what I hoped to find. How good of you to save me the effort.' She drew out her handgun. 'Pull out the gravel. Let's see if your guess was right.'

CHAPTER THIRTY-EIGHT

Eve crouched down and did as Marina asked, tugging on the gravel bag with shaking hands. What would happen to her? Other than Robin, no one knew where she was, and he had no idea Marina was a threat. Maybe he was out of contact because he was busy following up on Russell Rathbone and Tina Adcock. She'd sent him off in the wrong direction.

There was nothing under the hare.

'That's a shame. The owl?'

Eve shook her head. 'I've already looked.' Her voice trembled.

'So, we try the duck, right?' Marina gestured with the gun. 'And I hope we get lucky this time. Otherwise I need to carry on with my search. Either way, I won't be requiring your company, so once we're done with the ornaments you and I will take a little walk together. So good to know the villagers are still over at St Peter's.' She smiled again.

Why hadn't Eve realised how dangerous she was? She'd felt uneasy around her right from the off – and she was plenty ruthless enough to manage both deaths. Eve just hadn't worked out her motive.

'Get on with it.'

Eve crouched down slowly next to the duck and tipped it over, making the removal of the gravel bag take as long as possible. What was Marina's part in all this? She likely smoked cannabis, and she had come from Saxford St Peter originally…

'So you're involved in the local drugs operation too? You're connected to Tina Adcock?'

Marina shook her head slowly. 'You have no idea, do you? I don't need to get my hands dirty, selling drugs. I enjoy the odd joint, but dealing? Why would I? I've got my own successful business, in case you hadn't noticed – in a very different area of horticulture.'

Eve felt sick. Up inside the duck's upper body, beyond where the gravel had been, was a plastic bag. She drew it out.

A mobile, and a flash drive.

Marina held out her free hand. 'Thank you. And I'll have *your* phone too.'

Eve had no choice but to pass it over. Robin still hadn't returned her call. What the heck could she do to get out of this? She must keep Marina talking. It was possible Robin would come to the cottage if she didn't answer her phone. 'So the mobile and the flash drive contain evidence that the police could use to arrest Tina Adcock?' *Or do I have that completely wrong too?*

She still couldn't work out why Marina was so desperate to find the cache – or why she'd killed Ashton.

The business manager's jaw was taut, her eyes hard. 'The mobile, yes, from what Ashton said. He didn't mention the flash drive,' the edge to her voice had become more pronounced, 'but I rather think I know what I'll find on that.' When she pointed the gun at Eve there was a look of pure hatred in her eyes. Eve felt she was still thinking of Ashton. 'Time for that walk I mentioned. Put the gravel back inside the duck first, then tip it upright.'

As she worked, Eve tried to focus. She had to delay their progress, so Robin had a chance to catch them up. But he could be anywhere. And who knew how long it would be before he got her message. She felt panic bite and made a desperate effort to concentrate. She needed to hold it together.

So, Marina wasn't involved in Tina's cannabis operation, but she'd still wanted Ashton's cache of evidence. And she'd presumably killed him for it, and Howard too, to keep him quiet. What was on that flash drive?

Eve had set the duck the right way up again, and Marina gestured towards the garden gate. 'Let's get going.'

There was nothing she could do. Hope faded as she walked through to the front garden. She tried to apply her training as a journalist to battle through the fear.

Motivations. She needed to look at those. She couldn't guess why Marina had killed Ashton, but she had a good idea what drove her more broadly. Her career and her standing. She'd built Outside In, relying on Ashton for his contacts and the easy way he had with people, but providing everything else herself: the horticultural know-how and management skills. She'd even arranged bank loans while Ashton was away, working as a roadie. She'd probably spent endless hours slaving while he'd partied with the likes of Ronnie Randall.

'Ashton had information that threatened the future of Outside In?' Or possibly Marina's future. She'd see them as one and the same. It was the only solution that made sense.

Marina was behind her, forcing her across Heath Lane. 'He'd used his position in the company to steal incriminating evidence from Tina Adcock. And he proposed to take it to the police. It would have been front-page news in every tabloid paper in the land. *Outside In uses access to private house to bust drugs operation in rural Suffolk.* No client would have trusted us again.' Eve felt Marina's gun at her back and her legs shook as they entered the woods. She stepped over a tree root and ducked to avoid a branch. 'Surely it wouldn't put clients off if they had nothing to hide.'

'You really are an innocent. Almost everyone has something to hide. Especially the rich and famous – and they're the sort we deal with.'

Suddenly, Eve's mind flew back to the phone call she'd made to a previous Outside In client – the one who'd sung the company's praises in the *Sunday Times*, but refused to talk to Eve. She'd almost forgotten about him. Originally, she'd guessed that maybe Ashton had blackmailed him, but then, when his real motives became clear, after her talk with Amber Ingram, she'd failed to revisit that evidence. If Ashton hadn't been a blackmailer…

'Wait. You once blackmailed Outside In's customers? You were worried they might speak up if they saw the article about Tina Adcock?'

'My, you're thorough. I see you didn't stick to the list of clients I told you to interview then. I might have known.' She gave an impatient sigh. 'Yes, I did. Only right at the beginning, when we were struggling. I realised the business would go under if I didn't act. I did it anonymously. The clients would have guessed it was us – but they wouldn't have known if it was me or Ashton.'

For just an instant, Eve recalled her session with Marina at Monty's. 'When I interviewed you, I said I got to go inside my interviewees' houses too – and how much you can find out about a person that way.'

'That's right. For one moment I thought you were onto the truth – but you had no idea back then, did you?'

'You called the police anonymously to say I was going beyond my brief.'

'I was overcautious. I needn't have worried.'

Eve saw movement ahead: some small creature scurrying further into the woods. She felt so tense she might snap altogether. Could the animals and birds around them feel the fear coming off her?

'Those people deserved all they got,' Marina said. 'If they'd behaved themselves, I wouldn't have been able to touch them. And they could well afford what I asked. But can you imagine their reaction if they'd seen Ashton lauded in the press for prying into the affairs of yet another client, this time working on the right side of the law? They'd have been outraged.'

'You were worried it would make them take their own cases to the police?'

'Yes. There was a chance.'

But how big a one? Eve battled to think as they walked on. The way through the woods seemed endless. Had Marina really thought it necessary to kill Ashton to stop him taking his evidence to the police? True, if her fears were proved correct, her career would be over, but to resort to murder over something so uncertain…

And it still didn't explain what was on the flash drive.

Then suddenly she had it. 'You hadn't told Ashton you'd black-mailed the clients. It came out when you tried to persuade him not to take his evidence on Tina Adcock to the police. You thought he'd understand.' But Ashton had changed. After the spell in the young offenders' institute, it sounded as though he'd rethought his approach to life and hadn't looked back. He'd come home to Saxford with the aim of bringing Tina Adcock to justice, only for Marina to try to stop him, and to reveal his own business was built on criminal money.

'You sound almost pleased with yourself, which is pretty ironic given your situation. You finally worked it out! Yes, I told him the day I killed him, as a last resort. I'd already tried to persuade him to see sense on the Friday evening. I hoped he'd realise that just letting our clients see how vulnerable their secrets were would cause us trouble.'

'That was why you and Ashton argued so badly, when I overheard you, down by the estuary.' Eve remembered Marina's words: *You're creating problems when there's no need!*

'Yes. I was careless, but it seemed like we had the path to our-selves.' Her voice shook now – with anger. 'He just didn't get it. All he had to do was drop the idea of acting the hero, getting Tina

Adcock prosecuted. Someone else would have caught her eventually, and it wasn't his problem any more. But he wouldn't be told.' She spoke as though his death had been his own fault. 'He kept going on about the kids she was still grooming, and their futures. I knew at that point I'd have to confess to the blackmail, so he could see the real danger. I slept on it, but on Saturday I went ahead.'

There was no sign of Robin. Now, they were walking along a path that led through the woods towards the estuary.

What was her plan? She was too smart to risk another gunshot victim or faked suicide. Eve tried to maintain the conversation, but her throat was so dry she could hardly speak. She stumbled on the root of a tree.

'Keep going! And concentrate! I'm not leaving your body around in Saxford for people to find.'

Eve needed to ask more. If Marina was talking, she might not notice her trying to slow their pace. She guessed provoking her might be the best way to make her lose concentration.

'So Ashton didn't see things your way, when you finally admitted you'd blackmailed your own clients. I'm not surprised!'

'Don't push me!' Eve felt Marina's gun thrust up against her back again, and a lump rose in her throat. 'Ashton was blind! I was convinced he'd see my point of view. I managed the entire business side of Outside In and I knew we weren't making money fast enough to cover our debts when we started up. Ashton never bothered himself with those details. I ploughed all the money I extracted back into the business, so he benefitted too. He wouldn't have been the success he was without my actions.'

Eve clenched her fists, trying to keep control.

'But even when I confessed, he was *still* determined to carry on, and I could see the shock in his eyes. He was horrified by what I'd done. He said he'd have to think about his future and what he should do. I removed old financial records from our server as fast as I could, but I had a feeling he might have local copies that would show odd patterns of payments. Evidence against me. And I think he would have talked. I knew then that he'd have to die.'

They were headed towards the estuary. If they cut across now they'd get to the deserted end of Ferry Lane and Arthur's Jetty.

Where Matt Falconer's boat was moored. Had Marina got the keys? It would be easy enough to pilfer a set. She was staying at the pub, and Matt had taken her and her boyfriend out in the dinghy. Eve didn't know where they were kept, but Marina would. But how could she have known she'd need them in advance?

'You got Ashton and Howard into the woods to kill them.'

'I told Ashton I'd had a rethink. He was in the right. I wanted to make peace with him and work out the best way forward. He was quite trusting, despite all he'd been through. He had no idea what I was planning. As for Howard Green,' she gave a harsh laugh, 'he asked me to meet him there, then tried to get money out of me, bold as brass. He had weirdly old-fashioned ideas about women. I think he imagined I'd killed Ashton in some kind of fit of passion and that I'd never act in cold blood. How wrong he was.'

The thought of Marina forcing Howard up into the tree filled Eve's mind. She felt as though her legs might go out from under her. Her whole body quivered.

'The moment Howard contacted me I guessed he'd finally worked out I was guilty. I'd seen him go into Apple Tree Cottage just after I'd left. We so nearly bumped into each other. His death might have come much sooner, and been harder to explain. As it was, I was ready for him in the woods, with my gun, the rope in place and the fallen log prepared for him to climb. I hoped the investigation into Ashton's murder would end with him.'

The wind was still high, the noise levels in the woods more than enough to drown out their conversation. But there was no one to hear, anyway.

Eve could see the water up ahead now, through the trees. Tears pricked her eyes. Her children. Gus. Viv. She'd been so afraid of Tina Adcock and Russell Rathbone that she'd been blind to the danger under her nose.

'We're going for a ride, Eve. Up the coast and out to sea. I've used a boat like this before, but you'll be doing the driving, under my instruction. I'd rather keep my gun trained on you.' She smiled.

If Eve got aboard, she'd be lost. And that seemed unavoidable now. Marina's concentration was unwavering.

'Stand ahead of me, near the water. Don't move!'

Close to the point where the jetty met the land, Marina crouched down and reached out with her free hand, finding a small tin box that nestled just under one of the planks that was laid over dry land.

She chucked the tin to Eve, never once letting the direction of her gun waver. 'Open it.'

Eve did as she was told, almost dropping the container as her hands shook. The boat key was inside.

'The trip Zach and I made with Matt Falconer wasn't wasted after all,' Marina said. 'Fancy that! Climb aboard, Eve. I'm sure you'll be great at driving this thing. You're so practical.'

She made it sound like an insult. Eve's legs were like jelly as she clambered onto the boat. It was already pitching, even in the shelter of the river's mouth. She slipped and landed in the hull of the vessel. It was a simple affair, no larger than a rowboat with a tiller steer outboard motor at the back.

Marina would have to perform the same operation she had. Eve swallowed. She'd manage it better. Having gotten her story out, she'd regained control. She seemed confident and detached – in no doubt of her success. Adrenaline wouldn't make her clumsy. But it was still the only chance Eve had left. The only moment when Marina would have to divide her focus.

Eve looked around her desperately. There were life jackets under the seat. And a box too. She peered at the lettering on its side.

Distress flares. The parachute sort.

Eve's pulse quickened. Might they help her? But she had no idea how to set one off, and if she failed, she'd be done for. If she succeeded, what would Marina do? Kill her then and there? But that wouldn't help. A shot was just as likely to bring people running as the bright light of the flare. She'd more likely carry on with her escape plan. Unless anger overwhelmed her...

Marina's right foot was inside the hull of the boat, her left still on the shore.

Her heart thudding like a piledriver, Eve dove for a flare, fumbling desperately at the screw cap on its base.

Marina leaped towards her, losing her balance as she dragged her other foot on board the pitching boat.

Eve leaned precariously over the side of the vessel, flung the cap behind her and yanked the pull cord underneath. The flare shot high into the air.

As she turned back round, Marina had recovered. She thrust the gun at her, at point-blank range, in hands that shook with fury. It felt as though she was on a knife edge.

At last the woman reined in her rage. The blindingly brilliant light was out again already.

'No one will see your stupid signal. They'll all still be at the church. Put the key in the engine, then pull the starter at the top.'

Eve's attempt had failed. There was nothing more she could do. She made her movements as slow as she could. It was almost impossible to get the key in anyway, her hands shook so badly. She glanced over her shoulder and saw the impatient anger in Marina's eyes.

'Now pull the starter!'

She did it gingerly. Nothing happened.

'Pull it harder!'

Eve had turned at her voice. She was about to twist back again, all hope gone, when she glimpsed movement – to the left of Marina, back in the woods. Eve focused on Ferry Lane instead, to avoid alerting the woman, but there was movement there too. Each direction she looked in, someone looked back. The faces seemed to comprise half the attendees at the fundraiser.

Amongst them was Jim Thackeray. He'd ditched his cassock somewhere along the line and rolled up the sleeves of the black top he'd worn underneath. Viv was pink in the face and leaning over to get her breath. Even Simon was there, with a disgruntled Polly by his side. It looked as though the stiletto heel had come off her left shoe.

And behind them all was Robin Yardley.

'Drop your weapon!' It was the vicar who spoke, with a glance over his shoulder. 'The police are on their way.'

Marina looked around the semicircle of villagers. Eve watched her face. Would the woman try to use her as a bargaining chip?

'You've got nowhere to go,' Jim Thackeray said. 'There'll be police launches coming at you from all sides if you try to set off. And I should add that the Lord is also watching you very closely indeed.' He glanced up. 'It looks like thunder to me.'

A moment later, they could all hear the thrum of a boat's engine, brought in on the breeze.

It was fury Eve saw in Marina's eyes, not defeat. At last, she threw the gun out of the boat.

CHAPTER THIRTY-NINE

'Most of us were just making our way home from the roof launch thing when we saw the flare,' Viv said. 'Robin Yardley was out on the village green, rushing somewhere. I didn't spot him at first.' She frowned. 'I'd already started to wonder if you were okay. I tried to call you after you'd left and you weren't answering your phone, and of course we all knew you'd been digging about in some pretty dangerous stuff. Then Jim said he'd seen you looking anxious at the service.'

Eve remembered catching his eye.

'Before we knew it we were all surging through the village towards the flare. Jim stepped up to the plate good and proper, didn't he?' Her eyes were fond.

'He did indeed. I shall be sending a bottle of his favourite tipple and some heartfelt thanks his way.' But nothing could convey the gratitude she felt for his intervention.

They were sitting in Monty's being served Viv's Chocolate Intense selection by Angie and her student friend, Tammy, who was doing nicely now. The selection was Viv's standard cure for people who'd recently escaped mortal danger. After they'd finished, she was going to take Eve to the kitchen for some therapeutic baking tuition. They'd got the Easter Extravaganza the following Monday at Monty's: a cupcake hunt, and a bonnet competition. Viv said it was always utter chaos. But she'd promised to share her secret recipe for her favourite Easter cake: lemon, oranges, spices and a raspberry frosting. The following weekend was Easter itself, late this year, at the end of the school vacation.

'The police were a lot less effective than Jim.' Viv waved the cake she was holding. 'What was the hold-up with them?'

The seaborne reinforcements had come a short while after the vicar had called out his warning, but Boles and Palmer had taken longer.

'Something to do with Palmer, I expect. He probably hoped he'd seen the last of me.' What a disappointment it must have been, to find she'd come through alive…

'It was great that you got Marina talking. Do you know what progress the police have made?' Viv's blue eyes were alert.

'Not really.' Eve had given a full interview to DI Palmer and DS Boles, but it was Jim Thackeray and Robin she really needed to speak with now. Thanks would come first, but she had questions they might be able to answer too.

'Well,' Viv said, 'make sure I'm the first to know if you manage to prise the details out of anyone.'

She rolled her eyes.

'Oh, and Eve?'

'Yes?'

'What about a girls' night in tonight? And maybe a few sleepovers at Elizabeth's Cottage, until you know what's happening with Terrible Tina and Rat-face Rathbone?'

Eve had told her all about the ins and outs of Tina's drugs business, and that it wasn't over yet. She still felt under threat, and would do until they were both locked up. Viv's offer made her emotional. She opened her mouth to speak, worried that her voice might crack, but Viv cut across her.

'I know what you're thinking. I can see it in your face. Nothing would delight you more than having me as a house guest, but you can't imagine how to express your thanks. Well, don't worry, you don't have to. I want to come. If any dodgy characters turn up on your doorstep, I can frighten them away with my violent hair colour. And I can sleep in Simon's old room! His was bigger than mine and I was always insanely jealous.' She grinned. 'At last I can fulfil my dream.'

Eve laughed, feeling some of the tension seep out of her.

'Speaking of Simon, he was talking about dropping in on you too, so you might need added protection. I pointed out that he'd relinquished his visiting rights when he took up with Polly.'

Eve smiled. 'Put like that, you've talked me into it.' Her mind turned to Betty Foley. At least they had all the answers now. Thank goodness she'd be able to tell her how brave Ashton had been, and how much he'd cared for the young people Tina targeted. But the woman had lost so much. She voiced the thought.

'I know,' Viv said. 'It's appalling. We'll all rally round when she comes back. We can take her meals, and get her in here, and over to the Cross Keys. I was talking to Toby about it as a matter of fact. Villagers at the ready! Deploy! Even Moira's in on the act. Oh, speaking of Moira, I see you've cracked, by the way.'

'Excuse me?'

'She told me you've signed Robin up for regular gardening duty.'

How the heck had Moira found out? It wasn't as though Robin would have told her. 'Your parents' layout is beautiful. I don't want to lose it.'

Viv grinned. 'And then there are the other benefits.'

What was she talking about?

'He might not be chatty, but he's easy on the eye. And great with a hoe. So there you are, double benefits. Nice scenery, which will lead to nice scenery.'

Eve cocked her head. 'You do talk nonsense, you know that? So, are you going to show me this Easter cake recipe, or what?'

*

After her session at Monty's, Eve went to the village store. She was after whisky for the vicar. For Robin, she'd brought a bottle from her stores at Elizabeth's Cottage – something special a friend had brought back from France. She couldn't risk buying two bottles from Moira; she'd be bound to ask questions. She picked up the highest-end whisky the store had to sell, ready to head over to the vicarage. She was in no mood to answer any questions, and managed to get out of the storekeeper's clutches inside of five minutes; it was a cause for pride and celebration.

'My dear Eve, there's no call for this!' Jim Thackeray said as she took a seat in his spacious living room. 'I have to confess I took my lead from Robin Yardley.' His eyes were serious for a moment. 'I know you're aware of his background.'

She nodded. 'Well, to an extent.'

'We had the opportunity for a brief word on our way down Ferry Lane. Thankfully we are both reasonably fit, and could speak as we ran. Robin had already called reinforcements. I understand a message you left had put him on his guard. Whatever happened after that must have caused him to raise the alarm.'

Eve was still feeling weepy. She was so fond of the vicar and of Viv, and so grateful to Robin. She even felt more relaxed about Simon. What was the matter with her?

'It's a perfectly reasonable reaction,' Jim Thackeray said, seeing her tears and patting her arm. 'A drop of the right stuff is what you need.' He opened the bottle she'd bought.

'I should think that will finish me off all together. I'll be bawling my eyes out on the village green and everyone will wonder what you've said to me.'

The vicar laughed. 'Despite what Moira Squires thinks, I only ever drink in strict moderation, but at times like this, it's called for. I shall make you a nice cup of coffee to have alongside it.'

*

An hour later, Eve was sitting in Robin's warm kitchen, next to a fire kicking out a heartening heat, with a mug of hot chocolate in front of her.

'Sorry if I smell of whisky,' she said. 'I've been at the vicar's.'

Robin laughed. 'Good old Jim.'

She longed to ask how they knew each other. She was willing to bet the vicar knew more about Robin than anyone in Saxford, herself included. But she couldn't pry – not now. It would ruin his opinion of her. 'In fairness, I bought him the grog.'

'The pair of you, honestly! Though I guess you have quite a good excuse at the moment.'

'I got you something too: a bottle of Tempête des Marées. It's a fizzy cognac – you keep it in the freezer. My friend Sara brings me it from France.' She nodded to the tote bag she'd brought and found herself blushing. It was all Viv's fault. Her wisecrack about Robin being nice scenery was floating in her head.

'Tempête des Marées?'

'It translates as tidal storm. I thought it was especially apt after I escaped a woman called Marina onboard a pitching boat – thanks to you and Jim.'

He raised an eyebrow. 'I see your point. Would you like some now, alongside your chocolate?'

She hesitated. 'Better not, after the whisky. But let me know what you think of it.'

'I will.' There was a moment's silence. 'Thanks aren't necessary though,' Robin said at last. 'You know how much I miss my old job. If it wasn't for that I'd have left you to it, obviously.'

It broke the tension and she laughed. 'What happened, Robin?' she said. 'I mean, I know you were aware I might be in danger because of Tina Adcock, and there was the faint possibility that my hare-brained theory about Russell Rathbone was correct too. But to go from that to already having the police on their way when I set off that flare?'

'The timing was pretty tight, to be honest. I went to the village store. Moira had left the event at the church to reopen early, and I hadn't seen her in several days, so I was fresh meat. She was full of the gossip she'd managed to get out of Marina's boyfriend, Zach Campbell. It was all about Marina's ex, the guy she'd been seeing before Zach.'

'The rock star?' Eve remembered Zach mentioning how he was always away on tour, and then overhearing Moira regaling her friend with more related gossip. Something about the guy having problems, and being an alcoholic – and how it was all because of his career.

'Rock star?' Robin shook his head. 'No, this guy was in the forces. Came back from Afghanistan with post-traumatic stress disorder.'

'The forces?' Eve put down her hot chocolate and buried her head in her hands.

'What?'

'On tour! A tour of duty. Oh my goodness. Zach Campbell said it in front of me. But when I heard tour, I thought of a band.' And then a fresh realisation rushed over her. 'The gun?'

Robin nodded. 'Moira came out with some extraordinary story that Zach passed on, about how this ex-boyfriend had turned his service gun on Marina one day, before changing his mind and trying to shoot himself. He clearly never handed it in when he came home. And what would you have done in that situation, if you'd been Marina?'

'Taken it from him.'

Robin nodded. 'That was my conclusion. And although Tina Adcock seemed like a good fit for the double murder, I suddenly wondered if the real killer had been sitting under our noses all the time. I didn't know exactly what motive Marina might have, but it looked like she had means and opportunity.

'At first, I couldn't imagine how she'd have got back inside the Cross Keys without stirring Hetty up, but then it came to me. If she'd spent the night in Apple Tree Cottage, searching the place, she wouldn't have needed to. She could have sneaked straight into the breakfast room without anyone noticing she hadn't just come downstairs, so long as she entered the pub through the back door and kept her eyes open.'

It was true. Breakfast was open to non-residents; Hetty would be used to people coming and going at that time. 'That makes sense.' Eve thought about the sequence of events. 'Howard told me there were no keys on Ashton's body at around seven thirty in the morning, when he searched his pockets for cash. He'd have been over at Apple Tree Cottage five or ten minutes later. And Marina said she saw him arrive as she was making her way home. I'd guess she stayed all night, then sneaked off through the woods for an early breakfast. There would have been fewer people around then, than if she'd left it until later.' By eight or nine, you could count on several villagers nipping into the Cross Keys for their bacon and eggs. 'It would have looked as though she'd slept at the pub as usual. And then poor old Jo went out for a breath of fresh air, around nine thirty perhaps' – Toby did all the breakfast-time cooking, so she wouldn't have been needed – 'and found Ashton's body.'

Robin nodded. 'And I guess Marina adopted a similar approach after she'd killed Howard. His cottage is more central, so she might have left a little earlier to guard against being seen, but she could have hidden in the woods until it was breakfast time. Once I could see how she'd managed it, my thoughts came together in a rush. I stuck my head round the door of the church, but I couldn't see you or Marina, whereas the Adcocks and Rathbone were still there. At that point I took my phone out to contact you and saw you'd left me a voicemail. I must have been out of coverage when you rang. I tried you as soon as I'd listened to it, but there was no answer. And then I called my police contact on my way to Apple Tree Cottage. When I found you'd gone I ran back up Heath Lane.

And then I saw your flare and doubled back towards the estuary alongside the vicar.'

'Thanks. Just as well you're fit. And the police boats?'

'My contact and I guessed Marina might try to get you away from the village. She'd never get away with disposing of you in Saxford.' His gaze met hers. 'Sorry.'

She shook her head. 'You're a gardener. I'd expect you to call a spade a spade.'

A spark of amusement lit his eyes.

'Anyway, my police mate said he'd make sure all her escape routes were covered – including by sea as a precaution. When I saw the flare go up, I updated him as we ran.'

'Jim Thackeray says you told him how to handle the situation.'

Robin raised an eyebrow. 'He's a modest man.'

'No news on Tina Adcock or Russell Rathbone, I suppose?' It was horrible, the constant tension in her stomach at not being safe.

'I was going to call you if you hadn't dropped in. My contact tells me the phone in the cache of evidence Ashton collected is pure gold.' His eyes met hers. 'Tina Adcock's prints are all over it but it's clear of anyone else's. He must have used gloves.'

'Do you know if Carl knew what Tina was up to?' She pictured the angry look, tinged with fear, that she'd seen the Adcocks exchange.

'Not about the drugs, as far as anyone can tell. Looks like Tina had a separate bank account for all her proceeds. I'd guess she was planning on ending their marriage eventually. Jetting off to the sun maybe, and leaving her job at the school behind. But he's been questioned again now, and it's clear he knew about her liking for young men. He admits he thought she might have killed Ashton to keep him quiet about that.'

'So she must have been out when Ashton died. And he gave her a false alibi?'

'He says he was asleep, so he couldn't know for sure if she was home or not. But he didn't admit that to the police when he was first questioned. I can only assume Tina still has him hooked, so he protected her. And of course, he should have informed the school when he found out she was sleeping with her pupils, so he wasn't squeaky clean himself.'

'And what about Rathbone?' She was on the edge of her chair, hoping they had something to prove the lawyer had been involved.

'There were texts from another untraceable mobile on Tina's phone. They weren't explicit, but reading between the lines, it's clear they referred to new kids Tina should expect at the youth club: ones who were likely to agree to sell cannabis on to their friends. Other messages from the same number refer to payments. My contact's in no doubt those were the backhanders Rathbone was getting for helping her.'

'But there's no way of proving it was him Tina was messaging?' If he carried on operating unchecked, kids would still be in danger, and Eve wouldn't feel safe either.

'Well, it's very strong circumstantial evidence, given the kids were all contacts of his.'

'Of course.'

'But there's more too, thanks to you following the stolen-bike guy to that mailbox shop.'

Eve looked up at him; hope flickered in her chest as she saw his expression.

'The guy who works at the shop has been on the desk for years. Seen a lot of changes in his time and doesn't think much of them. He's not in charge and he worries his managers aren't doing due diligence on the people who rent their boxes. He's not spoken up before. My impression is he's worried about his job. But my contact caught him at the right time. He retires next week, so he agreed to make his concerns formal.

'On the back of that, the police viewed the outfit's CCTV. Rathbone was caught on camera, picking up a package from a mailbox. It matched the description you gave.'

'That's something.' But would it be enough?

Robin's eyes met hers. 'On the back of your testimony and the CCTV footage, the police brought Rathbone in to help with their enquiries. While he was there, they used Tina's disposable phone to call the number they guessed must belong to him.'

'And?'

'They could see his pocket vibrating. He might be wealthy, but I don't think he'll be able to buy his way out of this one.'

CHAPTER FORTY

Three Months Later

Eve and Viv were walking down to the beach, with Gus in tow. Or maybe it was they who were in tow; Gus was certainly well ahead of them.

Eve let the summer air fill her lungs, taking in the sweet scent of the honeysuckle carried on the warm breeze. She'd been feeling a lot more relaxed since Tina Adcock and Russell Rathbone had been charged with a series of drug offences. Tina's list was the length of your average roll of toilet paper. Robin had said their cases were watertight. As well as all the concrete proof they had, more circumstantial evidence had to come to light now. The police had interviewed a series of kids who were linked to both Rathbone and the Drop In. Several admitted Tina had groomed them to sell drugs. There were past cases too – the arrests Eve had marked on her map. Once again, the police found the youths involved had often been 'helped' by the lawyer.

Eve and Viv passed Apple Tree Cottage and spotted Betty Foley in the front garden, sharing a pot of tea at an outdoor table with a group of women who all had paperbacks open in front of them. Betty raised a hand and waved.

'I'm glad the book club's taken off,' Eve said, once they were out of earshot. 'It's great that everyone's rallied round, but poor Betty.'

'She was dealt a terrible hand,' Viv agreed. 'Thank goodness her aunt pulled through. Did you hear she's moving back to the UK once she's a bit stronger, so the pair of them can be closer?'

'No! That's good news.'

'I still can't believe Betty doesn't blame Howard for ripping her off,' Viv said, shaking her head. 'I would have been devastated. And livid.'

'Me too, but Betty's world view is different.' They'd had a long heart-to-heart since the woman's return to the UK; understandably, she'd wanted to know everything. 'She said she would have offered Howard her money if she'd known how difficult things were. She was upset that he hadn't confided in her, but not surprised. She said it would have hurt his pride too badly.'

'Blimey. Will she get any of the money back?'

'She was his sole beneficiary, so if there's anything left when his bills are paid, she'll get that. And the house he bought with her money will come straight to her now. It's mortgaged to the hilt, but her tenants are settled and happy. Hopefully they'll stay for years, and their rent will gradually mount up. And of course she'll get her share of Outside In's assets, once all the legalities are sorted out – that and anything else Ashton left her in his will.' The business was being wound up.

'I thought dealing with the aftermath in the village would be almost as hard for her as facing up to what Howard did,' Viv said. 'I mean, I know everyone's been hugely supportive, but all that gossip about the fraud, and the speculation about Ashton's motives.'

Eve had had the same fear. She thought back to the funerals. It was the vicar who'd steered things in the right direction. 'I could hug Jim Thackeray for the way he spoke about them.' She'd filled him in on her discoveries over the whisky and coffee they'd shared. By the time he'd finished his addresses in church, the villagers were in awe of Ashton's bravery and looking on Howard as a misguided fool rather than a self-centred criminal. Eve still couldn't get past what Howard had done, but the vicar's words had offered Betty some comfort, and the villagers shared her pride in her son. He was a local hero now, just like Elizabeth who'd once owned Eve's cottage, and tales of his exploits would pass into legend.

Ashton Tyler Foley, Artistic Director of Outside In

Childhood tearaway turned entrepreneur, Ashton Foley, whose extraordinary life story inspired so many, has died in Saxford St Peter, Suffolk. A woman has been arrested for his murder.

From the moment he was old enough to conduct a business transaction, Foley used his nous and creativity to make money. Aged sixteen, his easy charm and confidence helped him sell cannabis to his friends. Many adults in his world assumed he would continue down a criminal path, but his strength of character led him on a different route. After a spell in a young offenders' institute, he left Suffolk for London with new ideas for his future. By the time he was twenty-three, he'd travelled the world as a roadie for chart-topping bands, then teamed up with horticultural expert, Marina Shaw, to form the innovative indoor plant design company, Outside In.

The firm reflected Foley's personality. It was groundbreaking and showy, expensive and a little over the top, but with real passion, dedication and feeling at its core.

Many will remember Foley for his quirky charm, inspirational talks and colourful lifestyle, which were a hit with the media and clients alike. But though people often saw Foley as a bon viveur, who enjoyed painting the town red, he was much more than that. He seldom visited his family home, but he was still close to his mother, and a keen defender of her interests. And he never forgot his teenage years, and the adults with a duty of care who'd dragged him into serious trouble. He was determined they should be brought to justice. Rather than waiting for others to act, he chose a different route, born of key components of his character: bravery, impetuosity and independence. His attempts to find proof against them, and to save others from being groomed as he was, were ultimately successful, but led indirectly to his death.

Eve put down the copy of *Icon* magazine. She'd reread that opening so many times, wondering if she'd gotten it exactly right. Thank goodness she'd found out the truth about Ashton at last, piecing together what Heaven had said, which led her back to Amber Ingram. Obituary writing was like that sometimes: panning for information, picking out the true facts that caught in the sieve as rumours and conjecture washed away. She shook her head; she'd almost been thrown off course by her first impressions, and the stories of Ashton's past. She wouldn't let that happen again.

Gus had been sitting patiently next to her. Now he leaped up and put his front paws on her lap, his liquid brown eyes on hers. She gave him a cuddle.

'I know, Gus, glossy magazines aren't your thing. A good dose of fresh air is what we need. Let's go down to the estuary and watch the waders.'

A LETTER FROM CLARE

Thank you so much for reading *Mystery at Apple Tree Cottage*. I do hope you had as much fun working on the clues as I did! If you'd like to keep up to date with all of my latest releases, you can sign up at the following link. Your email address will never be shared, and you can unsubscribe at any time.

www.bookouture.com/clare-chase

The idea for this book started with thoughts of a stranger coming in to disrupt the normal routine of life in a small village. In the end, I decided it would be interesting to focus on someone who'd grown up locally, created an impression, then gone away for years and returned. How might people treat them when they came back? Who would be pleased to see them, and who might be unnerved by their reappearance? The inspiration for Outside In came from a visit to the University of Cambridge's botanic gardens. I loved the atmosphere in their fern room and the way having a concentration of plants in an enclosed space made me feel. (Like Eve, however, I haven't progressed further than buying geraniums for my windowsills!)

If you have time, I'd love it if you were able to write a review of *Mystery at Apple Tree Cottage*. Feedback is really valuable, and it also makes a huge difference in helping new readers discover my books for the first time.

Alternatively, if you'd like to contact me personally, you can reach me via my website, Facebook page, Twitter or Instagram. It's always great to hear from readers.

Again, thank you so much for deciding to spend some time reading *Mystery at Apple Tree Cottage*. I'm looking forward to sharing my next book with you very soon.

With all best wishes,
Clare x

@ClareChaseAuthor

@ClareChase_

www.clarechase.com

ACKNOWLEDGEMENTS

Much love and big thanks to Charlie, George and Ros for the pre-submission proofreading and feedback, encouragement, and cheerleading. And the same too, to Mum and Dad, Phil and Jenny, David and Pat, Warty, Andrea, Jen, the Westfield gang, Margaret, Shelly, Mark, cousin Lorna and a whole band of family and friends. And Sara-Ellen, thank you for the Tempête des Marées!

And then, at the heart of the publication process, huge thanks to my fantastic editor Ruth Tross for her incisive and inspiring ideas and friendly encouragement. I'm also truly grateful to Noelle Holten, for her phenomenal promotional work. Sending thanks too, to Peta Nightingale, Kim Nash, Alexandra Holmes and everyone involved in editing, book production and sales at Bookouture. I can't imagine being published and promoted by a better or nicer team.

Thanks to the fabulous Bookouture authors and other writer mates both online and IRL for their friendship. And a massive thank you, too, to the amazing book bloggers and reviewers who take the time to pass on their thoughts about my work. I really appreciate it.

And finally, thanks to you, the reader, for buying or borrowing this book!

Made in United States
North Haven, CT
12 May 2024

52414749R00171